Please address questions and book requests to: Harlequin Reader Service
U.S.: 3010 Walden Ave., P.O. Box 1325, Buffalo, NY 14269
CAN.: P.O. Box 609, Fort Erie, Ont. L2A 5X3

Born in the USA

COLORADO

DALLAS SCHULZE

Rafferty's Choice

Harlequin Books

TORONTO • NEW YORK • LONDON
AMSTERDAM • PARIS • SYDNEY • HAMBURG
STOCKHOLM • ATHENS • TOKYO • MILAN
MADRID • WARSAW • BUDAPEST • AUCKLAND

HARLEQUIN BOOKS
225 Duncan Mill Road, Don Mills,
Ontario, Canada M3B 3K9

ISBN 0-373-47156-4

RAFFERTY'S CHOICE

Dear Reader,

Writing a book is always an adventure. You can do outlines and character sketches and work out every detail in advance, but once you actually start telling the story, there are always surprises. It may be a new plot twist that suddenly pops up and catches you by surprise or a character who turns out to be something other than what you were expecting. Sometimes the surprises are nice and you pat yourself on your back for being so very clever. Sometimes the surprises are not so nice. Those are the days you think wistfully of becoming a short order cook or a coal miner.

By far the nicest surprise occurs when a secondary character comes so fully to life that she demands a story of her own. I've had this happen quite a few times, but the magic of it never fails to delight me. Becky, the child in this book, was just such a character. She started out in my book *Tell Me a Story*, and as soon as she spoke for the first time, she became such a real person that I knew I wanted to see more of her.

So here she is once again, making sure her father gets his life back on track, and getting herself a mother in the process. I hope you enjoy reading this story as much as I enjoyed writing it.

Best,

Dallas Schulze

Prologue

Amanda Leigh Bradford was making her escape. She'd planned carefully, making sure that everyone was out of the house before pulling her suitcase from the closet. It had been packed for nearly a week, ready for the first opportunity. Now that opportunity was here and she was going to make her getaway.

She eased the bedroom door open slowly. Lucky for her, no door in the Bradford mansion would ever dare creak. The hinges were silent, as silent as the house. Rosie would be in the kitchen at the back of the house, getting lunch ready. The maid had the day off. If she could just get past the gardener and down the driveway to where a taxi was waiting, her escape would be successful. Just a few minutes ago, she'd seen Carlos heading toward the rear of the property, a pair of shears in hand, which meant he should be out of the way, too.

The suitcase was heavy and she grunted with effort as she hefted it down the stairs. When she'd traveled before, there'd always been someone else to carry the luggage, someone else to open the doors. If she'd wanted, there would have been someone to carry *her* to the taxi.

But that was all going to change. Starting now, she was going to be on her own. No more servants, no more fussing. She'd left a note for her parents, explaining the reasons she was leaving. It wasn't anything she hadn't said before but perhaps this time they'd realize she meant it.

She set the suitcase down in the foyer and eased open the front door. This was a critical moment. If Rosie happened to come to the front of the house and see Amanda—or worse, see Amanda's suitcase—there'd be no escape.

Amanda glanced over her shoulder, as nervous as a thief. But the coast was clear and Amanda slipped out the front door, pulling the suitcase with her.

She dragged the elegant pigskin case across the slate porch, struggling to keep it from bumping down the stairs. Surely it had gotten heavier since she'd left her room. She wished she could have asked the cabdriver to pull up in front of the house but she hadn't dared.

Setting her teeth, she wrapped her slender hands around the handle of the suitcase and tugged it off the ground. It bumped against her jeans-clad leg, threatening to knock her off her feet. But she was determined to succeed; she hadn't gotten this far only to be stopped by an inanimate object.

By the time she reached the bottom of the long circular driveway, she was flushed and disheveled. If it hadn't been for the fact that the suitcase contained everything she thought she'd need to start her new life, she might have abandoned it in the shrubbery.

But the sight of the scruffy yellow cab gave new strength to her slender arms, and to her resolve. The driver was middle-aged and potbellied but he hefted the suitcase into the back as if it weighed no more than a pound or two.

Amanda sank onto the torn seat as he settled back behind the wheel.

"Where to, miss?"

"The airport, please."

She leaned back as the taxi pulled away from the curb. She was free.

Chapter One

Rafferty Traherne was looking for a housekeeper. A simple enough task, he would have thought. After all, with the job market in Denver somewhat depressed, qualified housekeepers should have been crawling out of the woodwork.

He shuffled the applications on his desk, looking at them without much enthusiasm. It had been a long day. A very long day, he amended. He couldn't, in all honesty, say that he hadn't had plenty of applicants for the position. This was the second day he'd conducted interviews and there had been plenty of women applying for the job, even a couple of men. Unfortunately none of them, male or female, was what he was looking for. He would have been hard-pressed to say just what that was but he knew he hadn't seen it yet.

He leaned back in his chair, reaching up to rub the knot of tension that seemed permanently lodged at the base of his neck. The two months since his housekeeper had left to move to Alaska had not been easy.

As one of three doctors in a medical clinic, Rafferty had been lucky in that his partners had been willing to pick up the night calls and weekend hours when he had to be home with Becky.

Sara and Michael had been more understanding than he'd had any business expecting, offering to work around his hours, giving him time with his daughter, time to try to make up to her for the years he hadn't been there.

But he couldn't expect his partners to shoulder more than their fair share forever. Really, what he needed was a live-in housekeeper, someone who'd be there so he'd be able to take emergency calls without leaving Becky alone.

He shook his head, dismissing the idea. The last housekeeper, Ms. Beckworth, had lived in. She'd worked for him for almost a year before deciding that she didn't like the room she'd been given as much as she liked the master bedroom. More particularly, the master bed—preferably with the master in it.

She hadn't been interested in anything as tawdry as an affair, she'd informed him. She was interested in marriage. A measure of Rafferty's desperation to keep a housekeeper was that he had actually given a moment's consideration to the suggestion. Sanity had returned before he could say anything he'd later regret.

Ms. Beckworth had departed for Alaska where the men were supposed to be interested in making commitments. Rafferty wished her well. But the incident had left him a little wary of engaging another live-in housekeeper.

He sighed and drew the stack of applications forward again. The truth was, Becky was probably more than capable of taking care of herself for the few hours after school; she seemed to have more common sense than most of the adults Rafferty knew. The thought brought with it a certain pang. There'd been too many years when Becky had had to be practical because, unfortunately, her mother hadn't been.

He pinched his fingers over the bridge of his nose. There was a headache building between his eyes. Becky had told him that she didn't need a baby-sitter. It was probably true but she'd already lost so much of her childhood. He was determined that she not grow up too fast.

Probably too late for that, he acknowledged ruefully. Sometimes he thought Becky must have been born old. At ten, there were moments when he felt she managed to make him feel as if she were the senior member of this family.

And that was part of the reason finding a housekeeper was so problematic. He didn't want someone who could just take care of the house and be there in case Becky needed something. He wanted someone who could...

Who could what?

Rafferty scowled at the stack of applications. He wanted someone who could teach Becky how to be a child, at least some of the time. What he really wanted was Mary Poppins. A little bit of popping in and out of sidewalk drawings would probably do Becky a world of good.

Surely there was someone out there who was not only trustworthy but who had a touch of whimsy in her, a bit of childlike spirit, just enough to remind his daughter that she was ten, not forty.

If there was such a person, he wasn't going to find anyone sitting here by himself. There was, he was fairly sure, only one applicant still waiting. He'd caught a glimpse of her when he called in the last woman, who'd turned out to be Atilla the Hun's first cousin. "Discipline, discipline, discipline. That's what children need, Dr. Traherne. Discipline in childhood creates order in later life."

Well, it might create order in Ms. Guvanstock's life but he had no intention of turning her loose with his daughter. He'd seen the nanny from hell to the door and now he was left with one last hope. If this woman wasn't right—and he wasn't overly optimistic about that likelihood—then he would have to start the whole tedious process over again tomorrow.

He sighed, wishing he'd put a bottle of aspirin in his desk. Well, there was no sense in putting off the inevitable. Shuffling the applications, he located the one that belonged to the woman waiting in the hallway.

Amanda Bradley. Age: 30. He frowned. She was on the young side. His thoughts had run more along the lines of a grandmotherly type. Experience: She claimed to have run a large household, including caring for two children. She'd done light nursing for an elderly woman and had worked as a teacher's aide at the elementary school level. Seemed like a lot of experience for someone so young, he thought.

Of course, if she really did have that much experience... Maybe someone young would be a good idea. Maybe Becky would find it easier to relate to her. Maybe Ms. Amanda Bradley would turn out to be the answer to his prayers.

"Hope springs eternal," he muttered aloud as he stood up.

That hope gained strength when he heard Becky's voice as he approached the door. The thick wood made it impossible to hear what she was saying but her tone was certainly animated. She had to be talking to Ms. Bradley, and from the sounds of it, she found her congenial, at the very least. Maybe, just maybe...

But then again, maybe not.

The hope flickered and faded when he opened the door and got a good look at the day's last applicant, the day's last hope.

She was too pretty...too young, too small...too pretty...too thin, too fragile...too pretty. Too everything. Her application had said thirty but she looked as if she was closer to nineteen. Masses of thick dark hair had been pinned up in a neat twist that looked too heavy for her slender neck to support. She was wearing a neatly tailored ivory dress and navy pumps; he didn't have to be an expert on women's clothing to recognize quality when he saw it.

Her head was turned away as she listened to Becky, who was telling her about some incident at school, so all he could see of her face was one smooth, fine-boned cheek and a surprisingly firm jaw. She held her purse in her lap, long, slender fingers resting against the navy leather. He frowned at the delicate bones of her wrist. She was too thin.

Just then, Becky glanced up and saw her father, her face breaking into a wide smile. Her companion turned as Becky jumped up and ran across the hall to him. Over Becky's head, Rafferty finished his appraisal of Ms. Bradley. Nothing he saw changed his mind about her unsuitability.

The firm jaw was topped by a sweetly curved mouth that looked very kissable. But he wasn't interested in kissable. He was interested in someone who could take care of Becky. She had a small, straight nose and a pair of the biggest, softest eyes he'd ever seen. Dark brown and thickly lashed, they were the final confirmation, if he needed one, that Ms. Bradley would never do.

Those eyes were too wide, too innocent, too vulnerable. Those were not the eyes of someone who could run a house and take care of a child. In fact, she looked as though she needed someone to take care of her. He couldn't imagine those eyes ever being stern. And though Becky was almost as perfect as it was possible for a child to be, he had to admit there were moments when a stern hand was in order.

Besides, she wasn't much taller than Becky herself. If she topped five feet by more than an inch he'd be surprised. Not that he was looking for Brunhilda the Muscle Woman but those thin arms would never manage to mop floors and scrub tile. If he hired her it would be like having two children in the house. Except that the figure beneath that prim white dress was slender but not at all childlike. And the fact that he was even noticing such a thing was another strike against her.

No, she certainly wouldn't do.

AMANDA WASN'T FEELING any more hopeful than he was. When she'd filled out the application, she'd stretched the truth so thin, it had more holes than substance. She'd soothed her guilty conscience with thoughts of how hard she'd work if she was lucky enough to get the job. Besides, how much could there be to taking care of a little girl and a house?

She'd never done much housework herself but she'd been watching Rosie and the maids all her life. It didn't look all that hard. She'd never done much cooking, either, but that's what cookbooks were for. And as for caring for a little girl, she'd been one herself once.

Sitting in the hallway for the last hour, she'd felt her confidence slipping. When she'd arrived, there'd been three other women there, the last of a long line of applicants, she was sure. They'd all been much older and they'd all looked terribly experienced. She'd added a few years to her age on the application and she'd done her best to look mature and responsible. But the other applicants hadn't had to lie. They'd all looked as if they were born to be housekeepers, destined to inspire confidence in the hearts of prospective employers.

The other women spoke neither to her nor to one another, leaving Amanda nothing to do but think of half a hundred reasons why she was completely unsuited for this job. By the time the last applicant had left the study, she'd been about ready to sneak out. Going through with the interview would only be humiliating.

And then Becky had pushed open the front door, whirling into the hall like a cool breeze. She'd stopped when she'd spotted Amanda, studying her for a moment in a disconcertingly adult fashion. Amanda had studied her right back. Becky apparently liked what she saw because she dropped her book bag and came over to sit next to her, holding out her hand and introducing herself.

They'd talked for only a few minutes but it had been long enough for Amanda to feel a little of her confidence creeping back. She *could* take care of this oddly adult little girl, she knew she could. If only she was given the chance.

Now, looking at her potential employer, that chance seemed more distant than ever.

He was a big man. Not just tall but broad. With those thickly muscled shoulders, he looked more like a stevedore than a doctor. Though he couldn't have been much more than thirty-five, his hair was steel-gray, thick and falling into a wave over his forehead. His eyes were gray too, a lighter shade than his hair, cool and intense.

He was, she supposed, attractive. Or he would have been

if he didn't look quite so intimidating. She swallowed and drew herself up straighter, wishing she were a few inches taller, a few years older and a lot more self-assured.

"Ms. Bradley?"

"I beg your pardon? I mean, yes. Yes, I'm Ms. Bradley." *Brilliant, just brilliant, Amanda. You win the prize for intelligent responses. Why don't you just wear a tag that says Bradley isn't your real name?*

"I'm Rafferty Traherne."

She stepped forward to take the hand he held out, and her fingers vanished inside his. His grip was strong and dry. There was nothing she hated more than a damp, wimpy handshake. For a moment, with her fingers lost in his, she felt an odd tingle run up her arm, an awareness she'd never felt before. But the contact was gone so quickly, it was easy to dismiss the feeling as imagination.

"I'm pleased to meet you, Dr. Traherne." She restrained the urge to curtsy. Not that he seemed to be trying to intimidate her. But he was so...so big, so there.

"We've been talking, Daddy." Becky looked up at her father, both of her hands clutching one of his as she leaned back on her heels. Effortlessly Rafferty supported her weight. Amanda rather thought he could have supported two or three Beckys without noticing it. "Amanda says she's never learned how to ride a bike. I said I could teach her."

Great, thought Amanda. *Now he'll know for sure that he shouldn't hire you. What kind of a housekeeper-nanny can't even ride a bike?*

Somewhere in the back of her mind, a small voice suggested that bike riding was probably not a prime requirement but Amanda was so deep in despair, she ignored it.

"She says she knows how to cut out paper dolls, though," Becky continued. "Real ones, not the funny-looking ones you cut out. Daddy doesn't know much about paper dolls," Becky added in an aside to Amanda.

"One of the many drawbacks that come of having been born a boy, I guess," Rafferty suggested with a smile.

He looked much less stern when he smiled and Amanda smiled back, feeling a tiny flicker of hope. She wasn't likely to get the job, but at least there was reason to believe he'd be kind when he told her how hopelessly unsuitable she was.

That shy smile was really quite attractive, Rafferty thought. He had no trouble recognizing the flicker of attraction he felt. And that was another strike against her, as far as he was concerned. The last thing he wanted was a housekeeper he found attractive. Especially not one who looked so lost and vulnerable.

Becky's mother had had that same look, helpless and fragile. But she'd had the strength to run away with their daughter and keep Becky from him for four long years. He'd had his child's infancy taken away from him and Becky had grown up far too quickly. As she had said on one of the rare occasions she talked about those years with her mother, someone had to be practical and Maryanne Traherne hadn't been capable of it.

No, he had no intention of getting involved with another vulnerable woman. If he ever got serious about a woman again—and it was a very big "if"—it would be with someone tough enough to take care of herself. No more wounded birds. Not that he knew for a fact that Amanda Bradley was a wounded bird but he had his suspicions.

"Are you going to interview her, Daddy? Can I watch?" Becky's questions snapped him out of his thoughts. How long had he been standing here staring at the poor woman? Long enough to bring a tinge of color to her cheeks, he noted. Considering the way he was acting, chances were she wouldn't want to work for him anyway.

"Yes, I'm going to interview her, and no, you can't watch. I doubt Ms. Bradley wants an audience."

"Oh, I don't mind," Amanda said. Then it occurred to her that he probably hadn't been excluding Becky for her sake as much as for his own. "I mean, it's up to you. It really doesn't matter to me."

Think before you speak, Amanda. Not that you have any

*chance at this job anyway, but there's no need to leave him
with the impression that you're a total idiot.*

"Please, Daddy, please. She doesn't mind. And you're
always saying that I should experience lots of stuff."

"Are you planning on conducting interviews any time
soon, urchin?"

"You never know," she said solemnly. "Suppose tomorrow you caught some ghastly disease like malaria or
yellow fever. And you were out of your head with fever
and delirious and stuff. I'd have to hire a nurse and how
would I know how to do it if I'd never seen it done before?"

Amanda and Rafferty both listened in fascination to the
scenario Becky drew, a scenario she appeared to find quite
appealing. Glancing at Amanda, Rafferty caught the glint
of humor in her eyes and his own smile deepened.

"I suspect if some terrible illness should befall me—
though I have to tell you I haven't seen a case of yellow
fever in Denver in quite a while—your Aunt Claire would
probably be conducting the interviews."

"But suppose it was an epidemic and Aunt Claire was
sick, too?"

Rafferty laughed, knowing when he was beat. Becky
could carry on this kind of hypothetical argument for hours.
"The word is *epidemic*. And I don't know a disease in the
world that would dare come near your Aunt Claire. But
you can sit in on the interview if Ms. Bradley is sure she
doesn't mind."

"I don't mind." Amanda smiled at Becky. The little
girl's presence might help cushion the blow of rejection. It
was too bad, really, that she wasn't going to get the job.
She really liked Becky.

As far as Rafferty was concerned, the interview would
just be a formality. There was no way this girl was what
he was looking for. And girl seemed a more appropriate
word than woman. If she was thirty as she'd indicated on
her application, he was Clark Gable.

Seated across the desk from her, he asked her questions,

paying only perfunctory attention to her answers. Everything about her spoke of money, even the way she sat—knees together, ankles tilted slightly to one side, her hands held loosely in her lap. What on earth was a girl like this doing applying for a job as a housekeeper? She looked far more suited to hiring one than to being one.

It was too bad really. She'd seemed so comfortable with Becky and Becky with her. In fact, Becky was even now giving him what she fondly believed were subtle hand signals indicating that she liked this applicant, which was more than could be said for the others she'd met.

But the decision couldn't be Becky's alone. He was the parent here. He was the one who had to carefully weigh the practicalities, make sure that his child would be in proper hands. And Amanda Bradley's hands were definitely not the proper ones.

She was saying something about her past experience—almost certainly fictitious—but he wasn't really listening. As she spoke, she lifted one hand to push back a lock of hair that had slipped loose and he was struck again by how fragile she was. Was she just carrying the dieting too far or was it that she couldn't afford to eat decently? He frowned, unaware that the expression made Amanda even more nervous.

THIS INTERVIEW WASN'T GOING at all the way she'd expected. Dr. Traherne asked her questions but he didn't seem to pay much attention to the answers. And she'd worked so hard to make the answers plausible.

She'd even thought up an explanation for the quality of her clothes, on the off chance that he was observant enough to notice that they weren't the sort of things you'd expect a housekeeper to be wearing. She was planning to say that a former employer had been gracious enough to give her some rather elegant castoffs. Wasn't it lucky that she and the woman were the same size? But he didn't ask about her clothes.

And to add to Amanda's uneasiness, Becky was sitting

in a chair just to her left and a little behind her. From the corner of her eye, Amanda caught occasional twitching movements and she was beginning to wonder if Becky had some physical problem about which Amanda hadn't been informed.

It was one thing to claim skills she didn't exactly have in order to get a job taking care of a *healthy* ten-year-old. Something else entirely to take on responsibilities for a child with a disability.

Not that it mattered, because she certainly wasn't going to get this job. She let her voice trail off, her fingers knotted around the soft leather of her purse. Foolishly she'd been counting on getting this job. If she didn't find work soon, she didn't know what she was going to do.

In the nearly two months since she'd left home, she'd learned one major lesson: money never went as far as you thought it would. And jobs weren't easy to come by. The cash she'd drawn out of her account when she'd left was dwindling at a frightening rate.

If she didn't find a way to replenish her cash flow soon, she'd be forced to go home with her tail between her legs. And she'd almost sooner starve than admit that her parents were right, that she couldn't manage on her own.

She straightened her spine and raised her chin. No. She wasn't going to do that. If this job didn't work out, there'd be another one. Gram had always said that if you just kept plugging something was bound to go your way. And if there was one thing she'd inherited from her maternal grandmother, it was sheer stubbornness.

RAFFERTY WATCHED the expressions flicker across Amanda's face and wondered what she was thinking. For a moment, she'd looked almost despairing and then she'd straightened and that fine-boned jaw had firmed—most attractively, he noticed. Those wide brown eyes held a determined glint that seemed at odds with their delicate setting.

He glanced at Becky who was all but doing headstands

to try to get his attention. The grimaces she obviously thought were subtle made her look as though she had a nearly fatal twitch. Obviously she'd already decided that Amanda Bradley was perfect housekeeper material.

She probably knew a pushover when she saw one, he thought cynically, well-aware that his daughter was not above a bit of manipulation if she thought she could get away with it. Still, with that chin, he didn't think Amanda would be quite as much of a pushover as he had at first.

Of course, she was lying on a number of issues. Her age, her experience—her name, for all he knew. But Becky liked her and he'd learned that Becky was a shrewd judge of character. And she hadn't talked down to the child the way so many adults felt obliged to do.

He shifted his attention back to Amanda, whose fingers were mangling her purse. If only she'd been a bit older, a little less delicate and a whole lot less attractive... She was watching him, her chin raised as if to show that this interview wasn't vital to her. But was it his imagination, or was there a hint of desperation in those wide brown eyes? Did she need this job, need the money? No, he responded to himself. Someone dressed the way she was wasn't likely to be penniless. Still, she did look as if she hadn't had a decent meal in weeks.

"Would you join me for dinner tonight?"

The question came out of nowhere, breaking the silence abruptly, startling Rafferty almost as much as it did his daughter and Amanda. Becky stopped her grimacing and gawked at her father. Amanda's eyes widened in surprise. She stared at him for a moment before chill hauteur stole over her face, making her, for a moment, look almost as old as she'd claimed to be.

"No, thank you." Clearly insulted she stood up, her slender body tensed.

It hit Rafferty suddenly that the invitation must have seemed like a cheap come-on, delivered in front of a ten-year-old, no less.

"Good day, Dr. Traherne."

He stood up, pushing his chair back with an abrupt movement.

"Wait." She had already turned away but she turned back, raising one eyebrow in haughty inquiry. How such a softly pretty face could look so cold, he couldn't imagine. The sudden change from wounded dove to offended woman threw him off balance. He found himself stammering like a nervous fifteen-year-old.

"I just meant—I thought—I meant with Becky and me, of course." Even though the chill eased, the suspicion didn't leave her eyes. "I thought you might like to celebrate your new job. That is, if you're still interested in taking us on."

Becky squealed with delight but Rafferty didn't take his eyes off Amanda Bradley. Emotions flickered across her open face. Surprise, shock, then pleasure. The color rose in her cheeks as she smiled at him, such a sweet smile that Rafferty felt as if sunshine had just flooded the room.

He had the feeling that his life was never going to be quite the same again.

Chapter Two

Seated across the table from Rafferty, Mandy restrained the urge to pinch herself. She had a job. She was actually going to get paid a real salary. The thought brought with it a glow of satisfaction. She'd set out to prove that she could make it on her own and she'd begun to doubt it herself these past weeks. But now she had a job and all she had to do was prove herself capable.

"The food here isn't fancy but it's good," Rafferty said, shaking her out of her thoughts.

"It smells delicious," Mandy said, giving him that shy smile that made him disturbingly aware of how attractive she was.

"The chili size is the best in the world," Becky told her. Her tone made it clear that, as far as she was concerned, a restaurant could be judged on its chili size alone.

"I don't think I've ever had chili size," Mandy said doubtfully.

"It's a disgusting concoction of hamburger and chili," Rafferty said. "Only truck drivers and ten-year-olds actually eat the stuff." He reached over to ruffle Becky's hair. She grinned at him, not in the least disturbed by his opinion of her taste in cuisine.

In the end, Mandy decided she wasn't quite up to trying the chili size. She settled for meat loaf and gravy. She'd never been to a place like Hall's Coffee Shop and she found it intriguing. When her parents went out to eat, their choice of restaurant was generally based on some sort of star system that seemed to require wine stewards and waiters with towels over their arms.

Hall's wasn't likely to earn any stars for the decor, which hovered somewhere between Early American kitsch and the current trend toward Southwestern. The waitresses wore jeans and T-shirts with only their aprons to differentiate them from the customers.

"Where are you from?" Becky's question interrupted Mandy's visual exploration.

"You shouldn't ask personal questions, Becky," Rafferty told his daughter.

"That's all right," Mandy said. "I don't mind. I'm from Philadelphia."

"That's in Pennsylvania," Becky said, her tone suggesting that Mandy might not have known this.

"Yes."

"How long have you been in Denver?" That was Rafferty. As long as his new housekeeper didn't mind answering questions, he had to admit to a little curiosity of his own.

"About two months."

"Summer here must have been a bit of a shock after summers in Philly. No humidity here."

"I can't say I've missed that. It's so dry here, though. It took me a while to get used to it. My skin felt terribly dry at first."

Rafferty's eyes lingered on the smooth curve of her cheek. Her skin didn't look dry. It looked silky smooth. Would it feel as soft as it looked? He pushed the thought away. Ms. Amanda Bradley was his employee now. Whether her skin was as soft as the petals of a rose was certainly none of his concern.

"How come you moved to Denver?" Becky asked, reaching for her milk shake as the waitress set it on the table.

"I always wanted to see what the Wild West looked like, I guess," Mandy said, her eyes smiling.

"You mean cowboys and Indians and stuff?" Becky licked at the chocolate mustache that now decorated her upper lip. "We got quite a few cowboys but there aren't any Indians. And I don't see how come they call them cowboys when I've never seen any of them near a cow."

Rafferty and Mandy exchanged an amused glance at her disgruntled expression. The waitress brought their meals then, saving them the necessity of trying to explain the concept of urban cowboys to Becky.

The food was, as Rafferty had promised, very good. Nothing like the exquisite meals Rosie prepared at home, but a far sight better than the canned and frozen food Mandy had been living on for almost two months now. Amazing how her appetite had dipped along with her bank balance. It had been hard to eat when she thought she might have to go whimpering home, admitting defeat.

Rafferty watched her tuck into the meat loaf and mashed potatoes, satisfied that, tonight at least, she was going to get enough to eat. He studied her surreptitiously, wondering, for the hundredth time, if he'd been crazy to hire her. He'd been looking for someone who could be a companion to Becky but at the same time exert some authority when it was called for. Looking at Mandy's delicate features, *authority* was not the first word to come to mind.

And what about the simpler aspects of the job? Taking care of Becky was certainly top priority but taking care of the house was a big part of the job description. Mandy's soft, slender hands looked as though they'd never washed a dish.

He frowned down at his plate. Maybe he could hire someone to handle some of the cleaning. The irony of the thought struck him. He'd just hired a housekeeper and now he was thinking about hiring someone to keep house so Amanda wouldn't have to get dishpan hands. He shook his head, his mouth twisting ruefully.

"Don't mind Daddy. He goes off into these moods once

in a while." Becky's voice dragged Rafferty back to the moment, making him realize that it must have been obvious that he'd been distracted. "And don't worry—we don't think he's dangerous," Becky added kindly, sliding her father a sly look.

Rafferty gave her a ferocious look that provoked a not-terribly-frightened giggle. He turned to Mandy, his expression serious. "I forgot to mention that part of your duties will be to beat my daughter at least once a day—twice if your arm holds out."

Mandy nodded, as if there were nothing unusual in this request. "Of course, Dr. Traherne. Shall I lock her in the attic, too?"

Rafferty appeared to consider the idea and finally shook his head. "No. It's a quiet neighborhood and her shrieks would probably disturb the neighbors."

"You could put me in the basement," Becky offered helpfully. She dipped her last French fry in catsup and popped it into her mouth.

"And disturb the spiders?" Rafferty raised his eyebrows. "Certainly not."

"Spiders?" Mandy questioned uneasily. The word alone made her skin crawl. If she had a phobia, it was spiders.

"Jillions of 'em," Becky told her with relish. "Some are as big as cats."

"Cats?" Mandy swallowed. Undoubtedly Becky was exaggerating. Spiders didn't get as big as cats. Did they?

"Don't pay any attention to her, Ms. Bradley. The basement contains more broken appliances and dust than anything else. If there are any spiders down there, they're no doubt the common garden variety. Nothing dangerous. And none of them are as big as a cat," he added, with a quelling look at his daughter. Becky shrugged her innocence, turning her attention to the last of her milk shake.

"I'm relieved to hear it." Mandy pushed the thought of eight-legged crawly things out of her mind. There were other, more pleasant things to think about. Like the fact that she had a job. Like the fact that her employer had a wonderful smile.

Not that the quality of his smile had any relevance at all, she reminded herself sternly. She couldn't, however, help but notice such things.

Watching him argue with his daughter over whether she had room for a piece of pie, Mandy had to admit that the thought of working for a man like Rafferty Traherne was not at all displeasing.

AN HOUR LATER, Rafferty pulled the car up next to the curb in front of Mandy's apartment building. It was an uninspired effort from an architectural standpoint but at least the neighborhood was respectable. Sliding out of the Jeep, he came around the front of the vehicle to the passenger side.

Mandy finished her conversation with Becky, who was in the back seat. She turned as Rafferty opened her car door. In the twilight, he looked menacingly large. His shoulders seemed to fill her vision. The fading light turned his hair from steel-gray to near black and shadowed his eyes.

For an instant, she was vividly aware of his size, of the strength in those wide hands. She couldn't remember ever knowing anyone who was quite so…male.

She hesitated a moment before taking the hand he held out to her. His fingers closed over hers, strong and warm. She was grateful for his support as she eased her way out of the Jeep. Her narrow skirt hadn't been designed with the vehicle's high seat in mind. Solidly on the ground, she wondered if it was her imagination that he held her hand an instant longer than was necessary.

"Do you have a car?" he asked, as the thought just occurred to him. He pushed his hands into the pockets of his jeans, looking down at her with a faint frown drawing his eyebrows together.

"No. Does it matter?"

"How are you going to get to work?"

"The buses are quite good," she offered. She crossed her fingers behind her back in a childish gesture, hoping she wasn't about to lose her first job before she'd even had a chance to start.

"I don't like the idea of you being stuck at the house without a car. What if there was some emergency with Becky?"

Mandy felt her heart sink. She'd just gotten used to the idea of having a job and now it might be slipping away from her.

"I've got a compact in the garage that I almost never use," Rafferty said slowly. "You can use that."

Something in his tone of voice made her wonder if he hadn't been hoping that her lack of transportation would be a good reason to change his mind about hiring her. She knew he must still have some doubts. She wished he didn't ever have to find out how well-founded his doubts were.

Mandy's smile was tentative—she hoped, reassuring. "Thank you, Dr. Traherne. I'll be very careful with it."

Rafferty's smile was slow, but quite wide enough to banish the doubt in his eyes. "Since we're going to be seeing a lot of each other, maybe you'd better call me Rafferty."

UNDRESSING FOR BED later that night, Mandy considered the idea of seeing a lot of Rafferty Traherne. The thought held more appeal than she wanted to admit. She didn't need the complication of being attracted to her employer. She just wanted to do a good job and prove, to herself more than anyone else, that she didn't need to be wrapped in cotton to survive.

She slipped the dress onto a hanger, frowning at the creases the wire put in the shoulders. She missed the padded hangers that filled her closet at home. In fact, there were a lot of things she missed about her old home. But they were minor compared to the freedom she'd gained.

It was a pity she couldn't make her family understand why she'd had to take such a drastic step. She could almost hear her mother's voice: if she wanted to work, why did she have to leave home to do it? Her mother could have found her a position on a committee with one of her many charities. There would have been someone there to drive her to her appointments and she could have stayed at home with people who loved her, people who could take care of her.

Mandy slid her arms into a pale pink silk robe, knotting the belt around her narrow waist. The point was, she didn't want people to take care of her. She was twenty-four years old. It was time she found out whether she could take care of herself.

Barefoot, she padded into the tiny kitchen and tugged open the refrigerator door. She hadn't done too badly so far, she thought, frowning at the sparsely filled shelves. Pulling out a bottle of orange juice, she considered her accomplishments: she'd gotten herself across half a continent, maybe not the accomplishment it would have been a hundred years ago but not bad for a first effort; she'd found an apartment and managed to keep from starving to death; and, finally, she'd gotten herself a job.

She grinned, lifting her glass in a toast to herself. It was too bad Gram wasn't here to see it, she thought, her smile fading. But if Gram hadn't died, Mandy would never have left Pennsylvania. Her maternal grandmother had been the one person in her life who hadn't smothered her with concern. Gram had been the only one who'd encouraged her to reach for her dreams.

Mandy blinked back tears. Her grandmother had been her best friend, the one member of the family who understood Mandy's frustration, her reluctance to hurt her parents warring with her need to stand on her own two feet.

As far back as she could remember, her parents had been cautioning her not to tire herself, not to try to do too much. She understood their concern and schooled herself to be patient. After all, her mother had had three miscarriages before Mandy was conceived. Then, she'd spent eight months in bed in order to ensure that this pregnancy would go to term.

Mandy had never doubted that she was loved and wanted. Since the doctors had advised her parents that another pregnancy would be unwise, they'd known from the start that she would be their only child. If they'd been a little over-protective, Mandy thought, it was understandable.

But all the care in the world couldn't prevent their precious little girl from developing rheumatic fever when she was six. And the fact that no one had realized how sick she was in time to prevent damage to her heart had only added to their guilt. After that, they'd all but drowned her in concern and care. Everything a child could possibly want was hers, as long as it didn't involve running or jumping or getting too excited.

If it hadn't been for a combination of stubborn independence on her part and Gram's common sense, Mandy would very likely have ended up becoming a thoroughly spoiled brat. But as determined as her parents had been to see that she wanted for nothing, Gram had been equally determined that her only grandchild grow into a well-rounded adult. It was Gram who'd introduced Mandy to the world of books, Gram who'd taught her never to view herself as limited in any way.

When Mandy turned sixteen, Gram had convinced her parents to buy her a car, and freedom had been within reach. But it had been abruptly cut short by a toddler who ran out into the street. Veering to avoid the child, a truck cut across the center divider and smashed into Mandy's car.

When she regained consciousness, the doctors had told her that she was very fortunate to be alive. They'd said it so emphatically that she'd known more was coming. There was. There had been some damage to her spine. It was possible she'd never walk again, certainly not without a walker.

Her mother had cried and her father had had that pinched look around his mouth that said he wished he could cry, too. Mandy had been numb, hardly absorbing the blow that had just been dealt her. It had been Gram, leaning on her cane in the background, who'd blown the gloom away.

"Stuff and nonsense," she'd said briskly. "Stop your sniveling, Pamela. Howard, get that look off your face." Having shocked her daughter and son-in-law into silence, she'd turned her attention to her granddaughter. "Don't you pay any attention to what the doctors say, Amanda Leigh."

The doctor had made a protesting sound and been promptly ignored. "You'll be dancing the Watusi again by Christmas, mark my words," Gram had told Mandy, her faded eyes fierce with determination. "No granddaughter of mine is going to give up without a fight."

And fight she had. Endless hours of physical therapy had filled her days with pain rewarded by an occasional triumph. Mandy didn't have any idea what the Watusi looked like and she certainly didn't dance it by that first Christmas after the accident. But by the next Christmas she was walking without a cane. Now the only trace of the accident was a slight limp when she got overly tired.

Mandy shook her head, putting the memories behind her. But all that was in the past now. She'd left home specifically because she wanted to get away from people who knew about the accident, who knew about her slightly quirky heart.

Rafferty Traherne saw her as a perfectly normal young woman. He trusted her to take care of his home and his daughter. And she was going to live up to that trust. Becky seemed to be a rather special little girl. And Rafferty? She frowned. Maybe it would be best not to think about her new employer in any personal way. Chances were, she wouldn't be seeing all that much of him anyway.

"I LIKE MANDY, Daddy." Becky dealt her sandy hair a glancing blow with the brush before setting it down. "I'm glad she's going to be our housekeeper."

"You are, huh?" Rafferty picked up the discarded hairbrush and sank onto the side of the bed. "Come here, urchin." He snagged her arm, drawing her to stand between his knees. "If we don't get some of these tangles out of your hair, we're going to have to shave your head in the morning."

Becky giggled, not in the least disturbed by the idea of being bald. Rafferty smiled, working the brush through the mop of baby-fine hair. These were the times he enjoyed the most, these quiet moments with his daughter. His sister Claire had told him to enjoy them while they lasted. Once children become teenagers, the quiet moments would disappear, swallowed by a barrage of loud music and a sort of sullen silence all children seemed to learn automatically at the onset of puberty.

Rafferty liked to think that, even in the midst of rampaging hormones, he and Becky would manage to keep open one or two lines of communication. But there were at least a couple of years before he had to start worrying about that. For now, she was still his little girl, even if at times she did seem almost as old as he was.

The brush slid through her hair without snagging in the smallest tangle. He dropped it on the bed and stood up, scooping her over his shoulder on the way up. She laughed as he dumped her into a heap in the middle of the bed. Her laughter was surely the sweetest sound in the world.

Her hair was already flying in a hundred different directions. By morning, it would need careful brushing again. Wearing a pair of pink-and-white striped pajamas, her face flushed with laughter, she looked like an advertisement for the joys of childhood. Feeling his chest tighten with emotion, Rafferty bent to drop a kiss on her forehead.

"I love you, urchin."

"I love you, too, Daddy."

She scooted under the covers, lying still while he tucked them carefully around her. She'd kick them off five minutes after he left the room. He knew it. She knew it. But it was a small ritual they'd developed. Sometimes he felt as if she was just indulging his need to fuss over her a little. And sometimes he thought maybe she liked the extra bit of fussing because she'd had so little of it when she was smaller.

"Do you ever think about Mama?"

Rafferty's fingers froze on the light switch. Where had that come from? His eyes slid to his daughter as his hand dropped from the switch. She rarely mentioned her mother, though she knew he was always open to anything she wanted to talk about.

"I think about her sometimes," he said slowly.

"Me, too." She plucked at the top of the blanket, her eyes on the aimless movement. "I miss her sometimes."

"That's only natural."

"But sometimes I don't miss her." Her eyes slanted up to his and then away. "I like living here with you, in a real house. Not moving all the time. Does that mean I'm not sorry she's dead?"

"Of course not." Rafferty sat down on the edge of the bed, groping for the words to reassure her. "Loving someone doesn't mean you have to like everything they do. Just because you like being here doesn't mean you didn't love your mom or that you're not sorry she's gone. I know you loved her very much. And she loved you, too."

Becky nodded, her eyes still on her hand tugging at the blanket. "You know, when I first saw Mandy, she reminded me of Mama."

Rafferty remembered how his first impression of Mandy had been of fragility, the same fine-boned beauty his wife had possessed.

"Did she" was all he said.

"But then we talked a little and she wasn't at all like Mama."

"Did you want her to be?" he questioned carefully.

There was a brief pause and then Becky shook her head. "No. Mandy talked to me as if I were a grown-up. I liked her."

"Well, then I guess it's a good thing I hired her, isn't it?"

"Yeah. I'm glad." She yawned. "I liked her."

"Good." He bent to kiss her. She smelled of baby powder and toothpaste and crayons, a unique combination that seemed to be hers alone. He hesitated in the doorway. With the lamp off, she was little more than a lump under the covers. "Good night, Becky."

"Good night, Daddy." The words were already slurred with sleep.

He pulled the door shut. When she'd first come to live with him, she'd had to have the door open and, on more than one occasion, she'd crept across the hall and slipped into his bed. It had taken a while but now she was comfortable with the door shut.

Rafferty wandered downstairs. Going into his study, he sank into the big leather chair that sat in front of the fireplace. In a few weeks it would be cool enough in the evenings to start having a fire again. First, the weather would chill and then, if they were lucky, there'd be a stretch of warm weather. Indian summer, surely the most beautiful time of the year.

He'd take Becky up into the mountains again. The sight of the aspens turning the mountainsides to pure gold was an incredible experience. It was one of the things he'd thought about during the years after Maryanne had taken Becky away. He hadn't made it into the mountains once during that time. A sort of silly promise to himself—that he wouldn't see the quaking aspens until he could see them with his daughter.

It had been worth the wait. Seeing the shivering gold veil through Becky's eyes had helped wipe away the years they'd been apart.

Leaning his head back, he stared into the empty fireplace. It had been three years since he'd gotten his daughter back. Three years of being a father. Three wonderful years. But nothing could ever erase the heartache of the years when he hadn't seen her, hadn't even known if she was alive.

His hand clenched on the arm of the chair. He'd told himself time and again that he should forgive Maryanne, that she'd been young and foolish, hardly more than a child herself, at least mentally. She hadn't meant to hurt him.

He suspected she'd even regretted having run away, tak-

ing their child with her. And in the end, her foolishness
had cost her her life. A blow to the head—whether delib-
erate or accidental the coroner couldn't be sure—and sweet,
foolish Maryanne was dead.

He should, he supposed, have spent more time grieving
for her. He'd been sorry. Not even in his most intense moments of rage had he wished her dead. But his concern had
been for Becky, for the childhood she'd lost. His pain had
been for how quickly she'd had to grow up, trying to shoulder the responsibilities her mother hadn't been capable of
coping with. His grief had been for the years the two of
them had lost.

She'd been a toddler when Maryanne had taken her
away. When he found her again, she was an unnaturally
self-possessed little girl. Six and a half going on thirty-six,
it had seemed.

Amanda Bradley definitely bore a certain physical resemblance to Maryanne. Was it wishful thinking on his part
that put a strength in her face that Becky's mother had
never possessed?

He wasn't quite sure what it was that had made him hire
her. Certainly there'd been others who were more qualified,
who had references, who hadn't lied about their ages. But
Becky hadn't responded to any of them. *He* hadn't responded to any of them.

Maybe she could teach his daughter how to be more of
a child. And if she could do that, then Ms. Amanda Bradley
would be worth any salary he paid her. If she could cook
and clean, too, he'd consider it a bonus.

The truth was, anybody could clean a house. It took
someone special to make a little girl laugh. He was hoping
Mandy might be that special someone.

Purely for Becky's sake, of course.

Chapter Three

Mandy woke for her first day at her first job filled with confidence. The confidence was only slightly marred by the fact that she was so nervous she felt a little sick to her stomach.

While getting dressed, she gave herself a pep talk. There was absolutely nothing to be nervous about. She was perfectly capable of cleaning a house and looking after a child.

She was equally certain her case of nerves had nothing to do with the fact that Rafferty had said he'd be staying home for the first few days after she started work. He said he had paperwork to do and that he wanted to be available if she had any questions. No doubt he also wanted to keep an eye on his new housekeeper. A perfectly understandable precaution, she thought, after all, she was a stranger.

She didn't mind if he wanted to observe her, she told her reflection in the mirror. That was just an added challenge. She'd prove to him that he'd made the right choice when he'd hired her. She might not have done any housekeeping but she didn't doubt that she'd get the hang of it fairly quickly—how hard could it be? She would have preferred some time to make mistakes without Rafferty there to witness them but his presence simply meant that she couldn't make any mistakes.

A challenge, she told the white-faced woman in the mirror firmly.

She was so worried about being late that she took an earlier bus, with the result that she had nearly forty minutes to kill before it was time to walk the few blocks to the Traherne house. Forty minutes to ponder all the mistakes she could make.

By the time she arrived on the doorstep, she was so keyed up she wouldn't have been surprised if, in answer to her knock, Rafferty slipped a note under the door telling her she was fired.

He did no such thing, of course.

"Good morning."

"Good morning." Mandy managed what she hoped would pass for a confident smile. There was a knot in her stomach and her palms felt clammy. *What on earth had made me think I was qualified for a job like this?*

"Becky's still in bed. She only goes to school half days this week. She'll probably get up at around ten or so."

He stepped back as he spoke and Mandy entered the hall. The air felt warm against her cold face. The early morning had carried more than a hint of winter's chill.

"It's just as well she's not up yet," Rafferty continued as he shut the door. "It'll give me a chance to show you around the house, give you an idea of where everything is. We didn't discuss the job in as much detail as we could have last night. I'm sure you've got a lot of questions."

"Yes, of course," she mumbled, hoping he wouldn't ask her what they were. She tugged off her gloves, pushing them into her coat pocket.

"Here, let me take your coat." Mandy was already shrugging out of the garment when he spoke. She turned to smile her thanks at the same moment he reached to grasp the shoulder of the coat. Instead of a handful of pale cashmere, he found silky dark hair. The tips of his fingers brushed against the nape of her neck.

For an instant, neither of them moved.

Mandy told herself it was only the warm air against her cold skin that had made her feel flushed and tingly.

Rafferty told himself that it was just his imagination that

had made him think there was a jolt of awareness in the accidental touch.

THERE WASN'T TIME to think about the incident—if, indeed, it had been an incident. The coat safely hung in the hall closet, Rafferty led Mandy off on a tour of the house. She concentrated on his words, trying to ignore the width of his shoulders, the strength of those broad hands.

The house was large, though considerably smaller than the home she'd grown up in. Four bedrooms and three baths upstairs. One of the spare bedrooms was used as a guest room but the other had been converted into a home gym. Looking at the weight machine, Mandy was startled when her imagination presented her with a vivid image of Rafferty—muscles bulging—working out.

She forced the image away, reminding herself that he was her employer, nothing more. And that was exactly the way she wanted it to stay. She was relieved when they left the intimacy of the second floor for the more public rooms below.

Downstairs, there was a half bath, living room, formal dining room—almost never used, he told her—Rafferty's study, a large kitchen and a utility room.

Mandy eyed the kitchen as if she were a wrestler sizing up the enemy, which was pretty much how she felt. Housekeeping didn't worry her, but cooking was something else entirely. There was something very mysterious about throwing diverse elements into a pot and coming up with something appetizing.

Of course, she hadn't claimed to be a gourmet cook, so he could hardly expect Julia Child. But he no doubt expected someone who had a little more experience than she did. Unless he was willing to live exclusively on hot cocoa and cinnamon toast, she was going to have to expand her repertoire.

"I'll take care of my own breakfast since I'm a disgustingly early riser," he was saying. "Becky usually just has cereal, which she can manage to get for herself. But when it comes to actually cooking anything, you take your life in your hands if you allow her near the stove."

"Why?" Mandy's eyes were startled when she looked at him. Surely Becky was old enough to start learning how to cook.

Rafferty smiled. "It has nothing to do with her age. She's careful enough in the kitchen." He paused, his smile widening. Glancing over his shoulder to make sure the subject of the discussion hadn't arrived unexpectedly, he leaned toward Mandy.

"It's not *her* safety you have to worry about," he said in a confidential tone. "It's ours."

Mandy's eyes widened as possibilities flitted through her imagination. Was Becky a pyromaniac, never to be allowed near a flame, even if it was on a gas stove?

"Why?" she asked, lowering her voice to match his.

"She's a dreadful cook," he told her solemnly.

"Dreadful cook?" It took Mandy a moment to shift gears.

"Absolutely awful," he confirmed, his eyes lit with humor. "And the worst part is, she doesn't know it. Luckily for the state of my digestion, she doesn't particularly like to cook."

"She's that bad?" Mandy questioned, wondering if she should just quit right now or wait until he fired her after tasting her cooking.

"Worse." He leaned back against the counter, tucking his hands into the pockets of his jeans. "She believes that all doughs should be kneaded thoroughly and vigorously, including piecrusts and biscuits. All food should be *very* well-cooked, either boiled to death or roasted at high temperatures until it approximates the texture of shoe leather."

"Oh." Mandy hoped her smile didn't look as weak as it felt. Apparently you weren't supposed to knead piecrust and biscuits. She filed away that bit of information. She also dismissed any idea she might have had about getting Becky to help her learn to cook. She was obviously on her own in that department.

"Anyway, breakfast pretty much takes care of itself," Rafferty continued, wondering what he'd said to make his new housekeeper look so bleak. "Sandwiches and soup is fine for lunch. I'll join you if I'm home. But I generally don't come home for lunch when I'm at the office.

"Dinner is a little less settled, but I do try to keep regular hours. I think it's important for Becky. So I'm usually home around six o'clock and you can leave then. But as I told you yesterday, I really need someone whose hours are flexible enough to mesh with mine. If I get caught up in an emergency or have to assist one of the other doctors, I could be late. Obviously there's no way to give you any warning on nights like those. I'd need you to be able to stay here and make dinner for Becky."

"I understand. There's no problem. My hours are quite flexible." Her smile took her face from just pretty to downright lovely.

Of course, he noticed it in a purely academic way, Rafferty told himself. He'd lectured himself firmly on the need to keep his relationship with his new housekeeper strictly business. The important thing here was that Becky and the house were taken care of. He certainly wasn't going to do anything to jeopardize that.

If that meant not noticing that she had the softest, most beautiful mouth he'd ever seen or that her hair was like dark silk, made for a man to run his hands through, then he'd simply not notice those things.

He realized suddenly that he'd been staring and he looked away, clearing his throat. "Yes, well, I don't expect you to rearrange your life completely. If I have an emergency on a night when you have other plans, you can take Becky to my sister's house or the McCallister's. They're friends of ours and Becky's always welcome there."

"I don't think that will be necessary."

"You could have a date. Or something," he added hastily, not wanting it to sound as if he was probing into the state of her love life. Again, that fleeting smile that made him—most regrettably—want to kiss her.

"It won't be a problem, Dr. Traherne."

He wondered how she could be so sure. A woman as pretty as she was must surely go out often. If he'd met her under other circumstances, he might have asked her to dinner himself, a dinner that didn't include a talkative ten-year-old. But that was out of the question now.

Strictly business, he reminded himself. In fact, last names were a good idea. Dr. Traherne and Ms. Bradley sounded properly formal.

"Rafferty," he told her, pushing away from the counter. "Call me Rafferty. Dr. Traherne reminds me of the office."

"Rafferty," she agreed, with a smile. "What time do you want lunch?"

"One o'clock or so." He pulled his hands out of his pockets and glanced at his watch. A plain watch on a wide leather band, Mandy noticed. The wrist it encircled was broad, strong. Just like the rest of him. She couldn't help but notice his strength. It was pretty hard to ignore, really. It certainly didn't mean that she was attracted to him or anything that foolish.

"A present from Becky," he said, catching the direction of her look. Mandy shook off the inappropriate thoughts that were threatening to creep into her head. This was her employer. That's all he was.

"You two seem quite close," Mandy said. Becky was a safe enough topic. Her confidence had begun to return as he showed her around the house. There was nothing too intimidating about taking care of a home like this. She felt good about this job again. Capable.

"We are." Rafferty's simple statement said more than any elaborate speech. "Actually I don't know if I was really clear on that point when I hired you but the house-keeping and the cooking are all secondary to taking care of Becky."

"I understand you want me to keep an eye on her," Mandy assured him. Really, this job was going to be a piece of cake.

"Becky is actually pretty self-sufficient," Rafferty said.

"She'd probably do just fine being left on her own. Of course, I feel better knowing there's an adult on hand. But mainly I want you to offer her a little...companionship, I guess is the word. She spends a lot of time alone. I was hoping maybe you could encourage her to play more, to... Oh, I don't know."

He frowned, groping for the right words to describe what he meant. "To do girl stuff, I guess."

"Girl stuff?" Mandy felt her new confidence quiver uneasily.

"You know, dolls or trains or whatever little girls do these days. Take her shopping. Maybe you can talk her into a dress or two. Have fun with her." He waved one hand in a vague gesture that encompassed a whole range of things he couldn't find the words for.

"You want someone who can play with her," Mandy said, her expression unreadable.

"Not exactly..." he started to deny and then stopped. "Yeah, I suppose that's what I've got in mind," he admitted sheepishly. "I don't expect you to play dolls with her exactly but she seems too adult sometimes. I worry that maybe she's missing out on being a child."

"Some children are just more serious, you know."

"I know. And that's okay. It's just that she's growing up so fast. I want her to enjoy what's left of her childhood."

"I'll try," Mandy said slowly.

There was a short silence, which Rafferty broke. Glancing at his watch again, he moved toward the door. "Well, I've got paperwork to finish. I'll be in the study if you need me for anything. Don't hesitate to ask."

"I won't." Mandy uttered the lie without a blink, her smile fading as he left the room. She didn't dare ask him for help because she didn't know enough about being a housekeeper to know what was a reasonable question and what might give away her total ignorance.

Left alone in her new domain, she sank onto one of the

chairs flanking the oak table that dominated one end of the room. Her confidence lay in ruins around her.

Teach Becky to be a child again. It sounded so simple when he'd said it. He couldn't know that he was asking her to do something impossible. She'd never been a child herself. How was she supposed to help Becky rediscover the joys of something she herself had never experienced?

She wondered, not for the first time, if she'd bitten off more than she could chew. All of this was new. Taking care of a house, cooking, watching over a child. Any one of these responsibilities would have been a challenge but she was tackling all three at once. For a moment, the thought was overwhelming.

None of the housework seemed urgent. And she couldn't worry about Becky at the moment. Later, she could consider the irony in being hired to help Becky enjoy her childhood; her own childhood had been spent listening to her parents tell her to be careful, to slow down, not to run so fast. She'd never been allowed to forget her damaged heart. She'd found most of her adventures between the covers of books.

When it seems as though you're about to drown in things to do, just start off with the first step. The rest will follow easier than you think. Gram's words made Mandy straighten her spine.

Drawing in a deep breath, she considered her first step. Figuring out where things were and deciding what to fix for lunch. Sandwiches and soup, he'd said. The sandwiches were easy enough but he was sure to expect something more than the canned soup she'd been living on.

Frowning, she tried to remember what Rosie generally served for lunch. Instinct told her that lobster bisque wouldn't be right. Something more all-American, she thought. Something hearty. She didn't know much about kids but she guessed that Becky would have a pretty healthy appetite. And a man the size of Rafferty would surely need a fair amount of fuel.

She didn't think she'd ever seen a man as solid as her

new employer. He wasn't enormously tall—six foot or so. But he was solidly built. There was something about him that inspired confidence, that made her feel as if she could put herself in his hands and know that she'd be safe. Maybe it was the prematurely gray hair. Or the steadiness in those eyes.

Mandy shook her head and stood up. She didn't have time to be sitting here daydreaming about her employer. And that's all he was—all she wanted him to be. She wasn't interested in anything more personal. She was just here to do her job, nothing more, nothing less.

And part of her job was figuring out what to make for lunch. She crossed the room to the tote bag she'd brought with her. Rafferty had set it inside the kitchen door before they started their tour of the house. Setting it on the table, she pulled out the apron she'd bought the day before. It was plain white and very businesslike.

Slipping it on over her head, she belted it around the simple gray dress she'd chosen as being appropriate attire for a housekeeper. Rosie always wore a black dress with a neat white apron over it. But Mandy didn't own any black dresses. Besides, she had the feeling that Rafferty might find such clothing more peculiar than businesslike. After all, this was Denver, not Philadelphia. In the few weeks she'd spent here, she'd learned that Westerners were quite a bit more casual than she was used to.

Concealed at the bottom of the tote bag was the book she hoped would be her salvation. Glancing over her shoulder to make sure she was still alone, Mandy eased the treasure out of its hiding place. The title said it all: *Cooking for the Culinary Illiterate—A Kitchen Guide for the Inept, the Idiot and the Inexperienced.* She didn't really care which category she belonged in as long as the authors got her through her first lunch. Opening the book as if it were made of gold, she turned to the section on soups.

Half an hour later, she was reasonably satisfied that lunch was under control. There was some hamburger meat in the refrigerator and plenty of vegetables. A hearty meatball-vegetable soup was just the thing, she told herself briskly.

"What smells so good?"

Mandy started, slamming the cookbook shut and spinning around as guiltily as if she'd been caught stealing the silver. Lucky for her, Becky didn't notice her reaction since the little girl's attention was on the stove. "Soup, I hope," Mandy answered, sliding the cookbook out of sight behind a canister.

"Smells good." Becky pushed back her hair, turning those disconcertingly adult eyes in Mandy's direction. "You look like a housekeeper in a movie."

"Do I?" Mandy fingered the apron, which was already marked with stains from her morning's efforts. "Do you think I'm overdressed?"

Becky eyed her considering. "Well, you look nice and everything. But I wanted to show you my tree house and I don't think you're going to be comfortable climbing a tree in those shoes."

Mandy had never climbed a tree in her life but she didn't doubt that Becky was right. Rafferty had said that Becky was the most important thing and tree climbing definitely fit into the category of childish pleasures. He couldn't expect her to dress like a housekeeper and play like a ten-year-old.

"If the tree house will hold until tomorrow, I'll wear something more suited for tree climbing, okay?"

"Sure."

To Mandy's relief, Rafferty had been absolutely correct regarding his daughter's choice of breakfast. She didn't seem to expect any help as she got herself a bowl of cereal and settled down at the table.

"How come you're doing those in the sink?" Becky asked between bites of cereal. "Daddy always puts everything in the dishwasher. He says anything that can't go into a dishwasher is uncivilized."

Mandy looked up from the knife she'd been rinsing. Her

gaze skittered over the intimidatingly blank front panel of the dishwasher before settling on Becky.

"I...uh...I like doing dishes by hand," she offered finally. She could hardly admit that she had no idea how to run the dishwasher. You didn't need experience to run a sink full of water and add a little soap to it. Especially since the bottle was clearly marked Dishwashing Liquid.

Becky shrugged, as if allowing Mandy her idiosyncrasies. Mandy rinsed the last dish and set it on a towel on the counter before drying her hands. Slipping off her apron, she sat down across from Becky.

It was odd how Becky reminded her of herself at the same age. There was no real physical resemblance. Becky's sturdy body and square jaw were unlike the rather waiflike figure she'd been at ten. She wasn't exactly a pretty child but there was something appealing in the direct way her eyes met yours—gray eyes identical to her father's. That square jaw was a great deal like her father's, too. The same strength and determination, the same straightforward way of looking at a person.

"I'm glad you decided to work for Daddy and me," Becky told her. "I didn't much like any of the others."

"So I'm the best of a bad batch, huh?"

Becky grinned, revealing an endearing gap between her front teeth. "Kind of. But I think I'd have liked you even if the others hadn't been so drippy."

"Thank you." Mandy accepted the compliment with the ironic solemnity it deserved.

"That's one of the things I liked best," Becky said.

"What?"

"You smile with your eyes. Most of those others smiled with their mouths but their eyes didn't change. You could see that they were hoping I wasn't going to be around very much 'cause they didn't really like kids."

She finished her cereal, pushing the bowl away and folding her arms on the table in front of her. She fixed her serious gray eyes on Mandy. "Do you like kids?"

"Well, I guess I don't really know whether I do or not,"

Mandy said, sensing that a truthful answer would serve better than anything glib. "I haven't really spent much time around them, to tell you the truth. I always assumed that children were a lot like adults—you like some of them and you don't like others."

Becky considered that a moment before nodding. "That's true. After all, you can't like everybody. Like Lisa Sue Kilterman, for example. She was in my class last year. Nobody liked her. Even somebody who likes kids couldn't like her."

"Well, you can like all of the people some of the time and some of the people all of the time but you can't like all of the people all of the time," Mandy offered solemnly.

Becky's eyes met hers for a moment before she started to giggle. "You're very silly."

"Thank you," Mandy said, pleased.

WHEN SHE THOUGHT about it later, Mandy would wonder a little at how comfortable she'd been with Becky from the start. As if they'd known each other forever.

She'd been speaking no more than the truth when she'd said that she'd had little experience with children. Even when she was a child herself, her delicate health had kept her from building any strong ties to other children her age. She couldn't run and play the way they could. She didn't know how to jump rope or ride bikes or play tetherball.

She'd always been set apart, never a part of the usual activities.

Once she reached adulthood, she had almost no contact with children. Her parents' friends had children who were already grown up and had gone off to college or had started homes of their own.

But that lack of experience stood her in good stead with Becky. Mandy didn't know how to talk down to a child. She didn't realize that she wasn't supposed to treat Becky as her equal. She reacted to Becky just as she would have reacted to an adult, listening to what she had to say and responding in an intelligent fashion.

By lunchtime, the two of them had formed the beginning of a solid friendship. Though the tree house expedition had to be delayed as a result of inadequate attire, there was still a wealth of things to be seen. Rafferty had shown Mandy around the house but he'd missed some of the more important things.

Things like Becky's awe-inspiring collection of My Little Pony figures. She seemed rather shocked to learn that Mandy had never heard of My Little Pony, and for a moment, Mandy was afraid that her ignorance might have done her some irreparable harm in Becky's eyes. But Becky seemed to think that she was more to be pitied than censured.

When the time came for Mandy to go back down and finish her lunch preparations, Becky came downstairs with her. She opened a can of tomatoes while Mandy got the rest of the ingredients together. As it turned out, her presence was invaluable. While Mandy was searching for a knife to peel the potatoes, Becky got out the potato peeler and set to work with deft strokes.

Despite the fact that she felt Becky would probably have had an easier time preparing lunch than she had, Mandy's confidence had taken another swing upward. She and Becky had established the beginnings of a friendship, she'd learned her way around the house and the soup smelled positively delicious. She'd been right to take on this job.

The time and anxiety she'd spent on the soup was well-rewarded when she watched Rafferty eat—not one—but two bowlfuls. Obviously there really wasn't all that much to cooking a meal. If she just followed the instructions, she'd do all right. It took something of an effort to keep a smug smile from her face.

Seeing what a good, healthy meal she'd prepared must surely have allayed some of the anxiety Rafferty had felt about her abilities as a housekeeper.

TO TELL THE TRUTH, Rafferty barely tasted the soup until he was most of the way through the first bowl. He could have been eating gruel for all the attention he paid it. It had taken considerable willpower for him to remain in his study all morning, giving his daughter and the new housekeeper a chance to get acquainted.

He'd hired Amanda Bradley more or less on impulse, basing the decision on Becky's reaction to her rather than on her resumé. He'd had two days to debate the wisdom of that decision—two days to consider the responsibility he was handing Mandy.

When he'd heard Becky come downstairs, he'd had the urge to run out and snatch her up. How could he possibly have considered hiring a stranger to look after his only child?

But a housekeeper was a necessity. No matter how self-sufficient Becky was, he wasn't comfortable leaving her alone in the house. Becky had agreed, more to give him peace of mind than anything else. It had been one of the moments in their relationship when he'd had doubts about which one of them was the parent.

And if they were going to have a housekeeper, then he had to give Becky time to get to know the one he'd hired. So, he'd sat in his study, ignoring the stack of paperwork in front of him, his ears straining to hear every move the two of them made, trying to convince himself that he hadn't made an enormous mistake.

All his rationalizing hadn't reassured him; halfway through a bowl of soup, however, Rafferty could feel the tension draining out of him. Mandy didn't say much but Becky made up for her silence. Every other sentence started with "Mandy said" or "Mandy and I." It was obvious that Becky was happy with her. And since that was Rafferty's main concern, he relaxed in his chair and allowed himself to really taste the soup.

It finally dawned on him that it couldn't have come out of a can. It was too delicious. Helping himself to another serving, he wondered if maybe he'd misjudged Mandy's experience.

"This is wonderful, Mandy."

Mandy preened just a little as he returned to the table. Today soup. Tomorrow the sky was the limit. It had been foolish to worry about silly things like cooking and housekeeping. They were just as simple as she'd always suspected.

"It was no trouble," she said modestly.

"Well, it's great." Rafferty took another spoonful before lifting his eyes to her. "But you know, we usually just open a can of Campbell's."

Mandy felt as if she'd been hit by a truck. All that hard work and worry... She'd been sure Rafferty expected home-cooked meals. After all, Rosie would certainly never have served anything canned. But then Rosie hadn't been a single father, she reminded herself. If she'd thought about it, she would have realized that it was unlikely that Rafferty made soup from scratch every day.

Well, better that she do too much than too little, she told herself briskly. She'd rather he thought her overly conscientious than not conscientious enough.

Neither adult spoke much during lunch. Both were thinking about their first morning's interaction and deciding that they were quite pleased with it so far.

Mandy had the chance she needed to prove that she was quite capable of managing her own life.

Rafferty had the housekeeper he needed to look after his home and his daughter.

It was altogether a rather satisfactory arrangement.

They might not have felt quite so comfortable if either of them had known Becky's thoughts. Becky was also quite pleased with the way the morning had gone but she had her own reasons.

Becky knew her father was worried about how she and Mandy would get along. She could have just told him that she and Mandy were already becoming friends. But she knew that he, like most adults, rarely believed a simple statement. You had to repeat things several times to get through to them.

She and her best friend Amy Martin thought it might be

something to do with getting old—something went wrong in the connection between the ears and the brain and things just didn't register with adults.

So she did her best to make it real clear that she liked Mandy. She could practically see her father relaxing. He thought he was concealing his feelings but it was all there in that anxious look in his eyes. But now, she'd convinced him that Mandy was the greatest housekeeper ever. He and Mandy were even talking a little.

Becky's eyes flitted back and forth between the two adults. It was just perfect. She'd thought from the moment she saw Mandy that she'd be perfect for her dad. Now that she'd gotten a chance to know her a little better, she was sure of it.

She'd decided some time ago that he should marry again. He wouldn't be lonely anymore and she wouldn't mind having a stepmother, as long as she was nice. Besides, she rather liked the idea of having a baby sister. She'd even be willing to settle for a baby brother.

Eyeing her father and Mandy, she felt a glow of accomplishment. Phase one was a success. With a little help from her, she was sure it wouldn't take them too long to figure out that they were meant for each other.

Chapter Four

Her first day on the job had gone so well, Mandy's confidence took a precipitous bounce upward. She'd known all along that she could handle this job. She'd been foolish to doubt herself. She'd proven she could master the stove, if not yet the dishwasher and she'd made a good start on a friendship with Becky.

What could go wrong now?

It was a foolish question.

THE SECOND DAY ON THE JOB, she tripped over her own confidence and was reminded that things were often not quite as simple as they seemed.

Her first attempt at cooking had gone so well that she decided she was ready to move on to greater challenges. Becky was spending the morning with one of her friends. Rafferty had shut himself away in the study. And Mandy had the big kitchen to herself.

The weather was cool, hinting at the oncoming winter. The chill in the air made it seem like the perfect day to learn to bake. Nothing too fancy, she cautioned herself. A cake, maybe. Something to show Rafferty what a treasure he'd hired.

The cookbook she'd brought didn't give recipes for cakes or pastries. Its focus was on simple, nutritious meals to keep inept cooks from starving to death. Mandy, however, had already proven that she was hardly inept.

Fortunately—or unfortunately, depending on how you looked at it—there were two cookbooks tucked into the back of a cupboard. She doubted Rafferty even knew they were there.

It didn't take her long to find just the recipe she was looking for—a nice chocolate cake. Nothing too fancy but everyone loved chocolate cake. Wouldn't Becky and Rafferty be surprised when they saw it?

Surprised they were but not in quite the way Mandy had hoped. The recipe hadn't told her to measure the flour into the cup and then level it. On the theory that more is generally better than less, Mandy had scooped the flour out of the canister and added it to the batter in heaping cupfuls. No one had pointed out that there was a difference between baking soda and baking powder and that it was critical to make sure you had the right one. She didn't.

The recipe said to mix the batter until the flour and the liquids were blended. Mandy did so, stirring vigorously until they were extremely well blended. The result looked like a cake but it had roughly the weight and texture of a hockey puck.

Mandy served it after lunch, bringing it to the table with enormous pride. She served Rafferty and Becky first, watching expectantly for their reactions.

Rafferty, aware of Mandy's anxious gaze on him, struggled to keep his eyes from bulging when his teeth encountered an apparently unchewable substance. He reached casually for a glass of water, hoping liquid would help wash the cake down. But it seemed to swell in the presence of water, turning to paste in his mouth.

Mandy was watching him, the expression in her eyes hopeful. She reminded him of a puppy who'd just performed a particularly difficult trick and was hoping for a reward. Manfully he swallowed, forcing the cake down.

He glanced at Becky, a warning in his eyes. But he needn't have worried. Becky knew as well as he did that the cake was important to Mandy. Luckily she'd taken a smaller bite than her father and she managed to get it down with less trouble.

"How is it?" Mandy asked at last, unable to bear the suspense.

"Um," Rafferty mumbled noncommittally. To tell the truth, he wasn't sure his mouth would open.

"It's real...different," Becky offered.

Satisfied, Mandy lifted her own fork to her mouth and bit into the very first cake she'd ever baked. Her eyes widened as the texture registered. Next to assault her taste buds was the strange, acrid taste, reminiscent of burning rubber.

The recipe had said to melt the chocolate over boiling water but because she hadn't understood how to go about doing that, she'd set it directly over the heat. She'd thought it smelled a little odd when she scraped it out of the pan but what did she know about baking chocolate? She now had the strong suspicion it wasn't the only mistake she'd made.

She felt the color rising in her cheeks as she chewed her way through the gluey mass in her mouth. *Pride goes before a fall,* Gram had told her on more than one occasion, making it sound as if she'd invented the saying.

One reasonably good batch of soup did not a baker make.

She raised her eyes slowly to Rafferty's, uncertain of what to expect there. What she saw was profound sympathy.

"It didn't turn out very well," she said with brave understatement.

"It was a nice idea," he said firmly.

"You know, it bounces kinda nice," Becky offered, poking it with her fork.

THE THIRD DAY, Mandy approached her job with more caution. Chastened by the disaster with the cake, she decided to curb any urge she had to try to dazzle her employer with her homemaking skills.

She got up late and barely had time to catch her bus.

There'd been no time for breakfast and by the time she got to work, her stomach was sending up impolite inquiries. Becky was still in bed. Rafferty greeted her and then retreated to his study, leaving Mandy on her own.

A soft-boiled egg and a slice of toast would stave off starvation until lunch. Soft-boiled eggs were one of the few dishes she'd mastered during the weeks since leaving home. She got out an egg and was about to get out a saucepan when the microwave caught her eye.

She'd never used a microwave but she'd watched Becky cook a bowl of cereal yesterday morning. If a ten-year-old could operate it, she ought to be able to. There was no manual in sight and the battery of buttons made her hesitate for a moment but she squared her shoulders and set the egg on a plastic tray.

Setting the tray in the middle of the microwave, Mandy shut the door. A three-minute egg wouldn't take more than thirty seconds or so in a microwave, she was sure. Squinting at the buttons, she set it for high at thirty seconds and crossed her fingers.

It wasn't until she'd punched the button to start it that she realized she hadn't started the toast. Hurrying to the toaster, she popped the slice of bread down. She'd just picked up a plate and silverware when a muffled explosion sounded from the direction of the microwave.

With a startled shriek, she dropped the plate and silverware. A quick glance showed her that the microwave was still intact. Darting over to it, she pulled open the door. A small moan was all that escaped her. Apparently one did not cook eggs in a microwave. The egg had exploded quite violently, coating the inside of the oven with flecks of yolk and bits of shell.

"Something wrong?"

Mandy spun around, staring at Rafferty with wide eyes. She'd instinctively blocked his view of the oven with her body. How could she possibly tell him about this new disaster? After yesterday's cake, this would surely confirm that she didn't know her way around a kitchen.

"No. Nothing's wrong," she said firmly and untruthfully. She followed his gaze to the plate and silverware lying on the floor. Fortunately the plate hadn't broken.

"I thought I heard you scream," Rafferty said.

"I...ah...had just realized I was about to burn something. That's all." She gave him a bright smile. "Sorry I bothered you."

"No problem," he said slowly. He hesitated a moment before turning to leave. Mandy waited until she was sure he was out of sight before snatching a roll of paper towels off the counter.

All right, she thought. So she'd made some mistakes. There'd be no more.

THE FOURTH DAY on her new job, she was not foolish enough to attempt any more culinary feats or experiment with unfamiliar gadgetry. Instead, she decided it was time to tackle the laundry. Doing laundry had to be simpler than cooking.

She studied the machine carefully and decided that the buttons were straightforward enough. She understood permanent press, which went on one cycle. And everything else must be washed on the other cycle.

She sorted the laundry into neat piles, permanent press in one, everything else in another. Since efficiency was surely the watchword of a great housekeeper, Mandy decided to do everything on the large load setting. It would obviously take much less time to do two large loads than three or four smaller ones.

The first load contained two sets of sheets, four pair of rather large man-size jeans—never worn and in need of washing to soften some of the crispness—assorted items of male underclothing which she tried not to notice and half a dozen much smaller items from Becky's wardrobe, including one gloriously red T-shirt.

Satisfied that the tub was sufficiently full, she added detergent according to the instructions on the box and turned the machine on, confident that she'd successfully mastered yet another aspect of her new job. Today the laundry, to-morrow the dishwasher, she told herself.

Becky wasn't up yet when Mandy started the washer but she was there when it came time to empty it. Standing in the doorway of the utility room, she watched with awe as Mandy pulled out item after item.

The tub had been so full, it was almost impossible for the fabric to move around in the water. The result was sheets so wrinkled, they were crushed down to the size of pillowcases. But that wasn't the big problem. The big problem was that nothing was quite the same color as it had been when it had gone into the washer.

Some things were pale blue, some a light pink. Some items were a combination of the two. Mandy forgot her embarrassment over handling her employer's underwear when she pulled out jockey shorts that had once been white but were now a beautiful pastel pink.

"How come you put the colored stuff in with the whites?" Becky asked. There was no criticism in the question, only curiosity.

"Colored stuff in the whites?" Mandy looked at her. "You mean you're supposed to sort them by color? All the red stuff in one batch, all the green in another?"

"Well, mainly just all the colors in one load, all the whites in another. And you got to be real careful about things like my red T-shirt and Dad's new jeans," she added, coming forward to nudge the items in question with the toe of her sneaker. "They tend to bleed all over everything else, specially if you wash them in warm water."

Mandy didn't have to look at the machine to know that she'd used, not warm, but hot water. It had seemed logical for some reason that the hotter the water, the cleaner everything would get.

"I used hot water," she admitted despairingly.

"Wow!" Becky was impressed by this evidence of the thoroughness with which Mandy had screwed up. She picked up the red T-shirt, holding it up between her hands before breaking into a fit of giggles. The bright red had faded like a flower left to lie under a desert sun. And the size—Mandy closed her eyes but it didn't help. With luck, the shirt might have fit a rather thin infant. Slender as Becky was, she could never have gotten into it.

"It shrunk," Mandy said flatly.

"Yeah. But it'll fit one of my dolls now." Becky wasn't at all disturbed. Mandy only wished she could accept the disaster as calmly. But then, Becky didn't have to worry about her father deciding to fire *her* for incompetence.

"Did everything shrink, do you think?"

"Probably not." Becky frowned down at the damp clothing. "Dad's new jeans maybe. But jeans are s'posed to be tight. I think he'd look great in real tight jeans, don't you?"

Such was Mandy's distraction that she didn't notice the intense look Becky sent her, trying to gauge her reaction to the thought of Rafferty in skintight denim.

"Great," Mandy agreed absently, images of herself standing before a firing squad dancing in her head.

Well, she'd have to face Rafferty and putting it off wasn't going to change things. If she'd thought there was any hope of the dyes migrating to their proper places, she'd have stuffed everything back in the washer and never mentioned the disaster. But that wasn't going to happen.

She wondered how he would look when he sued her for destruction of wardrobe.

Rafferty listened solemnly to her tangled explanation of how the disaster had occurred. It had something to do with a different method of sorting laundry in Philadelphia. It struck him that they probably separated laundry pretty much the same in Pennsylvania as they did in Colorado but he didn't say anything.

He observed the evidence she'd brought, his eyes widening slightly when he was presented with the once-white shorts that were now a lovely shade of pale pink. He tried to imagine going to play racquetball and stripping off his jeans to reveal…that. The image simply wouldn't come into focus.

Still, they were only clothes. Fortunately since he could

afford to replace them, he and Becky weren't likely to be forced to go nude.

He saw Mandy out and then sat staring at the door she'd closed behind her. He felt a vague self-pity. Other people hired housekeepers who kept house. Where had he gone wrong?

She'll improve, he told himself.

But would she improve before she'd caused a citywide catastrophe?

ON THE FIFTH DAY, Mandy came to work determined to make no more mistakes.

This time, she really meant it.

She'd planned to vacuum today. After careful consideration, she decided not to change her plans. Vacuuming looked almost as simple as dusting. It couldn't be as complicated as the washing had turned out to be. Rafferty had mentioned that the switch on the vacuum cleaner was moody and occasionally had to be hit twice before it would go on or off. A minor inconvenience but nothing she couldn't deal with.

Lunch was out of the way, Becky was at school, and Rafferty was in his study. Mandy had been among the gainfully employed for nearly one full workweek and she'd had some successes to offset the perfectly understandable failures. She and Becky were fast becoming friends. Becky was an appealing child, easy to like. Rafferty was— Well, best not to spend too much time thinking about Rafferty, she thought.

Mandy carried the upright vacuum cleaner into the living room and put the plug into a wall socket. One tap of her toe and the machine roared to life. It seemed a good omen that it started on the first try. She pushed the machine forward. The thick fawn carpeting disappeared beneath the vacuum, emerging a moment later clean and fluffed, providing immediate gratification for her labors.

There was a pleasant rhythm to the task. Back and forth. Back and forth. She began to hum under her breath. Really, the housework wasn't too bad. Aside from the laundry, it was turning out to be just about as simple as she'd thought it would be.

Tomorrow was her first day off. She could do a little shopping. Maybe buy some more slacks, which were much more appropriate attire for the job than the dresses she'd planned to wear.

She would call her parents on Sunday. She'd called them every Sunday since she'd left, careful not to tell them where she was but wanting them to know she was all right. She frowned as she navigated the vacuum around the corner of the sofa.

The calls to her parents were emotionally draining. They simply couldn't understand why she'd had to leave home. Hadn't they given her everything she wanted? Hadn't they loved her and cared for her? That, of course, was part of the problem. Not that they'd loved her. But the part about giving her everything she wanted. She needed a chance to earn something on her own. And that they'd cared for her, that part was true, too. But their caring had nearly suffocated her.

Maybe when she told them she had a job, they'd stop worrying quite so much. The thought of her mother's reaction when she heard that her only child was working as a housekeeper made Mandy wince. But the fact that Rafferty was a doctor should reassure them somewhat.

Which brought her thoughts circling back to Rafferty. Funny, how often they did that. She'd never met anyone who radiated such quiet strength, such calm control. She'd liked him from the start but her admiration had grown over the past week. Watching him with Becky, she was impressed by the obvious affection between them.

She'd never doubted that her own father loved her but they'd never shared the kind of easy camaraderie that Becky and Rafferty did. Of course, she couldn't imagine her father sharing that kind of friendship with anyone. He was just too formal, too restrained for that sort of thing.

Mandy had never once seen her father looking anything

less than neatly tailored. She'd be willing to stake her life
on the fact that he didn't own a pair of jeans. On the rare
occasions that he took time off and relaxed, he wore crisp
trousers and custom-made sport shirts. She could remember
being vaguely shocked by the sight of her father's pale
arms beneath the sleeves of his shirts.

Rafferty, on the other hand, seemed to live in jeans.
Becky's comment, only half heard at the time, that he'd
look nice in tight jeans had proven to be true. He looked
very nice indeed. His shirts were as casual as the jeans, soft
cotton, chosen more for comfort than style. She didn't have
to close her eyes to picture the width of his chest, the way
his shoulders seemed to go on forever.

Lulled by the simple rhythm of the vacuuming, Mandy
let her thoughts wander. When the cord hung up on a table
leg, she turned to flip it loose with one hand. At the same
time, her other hand thrust the vacuum forward. She hadn't
realized how close to the front window she'd gotten.

Deep-blue drapes framed the window covered in ivory
sheers that preserved privacy without blocking the sunlight.
She'd never really noticed that the sheers had been hung a
little low, so that the light fabric actually rested on the
carpet. On the forward motion, the vacuum rolled across
the edge of the fabric.

With a gurgle of pleasure, the machine sucked up the
curtain, wrapping it around the spinning brush. Mandy, her
attention jerked back to the task at hand, tried to pull the
machine back. But having gotten hold of such a bounty,
the vacuum had no intention of releasing it. Humming with
pleasure, it continued to suck fabric in, winding it ever
tighter around the brush.

Mandy's toe found the power button and pushed but the
vacuum didn't even hiccup. A second and third frantic jab
with her foot yielded the same results, or lack thereof. The
machine was beginning to sound strained but it hadn't
given up on the curtains yet. A panicked glance upward
showed the curtain rod beginning to move.

With visions of the drapes collapsing around her head,

Mandy grabbed for the power cord and yanked. The cord tightened but nothing happened. She'd apparently wound it around some piece of furniture, and now, instead of pulling the plug from the wall, her tugging was simply tightening the cord around the furniture.

Despairing, she abandoned the cord and stumbled over the vacuum to grab for the fabric it was inexorably sucking into its maw. Maybe she could pull the curtains loose before they were ripped from the wall.

Rafferty might have been able to laugh when she dyed his shorts pink but he wasn't likely to be terribly amused when she tried to destroy his house.

RAFFERTY LEANED one shoulder against the edge of the bookcase and stared out the window. A stack of medical journals sat on his desk but he wasn't having much trouble ignoring them.

He heard the vacuum go on in the living room. So his new housekeeper was going to tackle the vacuum cleaner. His mouth twitched, remembering her stumbled explanation of how she'd come to dye his underwear pink.

He'd wanted to laugh. He'd wanted to tell her not to worry about it. And, most disconcertingly, he'd wanted to take her in his arms and kiss the worried look from her eyes.

It was not an urge he liked.

He was curious to know why Mandy had applied for a job for which she, quite obviously, wasn't qualified. It certainly wasn't for money. He'd be willing to bet his medical practice that Amanda Bradley had never known a day's poverty in her life. It wasn't just the expensive clothes. There was just something about her, a certain demeanor, that spoke of money.

The Trahernes were more than comfortably off but he suspected that Mandy's family, whoever they were, had big money. The kind that allowed them to raise a child who'd never done a load of laundry in her life.

He tilted his head, listening to the hum of the vacuum

in the next room. Did it sound odd? Strained, maybe? He was halfway across the room when there was a loud crash from the direction of the living room. He was out the door and in the next room in record time.

The source of the crash was immediately apparent. The sheers that had covered the front window were no longer in place. The rod had been pulled out of the wall and the drapes now lay on the carpet. Beneath the drapes was a large lump that was heaving in an alarming fashion. Half-swathed in sheer fabric, the vacuum cleaner continued to hum but the sound had taken on a grinding note and there was the faint, but definite scent of burning rubber.

Crossing the room in three long strides, Rafferty grabbed hold of one edge of the fallen curtains and pulled them back to reveal the tousled form of his housekeeper. Crouched on the floor, her face flushed with exertion, she had both hands wrapped around a wrinkled fold of drapery fabric and was engaged in a fierce tug of war with the vacuum, which appeared to have devoured several inches.

"Good God." Rafferty's stunned comment brought Mandy's head up. Startled, she released her hold on the curtain too quickly and sprawled backward onto the twisted mass of fabric. Triumphant, the vacuum's hum grew louder as if it sensed victory within its reach.

"What happened?" he asked, raising his voice so it could be heard over the sound of the machine.

"It won't shut off," she said, breathless from the struggle.

Rafferty didn't bother even trying the switch. Bending down, he grabbed hold of the cord. Whereas Mandy's civilized tug had failed to budge the plug from the socket, Rafferty didn't bother with civility. He yanked on the cord with all his considerable strength. The small table it had been encircling sprang up into the air like a startled hare. The lamp that had been on the table sailed higher still before beginning an almost slow-motion descent. Both table and lamp landed almost simultaneously, the table with a dull thud and the lamp with a sharper crack. The porcelain base broke into half a dozen pieces.

Rafferty and Mandy watched the drama in stunned silence. It was almost an anticlimax when the vacuum cleaner ground to a halt, the plug having at last parted company with the wall. With a last sullen mumble, the machine stopped, leaving dead silence behind.

"Are you all right?" Rafferty asked slowly. He bent to grasp Mandy's elbows, lifting her to her feet. Her hands clasped his forearms for a moment while she got her balance.

"I'm okay."

She reached up to smooth the hair out of her face. A short time ago, it had been contained in a neat French twist. It now looked like it had been blow-dried by a hurricane.

Sensing that rearranging her hair would be hopeless, she tried to tuck the bottom of her loose silk shirt back into the waist of her linen slacks. Vaguely she thought that, if she looked better, the mess that surrounded her might not look quite so bad.

"Thank you," she murmured.

"You're welcome." Rafferty looked nearly as dazed as she felt. "You're sure you're all right?"

"Fine. Thank you."

Now that the crisis had passed, it was hard to determine what to do in the aftermath. What she wanted to do was crawl under the sofa and stay there until Rafferty left. Instead, she straightened her shoulders, lifting her eyes to meet his.

"The vacuum cleaner tried to eat the drapes," she told him.

"So I noticed." Gray eyes shifted from the ruined window to the offending vacuum to the overturned table and broken lamp. "This place looks like the Broncos just held a practice on the carpet."

Mandy chewed on her lower lip. "I'm sorry. Naturally I'll pay to repair the damage."

"Why?" Rafferty raised his eyebrows. "It was my vacuum cleaner that did the dirty deed. And I'm the one who laid waste the table."

"But it was my fault for letting it get hold of the curtains in the first place," she insisted, determined to take responsibility.

"An accident." He shrugged the damage off. "I'm just glad you weren't hurt. When I saw you bouncing around under those curtains—" He broke off, his mouth twitching at the remembered image.

Mandy's eyes met his and she felt a smile curling her mouth, despite her best efforts to remain properly serious. "I guess it must have looked rather funny."

"Actually it looked like something The Three Stooges might have cooked up."

"Should I say 'nyuk, nyuk, nyuk' and give you a poke in the eye?" She smiled openly, drawn by the laughter in his eyes.

"I'd rather you didn't. I already feel a little shell-shocked."

"You look it. If you could have seen your face—" She pressed her fingers to her mouth, trying unsuccessfully to suppress a chuckle.

"You didn't look all that calm and composed yourself," he reminded her.

"And when you yanked on that cord and the table jumped up in the air—"

"I was panicked," he defended himself. "If I hadn't done something quick, that thing might have sucked both of us in."

"Just like in a cartoon."

"The Pink Panther, maybe," Rafferty suggested on a laugh.

The laughter cleared any lingering tension. Mandy looked around the room, her smile fading. "I really am sorry about the mess."

"Don't worry about it. The curtains can be rehung and the table is okay."

"The lamp isn't."

"That's all right," he said nonchalantly. "I never liked that lamp anyway."

"Really? If I'd known you didn't care for Grandmother Adams's lamp, I certainly wouldn't have told Mother to let you have it."

At the sound of the new voice, Rafferty and Mandy both spun toward the door, looking like a pair of guilty children caught in the midst of a pillow fight.

"Claire." Rafferty's voice was more surprised than welcoming.

"Rafferty." The strong voice made his name a mocking echo of his greeting. Dark eyebrows rose toward beautifully styled gray hair. Like her brother, Claire Traherne Desmond was prematurely gray. It wasn't the only resemblance between them but it was the strongest.

"Claire." Rafferty's tone held more warmth this time. "I wasn't expecting you. Was I?"

"No. I was in the area and thought I'd drop by to see how you and Becky are getting on. Mother told me that you'd hired a new housekeeper. I thought one of us should meet her."

Claire's dark eyes shifted from her brother to Mandy, missing nothing of the younger woman's disheveled hair and clothing. Clearly she'd already taken note of the debris-strewn battlefield. Mandy had to suppress the urge to shrink behind Rafferty's considerable bulk.

"Checking up on me?" Rafferty said, with a trace of irritation. "Claire has never quite grasped the idea that I'm a big boy," he told Mandy. "She thinks being six years older means that she has to protect me for the rest of my natural life."

"How ungentlemanly of you to say that it's six years. It's really only five and a half," she told Mandy. While her tone was cordial, her eyes remained watchful. Mandy doubted she was likely to win much approval in those eyes.

"Five years and eight months," Rafferty said, continuing what was obviously an ongoing argument between them. "Since you've poked your nose in, allow me to introduce you to my new housekeeper. Claire, this is Amanda Bradley. Amanda, this is my nosey, *older* sister, Claire Desmond.''

"Ms. Desmond," Mandy murmured, wondering if she should curtsy or merely throw herself on the carpet and admit her total unworthiness. There was something about Claire Desmond that suggested either action would be appropriate.

"I'm pleased to meet you, Ms. Bradley." Claire came farther into the room, eyeing the fallen table and the partially eaten drapes. "You have a unique method of doing housework, I must say."

Her tone held a touch of humor but there was enough bite left in the words to bring color to Mandy's cheeks.

"That's enough, Claire." Rafferty's tone held a warning that even his formidable sister didn't quite dare ignore.

"Of course, it's none of my business," she added.

"That's right. It isn't." Rafferty's smile carried an edge to it. "Mandy, would you please go tell Becky that her aunt is here?"

"Of course," she murmured, glad of an excuse to leave the room.

She slipped out the door with the feeling that she was leaving behind a potential battle zone.

Chapter Five

The silence stretched after Mandy's departure. Rafferty waited. Claire would hate to be the one who spoke first, feeling that it would put her at some disadvantage.

Of his two sisters, he was closest to Claire but there was no denying that his oldest sister could be a royal pain. When they were children, he'd thought her nosy and bossy. His opinion hadn't changed all that much now that he was an adult. She was accustomed to control and quite sure that she knew what was best for everyone, particularly the people she was fond of.

Their sister, Louise, had moved to Virginia right after her marriage. She'd told Rafferty that she was afraid to stay in Denver for fear Claire would organize her right out of her marriage to a rather laid-back artist.

Claire's husband was content to let her rule the roost, only stepping in when her managing tendencies threatened to jeopardize his business or entangle the family in a lawsuit. It still amazed Rafferty to see Claire meekly back down in the face of her husband's gentle suggestion that she might have gotten a trifle pushy.

Rafferty refused to move out of Colorado and refused to let Claire run his life, an attitude that caused her considerable frustration. Although she hadn't been able to manipulate him since before he'd entered high school, that still didn't stop Claire from trying.

When it got to the point that he was quite sure he was going to be forced to physical violence, Rafferty always remembered that Claire had been like a rock during those terrible weeks after Maryanne had disappeared with Becky.

It had been Claire who'd insisted that he eat. Claire who'd bullied him into going back to work when the weeks had dragged into months and it had begun to look as though he'd never see his daughter again. Underneath the bossiness, she had a heart of gold.

But that didn't mean he was going to let her start managing his life at this late date.

He waited for Claire to speak.

Claire waited for him to speak.

The silence stretched.

Catching the amused gleam in his eyes, Claire lifted her shoulders in an almost imperceptible shrug of surrender.

"So, that's your new housekeeper."

"Yup."

She waited, but he didn't elaborate. Her mouth tightened with annoyance. No one else could stand up to her the way Rafferty could. From the time he'd been her baby brother, he'd been able to read her like a book, and the knowledge of that annoyed her. What was worse, he knew it annoyed her and did it deliberately. Still, there were more important things at stake here than old sibling quarrels.

"Where did you find her? The local high school?"

"No. As far as I know, she's not a teacher."

"I meant she was there as a student," Claire snapped, her temper pushed to breaking point.

"Oh, Mandy's considerably older than that. Her application says she's thirty," he offered blandly.

"Bosh!" Claire's tone was brisk. She tossed her purse onto the sofa with more than necessary force. "If that girl's thirty, I'm Katharine Hepburn."

Rafferty recalled having a similar thought about Mandy's age but he wasn't going to admit that to his sister.

"I suppose you believe her," Claire went on, her tone expressing her disgust at the gullibility of men in general and him in particular. "One look at those big brown eyes and you'd probably have hired her even if she'd told you her name was Mata Hari."

"Oh, I think that might have given me pause. Would you like some iced tea?"

"I did not come here to sip iced tea, Rafferty."

"I know." His smile held amused affection. "You came to inspect my housekeeper. And having decided she's unsuitable, you're determined to browbeat me into seeing the error of my ways."

"I don't think I care for the term 'browbeat,'" Claire protested.

"I'm sure you don't. But it's exactly what you've got in mind. You know, I'm surprised that, after all these years, you haven't figured out yet that I'm determined to go my own way."

"You always were pigheaded, even when you were a boy," she grumbled.

"While you, of course, were the soul of sweet tractability," he said, his eyebrows raised.

"I like to think I was not an unreasonable child."

"Yes, I'm sure you would like to think that."

Annoyance flashed in her eyes, swiftly banished by humor. "Really, you're the most irritating person."

"I know."

Claire's smile brought a rare flash of beauty to her face. "I should detest you," she suggested very cordially.

"I know." Rafferty grinned at her, not at all repentant.

Claire's smile faded. "You needn't think that I'm going to let you distract me from what I want to say."

"Could anything?"

His dry sarcasm was ignored as she returned to the original subject with the tenacity of a bulldog.

"That girl is completely unsuitable."

"You can tell that after having spent two minutes in the same room?"

"It doesn't take an extensive acquaintance to see that she's inappropriate. One has only to look at the condition of this room to have grave doubts about her abilities as a housekeeper.''

Following her eyes around the scene of destruction, Rafferty found it impossible to come up with a strong comeback for that one. Wisely he didn't try.

"I wasn't looking for a Hazel. Mostly I needed someone to be here for Becky."

"Exactly." Claire's tone imbued the single word with profound meaning. "The really important issue here is Becky."

"Agreed. And I'm satisfied that Mandy will take good care of Becky."

"Rafferty, she's hardly more than a child herself, no matter what lies she put on her application."

"She's hardly a child, Claire. And Becky likes her."

"So you're letting a ten-year-old do the hiring these days?"

"Of course not." Despite his determination not to let her get to him, Rafferty's tone held a snap. She was hitting on the precise concerns he'd had when he'd hired Mandy. He drew a deep breath.

"Of course I didn't let Becky make the final decision. But I do think her opinion is important. After all, she's the one who'll be spending time with Mandy."

"I didn't say Becky shouldn't be consulted but surely she needs someone more mature. She's growing up. She needs someone who can be a good influence on her, help her grow up."

"Becky's already more grown-up than she should be," Rafferty snapped. He half turned from his sister, running one hand through his hair. "She doesn't need someone to teach her to grow up any faster than she already has."

There was a moment of silence. When Claire spoke, her voice was softer. "You know, you can't change what happened, Rafferty. It wasn't your fault Maryanne took Becky."

"Isn't it? If I hadn't gotten angry at Maryanne, she wouldn't have run away."

"If she hadn't been so immature, she wouldn't have run away like a child expecting to be punished." It was an old argument, one they'd had hundreds of times during the years after Maryanne had disappeared.

"It doesn't matter." Rafferty shrugged irritably. "I know I can't give Becky those years back. But I don't have to encourage her to grow up any faster."

"So you hired a playmate for her?" Claire arched one eyebrow.

"Of course not. But Mandy makes Becky laugh. Mandy is willing to help her cut out paper dolls, a skill I sorely lack. She doesn't talk down to her. I think it's good for Becky to have a woman around full-time. Furthermore, Becky's already grown fond of Mandy."

"And you?" Claire's eyes were shrewd.

"And me what?"

"Are you fond of her, too? The two of you looked rather cozy when I first came in."

"Oh, for heaven's sake, Claire!" Rafferty strode across the room, needing an outlet for his irritation. Turning, he fixed his sister with an annoyed glare. "We'd just had a fight with a vacuum cleaner, one we lost, as you can see. We were laughing, that's all. I've only known the woman a week."

"Okay." She lifted a placatory hand. "I'm sorry I brought it up."

"You should be."

"I suppose I'm taking my life in my hands by bringing this up—"

"Then don't," Rafferty suggested bluntly.

"—but I couldn't help noticing that she bears a fairly strong resemblance to Maryanne. Are you sure that isn't the reason you hired her? Maybe even the reason Becky took to her?"

"Considering the hell Maryanne put me through, I'd have to be something of a masochist to hire someone because they reminded me of her, wouldn't I?"

"You've always had a penchant for wounded birds and

stray puppies, Rafferty. I've often thought that was a good part of the reason you married Maryanne. She needed you.''

She paused to let that sink in before continuing, ignoring the warning in her brother's expression.

"Your Mandy has much the same look about her, that same fragile, helpless look that Maryanne wore. Just be sure you really know why you hired her.''

"Hullo, Aunt Claire.'' Becky's voice broke in before Rafferty could frame the words to tell Claire that she was imagining things. Looking over her shoulder, he saw Mandy standing in the doorway. Their eyes met. It was obvious that she'd heard at least a part of the conversation. Before he could decide just what expression lay in her eyes, she'd backed away.

Rafferty was startled by the strength of his urge to go after her, to reassure her. To tell her—tell her what? Shaken, he dragged his attention back to Becky and his sister. Why should he want to reassure Mandy of anything? She was just an employee, certainly nothing more.

WOUNDED BIRDS and lost puppies. The words lingered in Mandy's mind. Was that how she seemed? For all her brave words about striking out on her own and proving her independence, did she really seem like a lost soul? The thought stung.

And did she really look that much like the late Mrs. Traherne? She knew very little about Becky's mother. All Rafferty had told her was that his wife was dead. Mandy thought it was a tragedy that Becky had been so young when she'd lost her mother.

Becky had mentioned her mother once or twice in passing, leaving the impression that she'd adjusted to the loss. Mandy hadn't probed further. Hadn't honestly felt any strong urge to do so. But now that she'd been compared with the woman, she couldn't help but be curious about her.

Rafferty's sister had made her sound like a helpless puppy. Was that what she'd been? Had Rafferty loved her?

She was still pondering that question half an hour later when Becky found her in the backyard, absently pulling weeds from a flower bed. To tell the truth, she didn't know the difference between a weed and a flower. Her parents would have been horrified at the very thought of letting her grub in the dirt. And the gardener would have been equally horrified by the thought of letting anyone near his immaculate beds.

Mandy wasn't really weeding. It could more accurately be described as plucking. She plucked a leaf here, a ragged flower head there and shredded them into tiny pieces while she stared at nothing in particular.

The afternoon sun was warm, though the nights had begun to cool off. She'd had a hard time adapting to the clear dry mountain air. It was very different from the humid climate of Pennsylvania. At first, her skin had felt drawn, as if the air was sucking all the moisture from it. But she'd learned to use more moisturizer and drink more water and now she found the air invigorating.

Odd, how she'd begun to think of Denver as home. Not just as the place she'd run away to but as a place she'd chosen to live. The thought made her smile. She'd chosen her destination by closing her eyes and sticking a pin in the atlas. Since her first try had landed her in the middle of the Pacific, she'd adjusted her aim and tried again. Denver had been the nearest big city to the second pinhole.

"You shouldn't pay much attention to Aunt Claire," Becky said from behind her.

Mandy started. She hadn't heard the little girl approach. "What?"

"I said, you shouldn't pay much attention to Aunt Claire." Becky plopped down in the grass next to Mandy and reached for a bedraggled dandelion. "Daddy says her bark is much worse than her bite."

"Is it?" Mandy dusted off her hands, trying to keep the doubt from her expression.

"Most of the time." Becky began shredding the dandelion with methodical precision, setting each tiny piece on top of a fallen leaf. "She's real bossy. Most of the time, you just have to let her say what she wants but you don't pay too much attention to it."

"Is that what you do?" Mandy asked, amused.

"Usually." Becky nodded, her bangs flopping on her forehead. "Daddy says Aunt Claire can be real intim— intimul—"

"Intimidating?"

"Yeah. So people do what she says. When I first met her, I thought she was kinda scary. But when you get used to her, she's pretty nice."

"When you first met her?" Mandy tilted her head, questioning the odd phrase. "Didn't you know her when you were a baby? I thought your Dad had always lived here."

"He did. And I guess I knew Aunt Claire when I was a baby." Becky frowned, staring into the distance, as if trying to remember. She shook her head. "I don't remember her, though. I don't remember too much about the time before Mama took me away." She slanted a quick look at Mandy, her eyes holding a touch of defiance and a studied indifference.

"You must have been quite small," Mandy said, at last, uncertain whether Becky wanted to pursue the topic.

"Yeah. Daddy looked for us."

"I'm sure he did. He loves you very much." Mandy felt as if she were treading on quicksand. All her vague images of Becky's childhood had been thrown off balance. She was groping to fit this new information into the picture. Becky had obviously brought the subject up deliberately. Was it because she wanted to talk about it?

And, if so, would Rafferty want her talking about it with Mandy?

"My mom is dead," Becky said without looking at her.

"I know. You must miss her," Mandy said, groping for the right words.

"Yeah. Sometimes." Becky found another dandelion

and began the same careful destruction. "But I like living with my dad. Mom and me were always moving. She was afraid of the welfare people, afraid they'd take me away from her."

"She must have loved you very much."

Mandy felt as if she were stumbling through a mine field in the dark of night. This was an emotionally loaded subject, to say the least. It was now obvious to her that Becky wanted to talk about her mother, though Mandy didn't know why. Was she supposed to ask questions or just let Becky tell her whatever she wanted?

"I got back with Daddy after my mom died." Becky piled the remains of the second dandelion next to the first and then drew her knees up, wrapping her thin arms around them and she stared into the middle distance. "He came and got me in L.A."

"I've never been to California," Mandy said, when the silence stretched.

"It's okay." Becky shrugged. "There's no seasons or nuthin'. I like the snow at Christmas."

"Me, too." Mandy wrapped her arms around her up-drawn knees, echoing Becky's pose.

"I was staying with Mr. Flynn when Daddy came to get me."

"Mr. Flynn?"

"He's my friend. Him and Ann. Mama, she sometimes went away for a day or two. She knew I was big enough to take care of myself."

How old could she have been? Mandy wondered. *Six? Seven?*

"Only this one time she didn't come back when she was s'posed to. And I got scared the welfare people were going to take me away. Only then Mr. Flynn found me and he took care of me. Him and Ann. Mr. Flynn told me about my mom being dead. He said he'd take care of me. But then Daddy came and got me and I've been living here ever since."

It didn't take a genius to figure out that the stark little

story left a lot untold. Becky didn't mention how frightened she must have been. Mandy had heard her mention Flynn and Ann before and had assumed they were family friends. It seemed they were considerably more than that.

And just what had happened to Becky's mother? An accident? Suicide? Did Becky even know what had happened?

"How long were you away from your Dad?"

"Three years." Becky shrugged. "I didn't hardly remember him anymore. 'Cept that he liked to throw me up in the air sometimes."

Three years. Mandy's chest ached with pain for both of them. Poor Becky. No wonder she was so adult. She'd had to grow up in self-defense.

And Rafferty. He adored Becky. It must have been terrible for him to lose her that way. Three years of wondering. Three years of worrying.

She caught the sidelong look Becky threw her, the hint of uncertainty in those gray eyes, as if Becky was wondering about Mandy's reaction to what she'd been told. On an impulse, she reached out, encircling Becky's narrow shoulders with one arm and hugging her close.

"You know, I think you're a lucky little girl. A lot of people love you an awful lot."

Becky leaned against her confidingly. "Do a lot of people love you?"

Mandy thought about it, about the times she'd thought her parents were going to suffocate her with their concern. About Gram's brisk, no-nonsense way. There hadn't been a lot of outward show of affection in her childhood.

Her parents hadn't known how to show their love except by shielding her from life. And Gram hadn't been the sort for tender hugs and kisses. Sometimes, she'd felt that lack and she'd lavished her dolls with all the hugs she never got.

But she'd never doubted that her parents and her grandmother loved her. They might never have said the words but she'd always known they loved her.

"Yes," she said, answering Becky's question. "Yes, there are people who love me a lot."

"Who?" Becky snuggled closer against Mandy's side.

"Well, my parents love me a lot."

"Daddy takes me out for chili dogs sometimes and pretends he likes them, even when I know he doesn't. Do your parents do things like that?"

Over Becky's tousled head, Mandy grinned, trying to picture either of her parents with a chili dog in their hand.

"People show affection in different ways," she said. "My parents always tried to protect me, to make sure I didn't get hurt. That was their way of showing me that they loved me."

"It's nice having people love you."

Mandy had to swallow a sudden lump in her throat before she could get out an answer.

"Yes, it is. It's very nice."

RAFFERTY STOOD in an upstairs window, looking out at the pair in the yard. Becky was not normally the demonstrative type yet there she was, snuggled up against Mandy as if she'd known her all her life.

He turned away, disturbed by the sight. It was one of Claire's most annoying characteristics that she was often right. He didn't like the idea that this might be one of those occasions. *Was* Becky drawn to Mandy because of a superficial resemblance to Maryanne?

She'd seemed adjusted to her mother's death. Too well adjusted, perhaps? When he brought Becky home, Claire had suggested taking her to see a psychiatrist, someone trained to deal with children who were experiencing profound grief. It had seemed necessary, and Becky was willing to talk about her mother.

She'd cried when she found out her mother was dead. Not that he'd been there to see it. She'd been staying with Flynn McCallister then. When Maryanne had failed to come home from a weekend away, Becky had run away, fearing the "welfare people" would take her away.

She'd spent three days living on the streets before Flynn McCallister found her in an alley and took her in. It had been Flynn who'd had to tell Becky that her mother was never coming back.

Poor, foolish Maryanne. Her body had been found in one of the aqueducts that carved through Los Angeles. She'd died of a blow to the head, but whether it had been an accident or murder, the police couldn't be sure. She was dead, and as far as anyone knew, Becky was an orphan.

Years later, it still ate at Rafferty that he hadn't been there for Becky. *He* should have been the one to give Becky the awful news. She should have cried out her grief in *his* arms. Not that he wasn't grateful to Flynn. God knows, Becky had been blessed in finding someone like Flynn to protect her and take care of her. But it still hurt that Rafferty hadn't been there for his daughter.

His hands shoved in his pockets, Rafferty walked down the stairs. In his mind's eyes, he saw Mandy and Becky sitting on the grass, Becky tucked confidingly beneath Mandy's arm, Mandy's dark head bent over the little girl's.

He'd only known Mandy a week, but already the initial impression that she looked like Maryanne was fading. It was only a superficial resemblance anyway. And he'd already seen enough to know that there were more differences than similarities between his late wife and his new housekeeper.

There was a spark in Mandy, a fire that Maryanne had never possessed. Maryanne would never have dared apply for a job for which she was clearly unqualified and then try to brazen her way through it.

He had only to glance into the living room to see a reminder of just how unqualified Mandy was. If that didn't suffice, there was always the pink underwear he'd stuffed into the back of his drawer or the partially tie-dyed sheets now residing in the linen closet.

A smart man would no doubt confront Mandy with his knowledge that she'd exaggerated her skills in the house-

keeping department and he would demand an explanation.
A smart man would probably fire her.

A smart man wouldn't have hired her in the first place.

Rafferty stopped in the living-room doorway. His hands
still in his pockets, he studied the disaster-struck corner
where the vacuum sat, a partially ingested curtain sprawled
half over it.

What kind of idiot kept on a housekeeper who couldn't
keep house?

The kind who wanted to see his daughter happy more
than he wanted to see his house clean.

Chapter Six

When she took time to think about it, Mandy was amazed by how easily she settled into her new life. She'd been determined to prove she could make it on her own, but she'd had secret doubts. In the weeks between leaving her parents' home and being hired by Rafferty, she'd given serious consideration to the idea that maybe her parents had been right—maybe she couldn't manage on her own.

She'd also secretly wondered if maybe she'd hate working once she actually convinced someone to hire her. There were undoubtedly jobs she would have hated. She couldn't see herself working as a waitress or as a clerk in a department store. Of course, she hadn't really seen herself as a housekeeper until she was hired to be one.

The vacuum cleaner war had shown her that disaster could lurk in the most innocuous task. Mandy had taken the warning to heart. She still hadn't attempted to run the dishwasher. And as for the microwave—it sat unused on the kitchen counter.

She'd made an uneasy peace with the washing machine and could do laundry without too many surprises. Though she *had* melted Becky's windbreaker in the dryer. But since Becky claimed to have almost outgrown the garment, anyway, it couldn't be considered anything more than a minor accident.

Mandy's general rule was to avoid anything that required

her to flip a switch or punch a button. The only exception was the stove, with which she fancied she'd developed a certain rapport.

While the cleaning was filled with pitfalls, the cooking was generally a pleasure. She enjoyed the time spent in the kitchen. Simple tasks like chopping vegetables or tearing lettuce for salads gave her time to think. It was relaxing undemanding work. And one of the best things about cooking was that the mistakes simply disappeared down the garbage disposal.

By the time she celebrated her one-month anniversary as a member of the working class, Mandy no longer had any doubts that she'd made the right decision when she'd left home. It seemed as if she'd known Rafferty and Becky forever.

Philadelphia seemed faraway in both time and space, only coming into focus during her weekly phone calls to her parents. They still couldn't understand why she'd rather work as a servant than come home. Mandy's explanations might as well have been in Greek for all the impact they had.

As far as they could see, what she was doing made no sense. If she'd just come home, where they could take care of her, her mother would find her some position on one of her charitable boards, something that wouldn't be too taxing.

Despite her determination not to let them get to her, Mandy found the calls depressing. They were so genuinely worried about her, it was impossible to get angry. Their continued belief that she was hardly more than a helpless child nibbled at her confidence.

She still hadn't told them where she was, sure that, if they knew how to find her, they'd both be on the first plane to Denver, determined to take her home. She was equally determined to stay right where she was and build her own life but she knew how difficult it was to stand firm in the face of their overweening concern. If she'd been more successful in doing so, she wouldn't have been forced into doing something as fundamentally ridiculous as running away from home at the age of twenty-four.

Aside from the weekly calls to her parents, her life was going along exactly as she wanted. She liked her job and loved her new home. Denver was nothing like Philadelphia. The people who lived here took life less seriously. They seemed to have more time to play.

The weather was still warm but the air was beginning to feel like fall. In the mountains that loomed over the city, the aspens were starting to turn, washing whole mountainsides in shivering gold.

Mandy loved the hint of crispness in the morning air, the promise of colder weather just around the corner. She was even looking forward to the first snowfall, though it was going to make her travel back and forth to work less than pleasant.

Rafferty had gone back to the clinic a week after she'd come to work for him. Mandy viewed this as a vote of confidence, especially since he returned to his office the Monday after the incident with the vacuum. Becky had returned to school full days the week following that.

They'd settled into a routine. Mandy was there early enough in the morning to see Becky off to school. Rafferty left a few minutes after Becky. He made it a point to tell her if he expected to be home any later than usual. Twice a week he and his partners kept the clinic open late in the evening, providing for those who couldn't manage to get there during regular office hours. It meant that, at least once a week, Rafferty didn't get home until after eight o'clock.

Mandy didn't mind staying late. Really rather shy, she'd never learned how to make friends. She generally spent her time away from work alone. Although she was used to being alone, she had to admit to an occasional feeling of loneliness.

There were moments when she thought, somewhat wistfully, that it would be nice to have someone she could call up on the spur of the moment to go to dinner with her.

Lying in bed at night, she sometimes wondered what it

would be like to have someone special in her life, someone she could plan a future with.

But if she didn't know how to make friends, she certainly didn't know anything about dating. She couldn't even imagine how one met a man *to* date. And what kind of a man would she want to go out with?

A strong man but one who wasn't afraid to show a gentle side. A man who liked children, who had tolerance for the mistakes of others. A man with shoulders broad enough to rest her head on if she was feeling in need of support. A man with smoky gray eyes and a certain determination around the jawline. Rafferty Traherne.

She always forced her thoughts in another direction at that point in her imaginings. It was disconcerting to find Rafferty Traherne popping up in her fantasies. Certainly he had many wonderful qualities and there was no denying he was an attractive man—very attractive.

But he was her employer and she wasn't interested in him becoming anything else.

Not in the least interested.

"OH, I ALMOST forgot to tell you that you've got an invitation to a barbecue at the McCallisters'." Rafferty had the front door open when he remembered the invitation. Feeling the chill of the early October morning, he pushed the door shut again, turning to look at Mandy.

Really, it didn't seem fair that she should look quite so appealing so early in the morning. For over a month, he'd been trying assiduously not to see how attractive she was. He didn't want to notice the way certain light picked out red highlights in her dark hair. He didn't want to see the softness of her skin or the way her eyes always lit up an instant before she smiled.

She was here to do a job and that was his only interest in her. She was his employee. Nothing more and nothing less.

But not even the most determined blindness could prevent him from noticing her this morning. She'd been headed toward the kitchen. At his words, she'd paused, turning her head to look at him over one shoulder. Her hair was pulled back in its usual chignon but one dark strand had fallen loose to caress her neck.

Her pale gray slacks were the epitome of conservative good taste but Rafferty couldn't help but notice the way they hugged her derriere—a very nice derriere, he had to admit. In deference to the chilly morning, she was wearing a sweater but it was nothing like the sturdy cardigan one might expect to see a housekeeper wearing. This sweater was a deep raspberry-pink angora, so soft it seemed to cry out to be touched. He could almost feel the soft fuzziness under his fingers and the warm skin beneath.

"An invitation?"

His thoughts had wandered so far, it took Rafferty a moment to drag them back to their proper place.

"An invitation. To a barbecue." He sounded peculiar, even to his own ears. He cleared his throat, wishing he could clear his mind as easily. "You've heard Becky mention Flynn and Ann, I'm sure."

"Yes, of course. They're good friends of yours."

"That's right. You probably would have met them before this but they've been in Europe all summer. They just got back last week and they've invited us to their home on Sunday."

"I can understand that they want to see you and Becky. But I don't see why I've been included in the invitation." There was a slight pucker between her eyes. Rafferty shoved his hands into his pockets. What was it about her that made him want to stroke that small frown from her forehead?

"They called when they got home and Becky did nothing but talk about you. She made you sound like a combination of Mary Poppins and Superwoman. I think they're curious to meet such a paragon."

Mandy flushed beneath the smile in Rafferty's eyes. Really, did he have to be so attractive? The plain gray suit that should have looked dull and conservative, managed to emphasize the breadth of his shoulders instead. He was a doctor, for heaven's sake. Goodness knows, she'd known enough doctors in her time and she couldn't ever remember finding one of them even remotely sexy. So why didn't Rafferty Traherne remind her of hospitals and physical therapists? Why did she find herself more inclined to think of candlelight and soft music?

She dragged her thoughts back to the matter at hand. "Are you sure the McCallisters don't feel obligated to invite me?"

"Why would they feel obligated?"

"Well, maybe Becky made it sound as if she wanted me there."

"Are you implying that Becky might try to manipulate someone into doing what she wanted?" Rafferty looked suitably shocked by the notion.

"Of course not." Mandy's face remained solemn but there was laughter in her eyes and a suspicious tuck in her cheek. "I'm sure Becky would never dream of doing such a thing."

"Right. She merely hints people in the direction she thinks they should go."

His tone was full of such dry affection that Mandy's lips curved in a smile. She'd already learned that Becky was a born manager. She didn't lie or whine or throw tantrums to get people to do what she wanted. She believed in the power of reasoned argument. And she could, as Gram would have said, argue the stripes off a skunk, if she took a notion to do so.

"To answer your question—no, Becky did not browbeat Ann into including you in the invitation. The McCallisters are really more than friends. They're more like family. After hearing Becky talk about you, they want a chance to meet you."

"I don't know," Mandy wavered. She wanted to go. She was curious to meet the McCallisters, the people who'd taken care of Becky when her mother disappeared.

"Of course, Sunday is your day off. You probably have other plans."

"No, I'm not doing anything." It didn't occur to Mandy to equivocate. The truth was, her time was almost embarrassingly free.

"Well, if it's just that you're sick of us by Friday and can't face the thought of seeing us again before Monday, I'd understand."

"Oh, no." She hastened to reassure him and then caught the teasing light in his eyes. "I mean, it's not that. Of course, I couldn't blame you if you weren't too enthusiastic about having your housekeeper around on the weekend."

The words were light but there was a trace of anxiety behind them. Clearly she didn't want to push her way in where she thought she wasn't welcome. Again, Rafferty had that disconcerting urge to take her in his arms and kiss the insecurity away.

"Becky and I would both be very happy to have you join us. Actually I think they only invite me because they feel obligated. The person they really want to see is Becky. I'm generally left sitting by myself in a corner."

"Well, if you're sure you wouldn't mind," she said at last.

"It's a date then."

Mandy nodded, feeling a tingle of excitement. She stared at the door after it shut behind him.

A date. Not that he'd really meant a *date* date. He'd just meant that it was an appointment. But no one ever said "It's an appointment." Unless they wanted to sound like a fool. Saying it was a date was just one of those phrases that people used. It didn't mean anything at all. Still...

A date with Rafferty. The idea sounded very interesting.

THE MCCALLISTER HOME was an untidy sprawl of brick and wood. At least seventy years old, it showed signs of more than one addition over the years, apparently added at random as more space was needed. The result was a disarming mishmash of materials, styles and proportions.

Within minutes of entering the house, Mandy's uncertainty about her welcome disappeared. Its interior was only slightly more organized than the exterior. Apparently they'd bought the house right before leaving for Europe. The main component of the decor appeared to be boxes. There were boxes full of things and there were empty boxes and there were boxes that had been partially unpacked, abandoned in midstream and left to sit, their contents strewn about them.

She soon learned that the partially emptied boxes were the work of Flynn, while the empty boxes and the neat labels on all of them were a result of his wife's handiwork. Ann complained with mock bitterness that she'd married a man incapable of finishing anything.

Balancing their two-year-old daughter, Hannah Rebecca, on his hip, Flynn gave his wife a lazy smile and said that he never forgot to finish the really important things. Ann flushed a rather pretty shade of pink that negated the impact of the stern look she threw him.

It didn't take long to figure out that the McCallisters were a great deal like their house—a mixture of styles that somehow blended into a working whole. Ann, like Rafferty, was a doctor, though she hadn't practiced since before Hannah was born. She'd planned to go to veterinary school at Colorado State University, which was why their first home in the state had been in Fort Collins.

But after Hannah's birth, she'd decided she couldn't bear to leave her daughter, at least not until Hannah was ready for school.

The move to the rambling old house had been an impulse. Flynn had seen it and decided it was perfect for his family. Ann's argument that there was nothing wrong with the house they were living in had been halfhearted at best. She'd thought the house was as wonderful as her husband did but her more pragmatic nature suggested that there should be a more practical reason for a move than simply finding charm in a slightly run-down house. Flynn saw no reason to be practical about it at all.

As near as Mandy could tell, that pretty much summed up the differences in their views of the world. Ann was concerned about practicalities. She labeled boxes and when she'd started to unpack one, she hadn't stopped until she was finished with it. Flynn thought practicality an overrated virtue, didn't care if he didn't know what was in a particular box and only unpacked until he found whatever he'd been looking for at that particular moment.

Somehow, the two disparate views blended to make a happy family.

The temperature had dipped unseasonably low overnight. The night before, frost had crisped the edges of anything foolhardy enough to still be growing. Mandy assumed that the planned barbecue would have been canceled in favor of something indoors. But Flynn seemed indifferent to the cool air and threatening clouds.

"It looks like rain," Ann told him.

Flynn glanced at the clouds scudding across a wan sky. "Nah. It won't rain. I just got the grill fixed. We should christen it."

The grill was an ancient brick affair that leaned drunkenly to one side. Rafferty eyed it doubtfully. "Well, it's a sure bet you don't dare hit it with a champagne bottle. It'd probably collapse."

Flynn didn't waste energy looking offended. "It's perfectly sturdy." He kicked idly at one corner. A brick tumbled loose, leaving a black hole where it had been. There was a moment of silence while Flynn stared at the brick.

Mandy bit her lip, not wanting to offend her host by smiling. Ann felt no such concern. She giggled. Rafferty grinned widely at Flynn's disgusted expression. Becky shook her head, as if the foolishness of adults never failed to surprise her. Even little Hannah studied the brick with wide blue eyes, her round face solemn.

"Perfectly sturdy." Rafferty commented to no one in particular. "Did you do the brickwork yourself, Flynn?"

"Maybe I should have added more water to the cement." Flynn frowned thoughtfully and then dismissed the problem. He nudged the brick up against the barbecue and forgot about it.

It was, Mandy thought afterward, exactly what she'd always imagined family dinners might be like in families other than her own. No matter how hard she tried, she couldn't picture her father standing in front of a smoking fire wearing an apron that said Kiss Me, I'm Cute, with a leather jacket thrown on over the apron as protection against the chill and flipping hamburgers with the skill of a short-order cook.

The closest her father had ever come to anything of the sort was in ordering mesquite grilled salmon at a restaurant. Flynn, on the other hand, looked perfectly at home. He turned hamburgers and carried on a conversation with Becky and kept an eye on his small daughter, all without showing any sign of expending too much energy.

Rafferty sprawled in a rusted chaise longue nearby, playing a rather haphazard game of three-way toss with Becky and little Hannah. Hannah's throwing skills falling somewhat short of professional standard, a good part of the game consisted of Becky chasing the ball down.

"I swear that man doesn't know the meaning of the word sweat." Ann's exasperated comment made Mandy turn from the window. Her offer to help Ann with the rest of the meal had been accepted and the two women had been working companionably together until Mandy's attention had been caught by the scene outside. She'd been watching Rafferty but Ann's words made her turn her attention to Flynn.

"He does look pretty calm," she said.

"He could probably handle another fifty people without twitching an eyebrow," Ann said. "Now, I'm a nervous wreck for two days before guests arrive. He sleeps late and still manages to get three times as much work done as I do. I should divorce him."

Since she was looking at Flynn as if the sun rose and set in him, Mandy didn't think her threat was terribly serious.

She felt a pang of envy. What would it be like to love

someone the way Ann loved Flynn; to know that you were loved in return?

Resolutely she kept her eyes away from Rafferty.

HANNAH'S NAP TIME fell not long after lunch. Ann took the baby from Flynn with a stern warning to stay out of the baby's room. Hannah knew she never had any trouble convincing her father that she'd rather play than sleep.

When the television was tuned to a Broncos game, Mandy wandered outside. The air was cool and crisp, smelling of autumn and maybe the first hint of snow. The McCallister property was large, the land as overgrown and untidy as the house. Flynn had cleared an area near the house and put up a quick fence to keep Hannah in bounds.

A good-sized stream ran through the bottom of the property, bordered by cottonwoods and Queen Anne's lace. The stream was deep and narrow, with a swift current. While it added to the rural beauty of the property, it also meant that a good, solid fence was a priority.

Mandy tucked her hands deep into the pockets of her light jacket. Leaves crunched beneath her feet. Taking a deep breath, she let the quiet drift over her, feeling peaceful and contented.

"Not a football fan, I take it." Rafferty's voice preceded him. Mandy turned to watch him approach. She half smiled and shook her head in answer to his question.

"I don't really understand it. I suppose if I knew the rules, it wouldn't look quite so..." She let the sentence trail off, searching for a suitable word.

"Dumb?" Rafferty supplied.

"I didn't say that."

"No, but you thought it. You can't imagine why anyone would want to watch a bunch of large men beating each other up over a ball that doesn't even belong to any of them."

"Well..." She met his eyes and smiled, lifting her shoulders in a shrug. "Now that you mention it, it does seem to be a rather peculiar pastime."

"It is." He stopped beside her. "Remnants of a more primitive past, I'm sure."

"Aren't you a football fan?"

"Oh, I can enjoy a game now and then. I prefer to go to the stadium, though, when I can manage it. Becky and Flynn are arguing statistics, at the moment. Way above my head." He slanted her a laughing look.

"You could ask Becky to explain it to you," Mandy suggested.

"The problem is, she probably could. It's humiliating."

"She's a remarkable child," Mandy commented.

"I think so. Careful." Rafferty reached out to take her arm. "Flynn isn't sure just how stable the bank is right here."

Mandy let him draw her back from the edge of the stream, liking the feel of his hand on her arm. Even through the layers of clothing she wore, she could feel the strength of his grip.

"Ann says they're going to put up a fence first thing next spring," she commented, watching the water rush by.

"They're going to have to. Hannah's getting to the age where she's going to be almost impossible to watch all the time."

He sounded pensive. Glancing at him, Mandy wondered if he was thinking that Becky hadn't been much older than Hannah when her mother had run off with her.

"Becky told me about how she met Flynn." She said the words without thinking, wanting him to know that she knew what he'd gone through.

"Did she?" Rafferty tucked his hands into the pockets of his denim jacket, his eyes on the stream.

"It must have been terrible for you, not knowing where she was."

"It was hell." The stark statement had more impact than any elaborate speech.

"She was lucky to end up with people like Flynn and Ann."

"I know. I try not to think about what could have happened to her. She was so little."

"She and Flynn seem close," Mandy said, trying not to notice the way his shoulders seemed to stretch forever beneath his jacket.

"They are." Rafferty's smile held a self-deprecating twist. "If Flynn wasn't so damned likeable, I'd probably be jealous. But I'm so grateful he took care of her."

"Becky's a wonderful child. She has such a strong sense of herself—as if she knows exactly where she's going."

"I hope she keeps that characteristic as she grows up."

"I think she will. I can't quite picture Becky ever letting anyone push her around."

"You sound as if you know what that feels like." Rafferty turned his head to look at her, his eyes questioning.

"I'm a total wimp." She laughed softly. "I'm more the sort that lets life buffet them around, rather than taking it by the horns and whipping it into shape. That vacuum cleaner had my number from the minute we met."

"Oh, I don't know. That was one tough vacuum." Rafferty's smile was quiet. He reached out to brush back a lock of hair that had fallen against her cheek. It wasn't until he felt the dark, silky strand curl around his finger that he questioned the wisdom of the gesture.

Mandy's eyes met his and he knew he wasn't the only one who'd sensed the sudden change in the atmosphere. It was a change that had nothing to do with the cool breeze that had sprung up while they were talking or the clouds that were suddenly thicker overhead, diffusing the pale sunshine.

Instinctively his hand turned, his fingers warm against her cool cheek. Mandy felt her heart skip a beat. It was a casual touch but it seemed to hint at possibilities she could only imagine.

"I've always wondered if your skin could possibly be as soft as it looks." Rafferty hardly seemed aware of what he was saying.

"Is it?" She turned her face and his thumb brushed across her mouth.

"Even softer."

He was closer, though she hadn't noticed either of them moving. He was so close she could smell his after-shave, a crisp woodsy scent that made her feel almost dizzy. His thumb settled just under her lower lip.

Mandy saw his head lower toward her and her lashes seemed suddenly much too heavy. Her eyes closed as his mouth touched hers. His lips were cool and dry. But there was nothing cool about the shiver that ran up her spine.

Was it always like this when two people kissed? This flood of warmth? Or was it just Rafferty Traherne who evoked this response? Who could make her feel like this?

Rafferty's thumb exerted a gentle pressure on her chin, coaxing her lips to part. His tongue slipped out to stroke across the sensitive skin of her lower lip and Mandy felt her knees begin to dissolve. Her hands came up to clutch the open front of his jacket as his arm swept across her back, drawing her closer to the broad strength of his body.

The kiss deepened as if it had a will of its own. His tongue slid across hers, starting a tingling in the pit of her stomach that threatened to steal the last bit of strength from her legs. Her mouth opened to his, her head tilting back to allow him greater access.

Mandy was too inexperienced to realize that the spark that flared between them was hardly normal for a first kiss. But Rafferty knew. He'd kissed a few women in his time and he'd never experienced anything like this fire that sprang to life, a fire that had the potential to burn out of control.

Her body felt just as he'd imagined it would. Her skin was soft and her hair, which had somehow come undone, felt like tangled silk in his hands. He resented the thickness of their clothing keeping them apart.

This was not like a first kiss had ever been for him. Where was that feeling of tentative exploration? The uncertainty—was this the right thing to do? He felt none of that. He had no doubts that this was exactly where she belonged, exactly where he wanted to be.

And with this woman, of all women, that could be disastrous.

But the warning thought couldn't take hold. His mind was filled with the sweet scent of her, the warm taste of her. He could hold her forever.

So absorbed was he in the unexpected flare of desire, that it took several minutes for it to register that the skies had started to deliver what they'd been threatening all day. The rain started out slowly, a drop here and there that rapidly increased in pace and impact until they were suddenly in the midst of an icy downpour.

Cold rain dribbling under his collar reminded Rafferty of exactly where he was and just what he was doing. He was standing out in full view of God and everybody, kissing his housekeeper. His housekeeper, for heaven's sake—like some scene out of a bad Victorian novel.

When he lifted his head and looked down at Mandy, he almost forgot about the rain, the semi-public setting and the fact that he had no business kissing her in any weather. She looked as dazed as he felt, thick lashes lifting slowly to reveal wide brown eyes that held a look of stunned surprise.

"It's raining." His voice was husky and it took a conscious effort to loosen his arms from around her.

His frame had sheltered her from the change in the weather and she blinked in surprise as the first cold drops splashed on her cheeks. The dazed look left her eyes as she suddenly realized where they were. Her fingers released their hold on his jacket and she backed away a step.

"We should go in. We're going to get soaked," Rafferty said when she didn't show any signs of speaking.

As if the words were a signal, lightning cracked in the distance. Thunder followed on its heels and the clouds opened. It was like having a bucket of cold water poured over your head. The shock of it swept away the last lingering sparks of desire.

Without another word, they headed for the shelter of the house.

Stepping under the porch roof, they stopped to shake the worst of the rain off. When Mandy started to shrug out of her jacket, Rafferty reached to help her, an automatic gesture. His hands brushed against the back of her neck and the heat that flared from that light touch proved that the rainstorm had only subdued the new awareness, not drowned it.

He pulled his hand back as if it had been stung and Mandy finished shrugging out of her jacket without looking at him.

Neither of them noticed Becky, kneeling on the sofa in the living room with a clear view of the porch. But she'd been watching them and she saw the way her father jerked back from the casual contact. She saw the flush that came up in Mandy's cheeks.

Things couldn't have been working out better if she'd been able to arrange them herself. She'd be willing to bet a month's allowance that her father had kissed Mandy. It was too bad the rain had interrupted them.

She'd begun to wonder if she was going to have to do something drastic to make them notice each other. Something like maybe getting hit by a bus so they could comfort each other at her hospital bedside. But getting hit by a bus was a pretty risky proposition.

Faking some dread disease would have been great and she'd toyed with that plan. But she'd been forced to abandon it. One of the problems with having a doctor for a father was that it made it hard to pretend to be sick.

But it looked as if drastic measures weren't going to be necessary, after all. Now that they'd kissed, it wouldn't be long before they saw how perfect they were for each other. And then they'd get married and they could be a family.

She turned and flopped back down on the sofa, well pleased.

Chapter Seven

It didn't seem possible that one small kiss could change so much. But the kiss they'd shared at the McCallisters' created a tension between Rafferty and Mandy that neither wanted to acknowledge.

On the surface, everything continued just as it had before the visit to the McCallisters'. Mandy came to work every morning. She got Becky off to school. She cleaned the house and picked Becky up after school. Rafferty came home—early or late—and Mandy left. If Rafferty worked late, he always took her home, saving her the bus trip after dark.

They spoke to each other just as they had before the kiss. Their conversation was more rigidly confined perhaps, dealing strictly with Becky or household matters. Anyone observing them would have seen nothing untoward.

Most of the time Mandy almost managed to pretend that nothing had happened. After all, it wasn't as if anything significant had occurred. Men and women exchanged kisses all the time and it certainly didn't mean anything. Nothing had changed. If she felt a new awareness between them, it was undoubtedly her imagination.

But on the nights when Rafferty drove her home, all her logical arguments began to sound specious. It couldn't possibly be her imagination that made the interior of the Jeep seem much too small for the two of them.

They generally ran out of things to say halfway through the forty-minute drive. The remaining twenty minutes seemed to take twice as long as the first half of the trip. Mandy would stare out the windshield, pretending that she didn't know that she had only to stretch out her arm to touch Rafferty. And Rafferty watched the road with a fierce concentration more suited to the Indy 500 than normal city streets.

When she got out of the car in front of her apartment building, Mandy was relieved the ride was over and, at the same time, disappointed.

THE FIRST REAL SNOW of the year fell the second week of November. It fell overnight, turning the city into a picture postcard of soft white. But the enchantment faded quickly. Traffic was slowed and, in places, stopped altogether.

Mandy's bus was almost thirty minutes late getting to her stop. Up to now, she'd enjoyed the ten-block walk to the Traherne house. This morning, she was not looking forward to it. Rafferty would have already left for work and she'd barely have time to get Becky to school.

She frowned. She wasn't looking forward to driving the little compact that Rafferty had put at her disposal. The roads were so snowy. He'd put snow tires on it a week ago and it wasn't as if she hadn't driven in these conditions before but she hadn't enjoyed it.

She stood up as the bus lumbered to a halt at her stop. The door slid open, letting in a wave of cold air. Mandy stepped down carefully, planting one foot solidly on the snow-covered pavement before bringing the other foot down to join it and releasing her hold on the rail.

The doors swished shut behind her and the bus groaned a protest before sliding away from the curb. The air was cold but dry. Mandy glanced at the leaden sky before turning her coat collar up and tugging her gloves on a little tighter. She was going to be frozen solid by the time she got to work.

Maybe she should consider buying a car, something

suited to a Colorado winter. She'd have to take money out
of her trust fund and that would require one of her parents
to sign. Which meant they'd come and try to talk her into
going home.

But she was going to have to face them sooner or later.
Even if they did come here, they'd have to see that she'd
done quite well on her own. And just because they wanted
her to move back to Philadelphia didn't mean she had to
go. She wasn't a child anymore, after all. She'd proven she
could take care of herself.

"Mandy."

She'd just started forward when the sound of her name
made her turn. On the snow-covered sidewalk, it was a
foolish move. Feeling her foot start to slip, she threw out
her arms, trying to regain her balance. It only postponed
the inevitable. Her other foot slid out from under her and
she closed her eyes as she started to fall.

And then someone's arms closed around her and she was
caught close against a very broad, very masculine chest
encased in thick wool. For the space of several slow heart-
beats, she stayed still, incapable of moving.

In the split second when she'd felt herself falling, Mandy
had known pure terror. What if she injured her back again?
The doctors had never expected her to walk again and she'd
proved them wrong. But it had always seemed a fragile
miracle.

"Are you all right?" Rafferty's voice rumbled beneath
her ear.

"Yes." Her voice was weak. She knew she should move
away, stand without his support, prove that she really was
all right. But she didn't move.

Rafferty supported her slight weight easily, one hand
splayed across her lower back. Even wrapped in a thick
wool coat, she felt delicate, as if made of fine porcelain.
His pulse was still beating too fast, a remnant of the moment when he'd seen her start to fall. She'd looked so
frightened—terrified, really.

She pushed against his chest and his arms loosened reluctantly. He liked the feel of her in his arms, liked it a great deal more than he had any business doing.

"Thank you." Mandy brushed back a strand of hair that had escaped from her knit cap. "Your timing was impeccable."

"Well, you know what they say about preventive medicine. Better to prevent a fall than patch up a victim afterward." His tone was light but his eyes scanned her, seeing the pallor in her cheeks, the slight trembling in her hand.

"Well, I'm very grateful, even if you were just trying to save yourself some work." Her smile was a bit shaky.

"You're welcome. I parked the car down the street."

"I hate to sound rude but what are you doing here?" Mandy let him take her elbow, grateful for the extra support. The near fall had left her feeling a bit unsteady. His hand felt strong and solid, as if he'd never let her fall again.

"I didn't like the idea of you walking all the way to the house in this weather." They stopped next to the Jeep and he opened the door.

"Hi, Mandy." Becky leaned over from the back seat. "You okay?"

"I'm fine." Mandy climbed up into the passenger seat. Rafferty shut the door with a solid thunk before going around the front of the vehicle.

"Gee, Daddy sure did move fast when you started to fall." Becky's eyes were bright and interested, skipping from her father to Mandy as Rafferty settled into the driver's seat and started the engine. "Good thing he was there."

"Yes, it was," Mandy agreed. Her hands were still not quite steady.

"We waited a long time for your bus," Becky continued, sitting back and buckling her seat belt as Rafferty put the Jeep in gear and pulled away from the curb.

"The bus was late. It was really nice of you to come to pick me up," Mandy said, looking at Rafferty.

"It's too far to walk in this weather," he said, shrugging off her thanks.

"He was real concerned," Becky threw in from the back seat.

"Well, I would have been okay but I do appreciate it."

It was odd how the same gesture could seem quite different depending upon who made it. If it had been either of her parents who'd come to pick her up because they didn't want her to walk a few blocks, she would have thought they were being their usual overprotective selves. But Rafferty doing the same thing gave her a warm protected feeling inside.

There was no logical explanation for it. She'd given up trying to understand it by the time she was due to pick Becky up at school. The sun had come out and the snow was beginning to melt, leaving the roads full of slush to be splashed up by the tires.

Mandy drove slowly, her hands tight on the wheel. She was relieved when they got back to the house with no damage beyond mud-stained fenders.

There was a message from Rafferty on the answering machine, saying that there was an emergency and he'd be late, he hoped it wouldn't cause her any problems. He sounded hurried and distracted. Listening to the radio while she fixed dinner, Mandy realized why. A school bus had collided with a tractor trailer. Victims were being taken to a local hospital.

She fed Becky dinner and made sure her homework got done, despite Becky's suggestion that the first snow of the season deserved a celebration, the main component of which would be that she didn't have to do any homework. Mandy listened politely and agreed that it didn't seem quite fair, but as long as Becky's teacher had seen fit to give out homework, she really felt that Becky had to do it, first snow or not.

Rafferty still hadn't come home by the time Becky's bedtime approached. He'd never worked so late before but Mandy wasn't surprised. He was associated with the hospital the accident victims had been taken to. For all she knew, he might not be home before morning.

Becky had seen the reports of the accident and she was unusually quiet as she got ready for bed. She slipped between the sheets without protest, a disturbed expression in her eyes. Seeing her small face looking so solemn, Mandy felt a wave of affection wash over her. She sat down on the edge of the bed, taking one of Becky's hands in hers.

"I suppose you're a little old for bedtime stories," she said lightly.

"Yeah."

"Don't worry about anything. I'll be here until your dad gets home."

"I know." Becky plucked at the covers with her free hand.

"What is it, Becky?" Mandy asked softly. Unable to resist, she reached out to brush the tousled bangs from the little girl's forehead. "Are you thinking about the accident?"

"I guess."

"You want to talk about it?"

A shrug was Becky's answer. Mandy waited, remembering how hard it could be to find the right words when you were Becky's age.

"How come awful things like that happen?" Becky said at last, the words bursting from her. "Things like that bus getting hit and my mom dying?"

Mandy didn't answer immediately, seeking the right words. Apparently the bus accident had brought up old fears, old questions. How would Rafferty want her to handle this? Should she tell Becky to wait and let her father answer her questions? But Becky was clearly disturbed now and she deserved an answer now. The problem was there was no simple answer.

"I don't know," Mandy said at last, deciding that Becky deserved the truth. "When bad things happen, people always look for a reason and they almost never find it. I guess maybe there are some things that we just have to learn to accept, even when we don't understand them, even when it hurts.

"You know, when I was a few years older than you are, I was in a pretty bad accident. For a while, I thought I might never walk again. I spent quite a lot of time feeling really awful, sort of scared inside."

She paused, looking at Becky to make sure she hadn't lost her. The little girl's eyes were fixed on her, wide and serious.

"I thought I must have done something pretty terrible to have such an awful thing happen to me. Only I couldn't think of what I'd done. No matter how hard I tried, I couldn't think of anything."

"Did you ever figure it out?"

"Kind of. My grandmother told me that things just happened and there wasn't always a why to them. She said you just had to accept them and get on with your life and that spending a lot of time looking for reasons that weren't there was a waste of time and energy."

"Do you really believe that?"

"I do." Mandy nodded to emphasize her belief. "I believe it with all my heart."

Becky's eyes dropped to where her hand still lay in Mandy's. "Sometimes, I wonder if maybe I did something and that's why Mama died. Not so much anymore but when I was little I used to think that." Becky's mouth quivered for an instant before becoming firm again.

Mandy's heart twisted. She understood just what Becky was saying. Mandy hadn't lost her mother but how many times had she asked herself what she'd done to deserve being forever different? Why couldn't she run and play like the other children? What terrible sin had she committed to deserve a lifetime of punishment?

"You didn't do anything, Becky. When your mom died, it was just a terrible accident and it had nothing to do with you."

"I know." Becky shrugged, her eyes still lowered. "Most of the time, I guess."

"Well, you should know it all the time." Mandy tugged

gently on one thin braid. "You're a pretty terrific kid, Rebecca Traherne. Don't you ever forget it."

Mandy was caught off guard when Becky lunged up and caught her around the neck, her thin, young arms hugging her tightly for an instant.

"Thank you for staying with me, Mandy. I really like you."

"I like you, too, sweetie." Mandy returned the hug, feeling her eyes sting.

A few minutes later, she walked slowly down the stairs, playing the conversation over in her mind, hoping she'd done the right thing. Hoping Rafferty would have approved of her response to Becky's question.

She finished tidying the kitchen, casting a wary eye at the dishwasher she'd yet to use. Sooner or later, she supposed she was going to have to break down and put some dishes in it. After all, all over America, people used dishwashers and nothing disastrous happened. Eventually she'd have to tackle it. But not tonight. Tonight was not a night for new ventures.

The kitchen cleaned, she wandered into the living room and settled down on the sofa. Picking up the mound of yarn she somewhat optimistically thought of as a sweater, she began to knit.

She'd bought the pattern and the yarn not long after she'd started work, thinking it might be pleasant to have something to fill in odd bits of time. She didn't hold out too much hope for the wearability of the garment she was making but she found the rhythmic click of the needles soothing. She was hardly aware of dozing off.

THE GRANDFATHER CLOCK in his den was just striking two o'clock when Rafferty pushed open the front door. It had been one hell of a night. He was exhausted and, at the same time, much too wound up to go to bed.

He wanted a hot shower, a stiff drink and fifteen hours of sleep, not necessarily in that order. Most of all, he wanted to be able to forget the smell of blood and fear and the sound of children crying for comfort he couldn't always give.

He rubbed a hand over the back of his neck, feeling the tension in his shoulders. The drink was the most readily available of his wants. A snifter of cognac would go a long way toward reminding him that he was home.

Rafferty stopped dead in the doorway to the living room. Mandy was curled up on the sofa, fast asleep. A tangled mass of yarn lay in her lap, a pair of rather lethal-looking knitting needles the only clue to what she'd been doing.

He'd never seen anything prettier. She looked soft and inviting, her hair tousled around her shoulders. It tumbled halfway down her back like a dark silk curtain. It made her look younger, even more vulnerable and infinitely more appealing, which didn't seem possible.

He must have made some sound or maybe she heard the rapid beating of his heart, he thought whimsically. She stirred, her eyelashes brushing slightly against her cheeks before slowly lifting. She blinked when she saw him, her eyes soft and dazed, as if she wasn't quite sure where she was.

Awareness swept in and she struggled to her feet, brushing aside the Pendleton blanket she'd had draped across her lap. "Hi." Her voice was husky with sleep.

"Hi."

"You look tired."

"I am," he said simply. He shrugged out of his coat, tossing it onto the nearest chair. Arching his back, he was aware of a bone-deep exhaustion. "Sorry I didn't call."

"That's okay." Mandy tugged the hem of her ivory sweater over her burgundy slacks, aware that she must look like an unmade bed.

She slid a glance at him, clenching her fingers against the urge to reach out and smooth away the lines of tension that bracketed his mouth.

"There's soup, if you'd like some. And I could make you a sandwich."

"Soup sounds great," he admitted with a half smile.

He followed her into the kitchen, feeling the tension start to ease from his shoulders. There was something so peaceful about coming home to find someone waiting up for him.

The kitchen was dimly lit, only the light over the stove pushing back the shadows. Mandy set about warming the soup and waved Rafferty into a chair, moving around to gather a spoon and a napkin and pour a glass of milk.

It occurred to him that he should offer to help but he couldn't seem to call up the energy to say anything. It felt wonderful to be sitting in the quiet kitchen. There was no one yelling for more blood. No sobbing of frightened children. No demands from frantic parents for answers he couldn't give yet. No one cursing at the realization that a life was slipping away despite their best efforts.

His eyes snapped open when Mandy set the steaming bowl down in front of him. He hadn't thought he was hungry until the rich scent of chicken and vegetables wafted up to him. He picked up his spoon as Mandy set a plate with a slice of bread down beside him.

"Thanks. This looks wonderful."

She sat down across the table from him, waiting to speak until he'd eaten half the soup.

"Did you get a chance to eat at all?"

"No. Someone brought in some sandwiches around eight, I think. You saw the accident on the news?"

"Yes. They made it sound pretty bad."

"It *was* bad." He dipped the spoon into the soup but didn't lift it. "We lost two children and there's another one who may not make it through tomorrow," he said bleakly.

"Oh, Rafferty." She reached across the table to put her hand on his. "It must be awful when you can't help them."

Comfort flowed from the light touch and he drank it in. It had been a long time since there'd been someone there to help chase away the demons after a night like tonight.

"It's hell."

He pushed the rest of the soup away, his appetite gone. His hand turned, his fingers grasping hers. "The worst of it was that every time I looked at one of those kids, I saw Becky. I kept thinking how easily it could have been her.''

"Well it wasn't," Mandy told him briskly, trying not to notice that they were holding hands. "Becky is just fine. She tried to talk her way out of doing her homework tonight. She felt very strongly that the first real snow of the season deserved a celebration. And what more appropriate celebration than not doing her homework?''

Rafferty smiled, the lines of tension easing from around his eyes.

"What did you tell her?''

"I told her that I agreed with her but I couldn't go against her teacher. And since her teacher was so thoughtless as to assign homework, she was going to have to do it.''

"Did it work?''

"Well, she couldn't very well argue with me when I'd already told her I agreed with her. That made me just another hapless victim of fate.''

"I'll have to try and remember that one. You're very good with her.''

"She's a wonderful child." Mandy eased her hand away, pretending not to feel a pang of loss.

Rafferty leaned back in his chair, letting the last of the night's tensions drain away. He'd done everything he could for those kids. He'd learned a long time ago that you couldn't take all the responsibility for the survival of every patient. There came a point where you had to rely on a higher power.

It was so peaceful here. So quiet.

He dragged his eyes open as Mandy pushed her chair back and reached for his dishes. "I'll get those," he mumbled, trying to summon up the energy to get out of the chair.

"I've already got them." She rinsed them off and set them in the sink. "That's what you hired me for, remember?''

"Not at three in the morning.''

"I'll bill you for overtime," she promised lightly. "You look exhausted. Why don't you go to bed and I'll call a cab to take me home."

"Why don't you just stay here tonight," Rafferty suggested, pushing himself up from the table. "I don't like the idea of you going home at this hour of the night. I have a terrific housekeeper and I'm sure the guest room is made up," he added coaxingly, when she hesitated.

"It is." She *was* tired and she wasn't looking forward to a long, cold cab ride back to an empty apartment. She nodded. "All right."

She turned off the lamp in the living room, while Rafferty checked the lock on the front door. They started up the stairs together and Mandy was vividly aware of him beside her. The house was silent around them, adding to the feeling of intimacy. She found herself thinking about the kiss they'd shared, wondering if he ever thought about it.

"You know where everything is, I guess," Rafferty said as they reached the door to the guest room.

"Yes." Mandy cleared her throat.

Rafferty frowned down at her. "I could probably find you something to sleep in. I've got a few pink T-shirts, if nothing else."

Mandy smiled at the teasing reference. "That's okay. I'll manage."

He lingered a moment longer, those gray eyes enigmatic. "Well, good night, then."

"Good night." She pushed open the guest-room door. "Thanks again for looking after Becky tonight."

"You're welcome."

She shut the bedroom door behind her and leaned back against it. It was odd how, even tired as she was, something deep inside her responded to him.

RAFFERTY CLOSED THE DOOR of the master bedroom behind him. He didn't bother with a light. He didn't need it to find the bed. Tonight, he could have found the bed even if it had been moved to another room. He stripped off his clothes, dropping them on the floor with uncharacteristic untidiness.

The mattress yielded beneath him and he closed his eyes, thinking he'd never felt anything quite so wonderful in his entire life.

Except the feel of Mandy's hair sifting through his fingers.

His eyes popped open and he stared at the darkened ceiling. He was exhausted, physically and mentally. All he wanted was ten or twelve hours of sleep. He didn't want to think about the way Mandy's hair had felt or the way her eyes had warmed with concern for him or the fact that her skin looked as soft as those damned fuzzy sweaters she was so fond of wearing.

Groaning, he shut his eyes again, trying to make his mind go blank.

What was she sleeping in? The thought brought another groan but Rafferty couldn't force the image from his mind. He wasn't sure what was worse, the thought of her going to bed wearing one of his T-shirts or the thought of her going to bed wearing nothing at all.

Or maybe she was going to sleep in her underwear.

Cursing, he rolled onto his side, squeezing his eyes shut, not so much courting sleep as commanding it to come.

Would she wear her bra and panties? Or maybe one of those silky little camisoles? Or, still worse, one of those one-piece things that were cut high on the leg and designed to cling to every curve.

He turned onto his other side, punching the pillow up before smacking his head back down on it. Mandy was his housekeeper. He'd hired her to look after the house and take care of Becky. She'd done a pretty good job of both, all in all. Only a total idiot would jeopardize a terrific combination like that because his libido got in the way.

It was just proximity, really. There was nothing more to it than that. And if he repeated that two or three hundred times, he might come to believe it.

WAITING FOR RAFFERTY to wake the next morning, Mandy felt oddly self-conscious. It was silly because it wasn't as if there had been anything even slightly risqué in her spending the night here. Becky hadn't batted an eyelash when Mandy casually mentioned that Rafferty had gotten home so late the night before that it had seemed like a good idea for her to just stay here.

She hadn't slept well. Maybe it was the time she'd spent dozing on the sofa or the strange surroundings or the fact that she couldn't stop thinking about Rafferty being just down the hall. Whatever the reason, she had still awakened at her usual time.

Luckily she had her makeup in her purse. Not that she wore much, but a touch of mascara and a dab of lipstick went a long way toward making her feel put together. She'd taken time to rinse out her underwear before going to bed. Her sweater could survive another day of wear and her wool slacks recovered nicely after steaming in the bathroom while she showered.

She went about her morning, as if there was nothing unusual in the fact that Rafferty was still asleep. Warned that her father had gotten to bed very late, Becky tiptoed through her morning routine.

The streets were wet, but with typical Colorado perversity, the sun was shining brightly, as if winter were still months away. Dropping Becky off at school, Mandy drove home.

Rafferty didn't come downstairs until after ten o'clock. Mandy was in the kitchen, studying a recipe for bread and wondering if she dared tackle it. She'd heard the shower go off, so his appearance was no surprise. He was dressed except for his shoes.

He looked tired, the lines beside his mouth drawn a little deeper. Without speaking, she handed him a cup of coffee. He took a grateful swallow before murmuring his thanks.

"I could make you breakfast," she offered, hoping he wouldn't ask for anything beyond scrambled eggs, which was the only breakfast dish she'd mastered so far.

"No thanks." He leaned one hip against the counter, the cup cradled between his hands as if it were more precious than gold. "This will hold me just fine."

"Nutritionists claim that breakfast is the most important meal of the day," she commented.

"And they're absolutely right, which is why I'd advise any patient to eat a good breakfast. Doctors, however, are trained to run on pure caffeine. It's an actual metabolic change we go through in medical school."

Mandy raised her eyebrows in a skeptical but silent response. Rafferty met her eyes and shrugged, half smiling.

"I can't face food this morning. Did Becky get off okay?"

"Yes. The roads are pretty clear this morning."

"It figures." He glanced out the window at the pale blue sky and Mandy knew he was thinking that, if the weather had been like this the day before, the school bus accident might not have happened.

"Becky seemed to think that the fact you had slept past six a.m. was a sign that the world as she knows it might be coming to an end," she said, hoping to distract him. "She said you're an early bird."

"Guilty. I'm a relentless morning person."

"So am I but I didn't dare tell Becky that."

"Coward."

"I know. But I didn't want to destroy her illusions."

Rafferty swirled the coffee in his cup, his eyes on the aimless movement. "I really do appreciate your staying last night. It meant a lot to me to know that Becky was taken care of."

"I really didn't mind. She's a lot of fun."

"She has her moments," Rafferty admitted with a smile. "Quite a few of them."

Mandy leaned down to pick up a fallen towel and her hair swung forward. Maybe it was the fact that he'd had only a few hours of sleep. Or maybe it was the way the sunlight caught faint gold highlights in the rich brown waves. Rafferty wasn't sure what made him do it. He reached out and slid his fingers into her hair as she straightened.

Mandy froze, her startled eyes flying to his face, then quickly darting away. A voice in the back of his mind suggested that he should make some light remark and leave, pretend he hadn't just breached some invisible barrier.

"You have the most beautiful hair," he said quietly, feeling it sift through his fingers.

"It's just brown." She couldn't force out more than a whisper. His finger brushed against her neck and she felt the light touch all the way to the tips of her toes.

"It's so soft, like silk."

She could feel his gaze on her as surely as she could feel his hand in her hair. She swallowed hard, trying to sort through her tangled thoughts for the right response. Should she pull away? Or should she do what she wanted to do and lean into his touch?

She didn't have to make the decision. Rafferty seemed to suddenly remember where they were—who they were. Blinking as if coming out of a dream, he pulled his hand away.

"Sorry."

"It's all right," she told him, not sure it was all right at all.

He stared at the coffee cup in his other hand, as if not quite sure what it was or how it had come to be there. He set it down on the counter with a sharp click.

"I'd better get to work."

"Yes. Have a nice day," she said to his back as he retreated out the door.

Chapter Eight

Have a nice day? Mandy was still annoyed with herself twenty-four hours later. She ran the dusting rag over the surface of an end table with a vehemence at odds with the ordinary task.

"Have a nice day?" she muttered out loud. "Could you have come up with a more banal, ridiculous response?"

The man had been fondling her hair. He'd all but made love to her with his eyes and she'd said "Have a nice day."

She gave the table a last swipe before lifting the lamp back onto it. She scowled down at her handiwork. Maybe it was time to pull her head out of the sand and look at exactly what was going on here.

"Right. So would someone please explain what's going on?"

The lamp had no response. Sighing, Mandy picked up the furniture polish and left the room. She put away the polish and poured herself a cup of tea before sitting down at the kitchen table. She still needed to vacuum—Rafferty had had the switch repaired right after the drapes were re-hung—and she had to leave to pick up Becky in an hour. But a few minutes' thought wasn't going to put too big a dent in her schedule.

It was no longer possible to pretend that there was nothing between her and Rafferty but their work relationship. Just what else was there, she couldn't quite define. An attraction, certainly. An awareness she couldn't explain. She didn't have to see or hear him to know when he'd come into a room.

When she was with him she felt…she felt…

Just what did she feel?

She felt more alive than she ever had before. She felt as if all her life she'd been waiting to meet him.

Mandy shook her head, smiling at the thought. The main problem here was that she didn't have enough experience to know *what* to think. She'd had so little contact with men, aside from her father and his business associates. During the years when she would have been dating and getting to know the opposite sex, she'd been struggling to learn to walk again.

If she'd gone to college, she might have gotten some experience there. But she hadn't gone to college. The very thought of it had terrified her mother. And since she wasn't filled with a burning ambition to become a nuclear physicist or a structural engineer, it hadn't seemed that much of a hardship to give up.

So here she was, at the ripe old age of twenty-four and the only time she'd ever been kissed in her life was when Rafferty had kissed her. It was possible that the feelings he stirred in her owed more to normal sexual urges too long suppressed than they did to some romantic attraction to him specifically.

Mandy rolled the thought around before shaking her head. Somehow, she couldn't quite make herself believe that. If she went with that theory, she'd have to believe that what she felt for Rafferty was essentially a crush brought on by suppressed hormones. That she might have reacted the same way with any reasonably attractive man.

But what Rafferty made her feel was more than simple lust, though she was willing to admit to a good bit of that. She liked him. She liked his relationship with his daughter. She liked the way his eyes lit when he smiled, the way he ran his fingers through his hair when he was thinking about something. She liked his sense of humor. She liked—

She stood up, her chair scraping on the floor. The fact of the matter was, she liked altogether too much about Rafferty Traherne. And it wasn't overactive hormones. It would have been simpler if it was. She refused to let herself believe that she was falling in love with the man. She simply wasn't going to let that happen.

Glancing at the clock, Mandy realized she'd spent more time psychoanalyzing herself than she'd planned. The vacuuming was going to have to wait if she was to pick up Becky on time. She just had time to run down to the freezer in the basement and get out something for dinner.

She approached the basement door reluctantly. Ever since that first dinner when Becky had said the basement was full of spiders, some of them as big as a cat, she'd made it a point to avoid the place. She was fairly sure she could discount Becky's claims about the size of the basement's insect inhabitants and possibly the place wasn't actually *full* of arachnids. But it didn't take a big spider or a large quantity of them to make her uneasy. Spiders simply terrified her.

Luckily there wasn't much need for her to go into the basement. The only thing down there of any interest to her was the chest freezer. Even more luckily, Becky was more than willing to venture down the steep stairs and bring up whatever Mandy needed.

But Becky wasn't here. She could wait until Becky was home but that seemed like active cowardice, rather than the passive sort she'd been practicing. She was a grown woman. Was she really going to let the thought of a few little spiders keep her from doing her job? They were probably more frightened of her than she was of them.

Mandy gave herself a continuous pep talk as she pulled open the door and flipped on the light. The stairs looked much too steep and the basement looked much too dark. As Rafferty had said, it was filled with all the junk families seem to collect and never really have a place for. Things they never had a use for but could never quite get rid of.

She tiptoed down the stairs. The room smelled damp and

cool. A broken exercise bike sat beside a stack of magazines that perched on top of half a dozen paint cans. All along one wall there were shelves filled with assorted, unidentifiable objects. A pair of dusty skis leaned drunkenly next to the freezer that was her goal.

When she lifted the lid, icy air wafted up at her. Unlike the basement, the freezer was neatly organized. It didn't take long to find the chicken she wanted. The icy package clutched in one hand, she let the lid fall and turned to make her way back across the floor.

The stairs creaked under her feet like something out of an Alfred Hitchcock movie but the door beckoned ahead in the clean, dustless, spiderless light.

She was reaching for the doorknob with one hand, using the frozen chicken to push down the light switch with the other when she felt something brush across her hand. A small brown spider, perhaps disturbed by her movements, had dropped from the ceiling onto her fingers.

With a shriek, Mandy flung out her hand. The light snapped off as she smacked against it and the chicken went flying, landing somewhere in the rubble below. The sharp movement threw the spider off. It also threw off her balance. Aware of the steep stairs at her back, she grabbed for something to hold on to, which happened to be the doorknob she'd been reaching for. The door slammed shut with a crash that threatened to break the frame.

Frantic to escape the sudden darkness where who knew how many spiders might be lying in wait, Mandy pushed on the door, twisting the knob. But foolishly, she'd left the lock button turned when she opened the door. In closing, the door had locked itself, just as it had been designed to do.

She was locked into the basement, in the dark. There was no one home. No one to know where she was. No one to let her out.

She beat down the hysteria that threatened to overwhelm her. There was nothing to be afraid of. All she had to do was switch the light back on. There was bound to be a screwdriver somewhere in the debris below. She could either use it to work the lock or she could remove the doorknob—the whole damned door, if she had to.

Drawing a deep breath, Mandy reached for the spot she thought the switch might be. Her fingers brushed against the rough concrete. She felt to the right and then up and then down. And came into contact with something that moved.

With a cry, she jerked her hand back, clutching it against her chest. It was probably the same little spider she'd shaken off her hand and it was probably just as terrified as she was.

But it might not be the same spider. It might be another spider. A larger one.

"Stop it!" Her voice echoed oddly but it helped to calm the panic that was building up in her throat, threatening to choke her.

There was nothing to be afraid of. Most spiders were completely harmless. After all, if she did nothing to upset them, they had no reason to bother her. So all she had to do was try not to upset any of them.

RAFFERTY LEANED ACROSS the seat to push open the passenger door as Becky raced across the school yard toward the Jeep.

"Hi, Dad." She scrambled into the seat and reached for her seat belt.

"Hi, urchin." He waited until she was settled before shifting gears and stepping on the gas.

"Sorry I had to call you."

"That's okay. Mandy didn't call?"

"Nope. And she didn't answer the phone when I called home."

Rafferty nodded but the frown didn't leave his forehead. If there was one thing he'd learned about Mandy, it was that she was totally dependable. She'd never even been late picking Becky up. When Becky had called to tell him she was at school and Mandy hadn't shown up, he'd taken time to call the house before leaving to pick her up. Just as Becky said, no one had answered.

"Maybe she had a flat tire," Becky suggested, picking up on his concern.

"Probably."

But when he pulled the Jeep into the driveway, the car was sitting just where it always did. Which meant that, wherever Mandy was, she hadn't taken the car. Rafferty's stride was longer than usual as he crossed the yard, Becky trotting behind him.

It was probably nothing. Maybe a friend had come by and picked her up and she'd lost track of the time. Irresponsible as that would be, he'd much rather that be the case than some of the possibilities that were racing through his mind.

She just looked so damned fragile sometimes. He couldn't help but think of all the ways someone as small as she was could end up injured.

"Mandy?" He was calling her name as he thrust open the door.

"I'll check upstairs." Becky darted by him and ran up the stairs.

"Mandy?" Rafferty started for the kitchen, feeling a choking sensation in his throat. If anything had happened to her...

"Mandy?"

MANDY DIDN'T KNOW how long she'd been in the basement. She'd finally gathered the courage to try the light switch again but the bulb, with a malice inanimate objects were occasionally capable of, had come on only long enough to blow out with a decisive pop.

Groping for the doorknob had done her no good. It had refused to yield to her most determined assaults. After what seemed like hours, her legs had started to ache. She'd settled gingerly on the step, drawing her knees up to her chest and wrapping her arms around them. The air was cool and damp and she wished she'd grabbed a sweater before coming down. But then she hadn't expected to find herself locked in.

It wasn't just the physical discomfort that wore at her. It was the pictures her imagination painted. Every shift of air, every sound, presented possibilities on which her phobia fed. She imagined spiders everywhere.

How long would it be before someone found her? When she didn't pick Becky up at school, surely Becky would call her father. Rafferty would pick Becky up. Then they would come home and find her. He was welcome to fire her on the spot, just as long as he let her out of here.

She rested her forehead on her knees, squeezing her eyes shut. The darkness wasn't so bad with her eyes closed.

At first, when she heard Rafferty calling her name, she thought it was her imagination. She wanted it so desperately that she thought she was hallucinating. When she heard him the second time, she stumbled to her feet. She opened her mouth but no sound came out. It wasn't until he called her name the third time, that Mandy was able to force her voice to work.

"I'm in the basement! Please!" She fell against the door, no longer concerned with spiders, no longer concerned with anything except getting out into the light again.

"Please don't go away," she begged, hardly aware of the absurdity of thinking he was going to leave her locked in the basement.

The knob rattled and then the door was pulled open. Mandy tumbled through the opening, aware of glorious light spilling over her.

"Mandy!" Rafferty caught her when she stumbled, pulling her into his arms. "How long have you been in there?"

"Hours." Now that she was safe, she could only cling to him. "I went to get a chicken and then there was a spider and I dropped the chicken and the light blew out and the door was locked. And I didn't pick Becky up," she got out, choking back the urge to cry.

"It's all right. Becky's fine. Don't cry, love."

Neither of them noticed Becky enter the kitchen. Having

not found Mandy on the second floor, she'd come down-stairs to see if her father was having better luck. Seeing Mandy wrapped in her father's arms, Becky stopped short. A slow smile curved her mouth. Obviously Mandy was all right. Equally as obvious, her father was more than capable of comforting her. Grinning, she backed out as silently as she'd entered.

Rafferty was aware that his hand was not quite steady as he brushed it over Mandy's cheek. He had been so afraid that something terrible had happened to her. Finding her frightened but unharmed, he wanted to shake her, he wanted to yell at her for scaring him and he wanted to kiss the breath out of her.

Those beautiful brown eyes swimming with tears she was determined not to shed. Her cheeks were pale and her lips trembled. Damn it! Did she have to be so vulnerable? So damned beautiful?

"I've got you safe, now."

"I was so scared," she whispered. "It's stupid but I felt as if I would be locked in there forever."

"I'd have found you," he promised huskily.

Her face cupped in his hands, he bent to kiss a solitary tear from her cheek. Mandy closed her eyes, feeling the rough brush of his beard-roughened skin, the strength of his broad hands.

It seemed inevitable that his mouth should find hers, in-evitable that she should melt into him. There was more urgency in this kiss than there had been in the first. His mouth slanted across hers, his tongue demanding and re-ceiving entry. With a soft moan, she wound her arms around his neck.

If Rafferty's motive had been only to comfort her, that noble intention disappeared the moment he felt her re-sponse. His arms slid around her, drawing her closer. She fit against him as if made for him, as if they were two halves of one whole.

"Did you find her, Daddy?"

It took several moments for Becky's voice to register,

several seconds more for him to gather the strength to drag his mouth from Mandy's. Their eyes met, full of questions as his hands slid away. Becky was clattering down the stairs. The sound seemed unnaturally loud.

"Daddy?"

"We're in here, Becky." Rafferty had to clear his throat before he could get the words out. He turned as Becky trotted into the room, his wide frame shielding Mandy for a moment, giving her a chance to regain her composure before Becky saw her.

Feeling rather fragile, she stepped around Rafferty and gave Becky a smile that was only slightly shaky around the edges.

"I locked myself in the basement," she said, pleased that her voice was steady. "And I'm afraid I lost tonight's dinner somewhere between the skis and the paint cans."

WITH BECKY THERE, there was no chance to discuss what had happened. Mandy didn't know what she'd have said, anyway. That she always kissed men who rescued her from spider-filled basements? That she wished he'd taken her into his arms again and never let go? The truth was she didn't know what she felt.

Rafferty could have agreed with her on that point. The fear he'd felt when he thought something might have happened to her had certainly been more than he should have felt for someone who was, at most, a friend. Simple concern would have been more appropriate than the near terror he'd felt.

He could no longer pretend that she was nothing more to him than a housekeeper. But he wasn't quite ready to come up with another definition for her role in his life.

So they tried to pretend that nothing had happened, just as they'd done with the first kiss. It was even less effective this time around.

IT SEEMED AS IF, before she had time to draw a breath, Mandy was face-to-face with Thanksgiving. She'd been dreading the holiday, her first away from home. Her parents wanted her to come back to Pennsylvania but it was clear that they would view such a visit as a golden opportunity to convince her to come back for good.

Sometimes, she was amazed at how easily they managed to overlook what she'd accomplished; to remain deaf to what she told them. They simply refused to let go of their image of her as a helpless child, who needed to be protected. Maybe it was their way of feeling needed, of being sure that she loved them.

Mandy knew they were hurt by her continued refusal to come home. She still hadn't even told them where she was. It hurt her to know that she was causing them pain but she couldn't go back to the way things had been.

So she steeled herself against her mother's tearful pleas that she come home for the holiday. As soon as she'd put down the receiver, she shed a few tears herself. Her refusal to go home meant she'd be spending the holiday alone, a prospect that held very little appeal.

"BECKY TELLS ME you're not going home for Thanksgiving." It was the week before the holiday and Rafferty had lingered after Mandy arrived, something he hadn't done since the day she'd been locked in the basement.

"That's right." She measured tea into the pot, forcing her hand to remain steady. She didn't have to be looking at him to feel his eyes on her.

"If it's a matter of needing time off," he said slowly, "there's no problem there. I know Claire would be happy to look after Becky on the days I work."

"You're not taking the weekend off?" Mandy turned to look at him, trying not to notice how good he looked in the thick ivory sweater he wore over his shirt.

"Just Thursday. Since I'll be filling in at the hospital, I'd planned to ask Claire to look after Becky the rest of the weekend anyway. I guess we didn't discuss time off when

I hired you but I'm not such an ogre that I expect you to work right through the holidays.''

"I don't think you're an ogre," she told him. Her lips curved in a smile. The movement drew Rafferty's eyes and she felt the impact of his look as if it were an actual touch. The smile faded, her mouth unconsciously softening. Rafferty's eyes lifted to hers and the atmosphere was suddenly rife with tension.

For a moment, Mandy thought he might cross the room and pull her into his arms and she knew she'd melt like butter in the sun if he so much as touched her.

Sometimes it seemed as if the time since they'd last kissed could be measured in years rather than weeks. At others, it seemed only a heartbeat ago.

This was one of the times when she could almost feel the pressure of his mouth, feel the weight of his hands on her shoulders.

She wanted him to cross the few feet that separated them—wanted it so fiercely, she knew she'd be shocked at herself later. From the look in his eyes, she knew he was remembering, too. Had she leaned toward him? Had he taken a step toward her?

Behind her, the kettle began to squeal, the shrill sound shattering the tense moment. Mandy turned and picked up the kettle, her hand not quite steady as she poured the boiling water over the tea.

Behind her, Rafferty cleared his throat. "Well, anyway, if you need a few days off, there's no problem there."

"Thank you, but that won't be necessary." She set the lid on the teapot, making sure it was perfectly aligned before she turned to face him again. "In fact, if you'd like, I could take care of Becky that weekend."

The sexual tension had been shoved into the background again, not quite forgotten but possible to ignore.

"I wouldn't ask you to do that," he protested.

"You're not asking. I'm volunteering. I'd be happy to look after her."

He shoved his hands into his pockets, his eyes thoughtful. "Don't you have any plans? Friends or something?"

"Nothing," she admitted with forced cheer.

"What about Thanksgiving Day? Are you going out with anyone?"

"No." It was getting harder to sound cheerful. Did he have to rub her nose in her solitary circumstances?

"You're planning on spending the day alone?" he asked, beginning to frown.

"I don't mind," she lied.

"Well, I do."

She blinked at his blunt response. "I beg your pardon?"

"I mind you spending the day alone," he told her, a touch of belligerence coloring his voice.

"Why should you?"

"Because spending the holiday alone isn't a hell of a lot of fun."

"I suspect I'll survive."

He scowled at her for a moment, dark eyebrows hooked over gray eyes. "I've got a better idea. Why don't you spend the day with us?"

"You and Becky? Becky said you're going to your sister's for the day. That your whole family will be there."

"We are and they will. But you're more than welcome to join us."

"I couldn't." She shook her head. "I couldn't just push myself in like that."

"So let *me* push you in," he said, smiling.

"No, really. I don't think your sister liked me all that much the time we met and I'm sure she wouldn't like it at all if I just arrived on her doorstep. And I couldn't blame her."

"Claire's bark is a lot worse than her bite. Beneath that ironclad exterior beats a heart of marshmallow." He caught her disbelieving look and amended the statement. "Okay, it's not quite marshmallow but she's not as hard-nosed as she sounds. And she didn't dislike you. She wouldn't have approved of anyone she hadn't personally vetted and hired—not even Hazel. But as long as Becky's happy, that's all Claire really cares about.''

Mandy shook her head, unconvinced. "Your family isn't going to want a stranger around.''

"You're hardly a stranger. Come on, Mandy. I wouldn't suggest it if I thought you were going to be uncomfortable. You know Becky would love to have you there.''

"Where?" Becky stepped out of the doorway and ran to her father's side. He put one arm around her shoulders. "Where would I like to have Mandy?''

"Nowhere," Mandy said hastily.

"At Aunt Claire's for Thanksgiving," Rafferty said, overriding her.

"Yeah! That'd be neat!" Becky skipped out of her father's hold and crossed the room to grab Mandy's hand. "Say yes, Mandy. It'll be fun. My cousin Mark has a horse and everything. And there'll be tons of food. Everybody gets to eat until they're sick. Come on, Mandy. Say yes!''

Mandy looked from Becky's bright face and shining eyes to Rafferty, who was looking distinctly smug. He knew she might have been able to resist his arguments but Becky's coaxing would have melted a much harder heart than Mandy's.

"It's a family holiday," she protested weakly. "I wouldn't want to intrude.''

"You won't. Will she, Daddy?" Still holding Mandy's hand, Becky glanced over her shoulder for her father's corroboration.

"Of course she won't," Rafferty said promptly. He was grinning openly now.

"'Sides, you're practically family, anyway," Becky told Mandy. "Say you'll come with us, Mandy.''

In the end, Mandy couldn't stand firm against the combined weight of Becky's pleading and Rafferty's smile. It wasn't as if she'd been looking forward to spending a lonely holiday, anyway.

Becky felt a certain smug satisfaction at Mandy's capitulation. She was especially pleased that it had been her father's idea to invite Mandy to spend the holiday with them. It meant that he was beginning to think of Mandy as family.

Now, all he needed was a little nudge to start thinking of making her a permanent part of the family.

Chapter Nine

As it turned out, Rafferty had been telling the truth when he'd said his family wouldn't consider Mandy's presence an intrusion. His parents were predisposed to like her because of their granddaughter's enthusiasm for her.

Claire's husband turned out to be a quiet, soft-spoken man, whose gentle features and receding hairline seemed an odd match for his dynamic wife. Since Rafferty's other sister wasn't coming back to Colorado for the holiday, and Claire's children were amenable to any visitor, as long as the path to the table remained unblocked, that left Claire as the only potential stumbling block.

But though Claire did seem a bit reserved at first, she soon began to relax, at least as much as Mandy imagined she ever relaxed. Claire might have her reservations about her brother's housekeeper and his reasons for hiring her but she wasn't blind to the fact that her niece was happy and seemed to think Mandy was the greatest thing since peanut butter. If Becky was happy and Mandy had anything to do with that happiness, Claire was willing to swallow her own doubts.

It didn't seem to occur to anyone that inviting the housekeeper to share a family holiday was odd. Mandy tried to imagine how her parents would react if it was suggested that Rosie sit down to dinner with them.

The picture simply wouldn't come into focus. It wasn't

that they were snobs. They didn't consider Rosie beneath them. But in their world, there was a place for everything and everyone and the housekeeper did not sit down to dinner with the family.

The Trahernes had no such reservations. It wasn't a difference in financial position or social standing. The Traherne family had plenty of both. But they didn't have the same old-world reserve that characterized the Bradfords. The Bradfords of Philadelphia traced their ancestry back to the Mayflower.

The Trahernes traced theirs back to an indentured servant brought over from England, who'd served out his time and then proceeded to make a fortune during the Revolutionary War.

Pamela Bradford was on the board of several important charities. She took her committee work very seriously and had helped to raise thousands of dollars to aid the needy.

Lillian Traherne was also on the board of several charities but she was just as likely to be found serving soup to the needy as coaxing money out of sponsors to pay for it.

The way the Trahernes celebrated the holiday was quite different, also. Holidays in the Bradford home were generally somewhat restrained. The food was gourmet, the decorations were refined and the guests were elegantly dressed and spoke in modulated tones.

Claire Desmond served up plenty of wonderful food but elegance took a back seat to quantity and robust flavor. The decorations were a haphazard array of paper chains in appropriate autumn colors, lopsided turkeys created by the children and several slightly malformed pilgrims made out of modeling clay and painted in colors that dazzled the eye.

Flynn and Ann McCallister joined the gathering, as well as several other family friends, most of whom Mandy never quite managed to attach names to. Assorted children ran in and out of the house, playing and laughing. The adults either assisted in the preparations or kibitzed as suited their personalities and inclinations.

Controlled chaos ruled the day. It took Mandy a little

while to get used to it. But once she had, she found it rather exciting. It certainly was never boring.

It was long after dark when the gathering at last broke up and they set out for home. Mandy was pleasantly tired. She leaned her head back against the seat and relaxed. If she turned her head slightly, she could see Rafferty's hands on the wheel, strong and confident.

She'd enjoyed watching him with his family today. He'd shown endless patience with his nephews, who'd wanted his opinion on everything from science projects to how to properly shoe a horse.

The affection the Traherne clan felt for one another was an open, comfortable thing that everyone took for granted. It was a nice feeling, she thought, her eyes beginning to drift shut.

"Mandy. We're here." Rafferty's voice was quiet, rousing her from the light doze she'd drifted into. When she opened her eyes, she saw that he was leaning over her.

"I'm either very dull company or a terrific driver," he said quietly. "Becky's out like a light, too."

Drowsy, Mandy blinked at him, feeling warm and contented. He'd stopped under the street lamp in front of her apartment building. The light spilled over the dash but left most of the car interior in shadow. His eyes picked up the light, the pale gray irises looking like polished silver.

"I had a nice time," she told him.

"So did I." He reached up to brush a soft brown curl back from her forehead, his fingers lingering against her temple.

"Your family is very nice."

"They liked you, too. Mom seems to think I should double your salary."

"Does she?" His hair had fallen over his forehead and she reached up to brush it back into place.

"You look like a sleepy little girl," he told her, his voice hardly above a whisper, in deference to the child sleeping in the back seat.

"Do you think of me as a little girl?" she asked him,

knowing what his answer would be. Wrapped in darkness, with Becky asleep nearby, she felt safe flirting with him.

"Hardly." She caught the gleam of his teeth as he smiled. She felt his hand slip deeper into her hair, drawing her face up to his.

"I'm glad," she murmured as his mouth touched hers.

It was a warm kiss, full of promise but making no demands. There was heat, but it was a slow-burning kind of fire, the kind that promised to last. Mandy's fingers slid into Rafferty's hair, savoring the feel of it against her hand. Her mouth opened beneath his, her tongue coming up to fence with his in a gentle combat that had no winner and no loser.

Becky stirred in the back seat, muttering in her sleep. The small movement reminded them of where they were and Rafferty drew back. Only his hand lingered in her hair, and while his eyes were intent on hers, the darkness made it impossible to read anything in his expression.

Mandy felt a sense of loss at his withdrawal but she didn't offer any protest. She knew as well as he did that it was neither the time nor the place to continue this.

"I guess I'd better get in," she murmured as his fingers finally left her hair.

"I'll see you tomorrow."

The words sounded like a promise and Mandy hugged the thought to her as she hurried through the cold night air to her apartment. Rafferty waited until he saw that she was safely inside before pulling away from the curb.

Leaning back against the door, she listened to the sound of the Jeep's engine fade away. *See you tomorrow.* She liked the sound of the words.

It came to her suddenly that she'd begun to count on seeing Rafferty Traherne for quite a few tomorrows.

THE WEEKS BETWEEN Thanksgiving and Christmas flew by at a speed that seemed nothing short of miraculous. The week following Thanksgiving, Rafferty came down with a cold. He proved to be a somewhat grumpy patient.

Mandy dosed him with orange juice and chicken broth and ignored his ill temper. He refused to stay in bed, which would have probably accelerated his recovery. Instead, he holed up in the den, rather like a wounded wolf, she thought with some amusement.

Since the weather had become more erratic, with occasional snow flurries that made the buses less reliable, Rafferty had insisted that Mandy use the car he'd provided to drive back and forth to work. Having it at her disposal made it easier for her to stay late in the evenings, feeding Becky dinner and making sure she was tucked in at night.

After two or three days of hiding in the den and snapping at anyone who dared come near him, he'd recovered enough to be bored with his own company. Becky was only in school half a day all that week and she convinced her father that cutthroat games of Monopoly were the best medicine to help him along the road to recovery. Since Monopoly was obviously more entertaining with three players than it was with two, Mandy was roped into their games.

Seated around the kitchen table, they bought and sold enough property to make Donald Trump green with envy. Of the three of them, Becky had the best head for business and she triumphed over the adults in every game. Not even her father's whining complaints that he was an invalid and deserved a little compassion could convince her to show any mercy.

Mandy proved to be an appallingly bad player with a tendency to buy the properties no one else wanted because she felt sorry for them. Rafferty looked at her incredulously when she mentioned this as a motive for buying Baltic Avenue. She argued that surely compassion should be its own reward. While that might be true in other walks of life, in Monopoly, nice guys did finish last.

But not even bankruptcy could put a serious dent in her enjoyment. Broke and tossed ignominiously out of the game, she took as much pleasure in watching Rafferty and Becky fight it out to the end than she would have if she'd actually won.

Rafferty might have had a better chance at winning if at least half his concentration hadn't been on Mandy. It was a good thing they weren't playing poker because her face revealed every emotion. He'd have been able to read her cards just from the look in her eyes.

He wondered if it had occurred to her that, to anyone watching the three of them, they must look like a family. They were the very picture of the American ideal. Mother, father and child. A cozy house, the smell of dinner cooking on the stove. After supper, they'd sit and read or watch television and then they'd all go up to bed, Becky to her own room while he and Mandy—

He broke the thought off, dragging his attention back to the game board at Becky's crow of delight. Boardwalk with two hotels. It seemed there were hazards everywhere. Financial ruin on the game board and emotional pitfalls in the form of the woman sitting across the table from him.

Sooner or later, they were going to have to face what was growing between them. And there could be no more pretense that there wasn't something between them.

THE DAY RAFFERTY pronounced himself recovered, the McCallisters dropped by for a visit. Mandy was glad to see them. She and Ann had spent some time talking at Thanksgiving, furthering what Mandy hoped was the beginning of a genuine friendship.

Flynn was getting ready for a showing of his photographs due to open just after the first of the year. As it turned out, part of the reason for the visit was that Flynn wanted Mandy's permission to use a photograph he'd taken of her.

"Why on earth would you want a picture of me in your show?" Mandy asked incredulously. Out of the corner of her eye, she saw Rafferty frown.

"It's not a photograph of *you* precisely. Or at least that's not the reason I want to use it."

"Careful, Flynn, your tact is showing," Ann warned him dryly.

He grinned. "It isn't that I don't think you're devastatingly beautiful,'' he told Mandy expansively. Laughter made his eyes a bright, shining blue. "But it's really more the mood of the piece that I want in the show.''

"I suppose it makes me look awful.'' It was impossible *not* to respond to Flynn McCallister. Ann had said that her husband could charm the birds out of the trees and Mandy believed her. There was a mischievous sparkle in those eyes that made it impossible to remain immune.

"It wouldn't be possible to make you look less than wonderful,'' he told her, still with laughter in his eyes.

Ann groaned and rolled her eyes in silent commentary. Rafferty continued to frown.

"I brought a copy of the photo I want to use,'' Flynn said, reaching for the folder he'd laid on the table.

Mandy took the picture from him, feeling her breath catch when she saw it. He'd taken the picture the day she'd gone to his house with Rafferty and Becky. She remembered that he'd had his camera out and he'd taken any number of pictures of Becky and Hannah.

At first, she'd been self-consciously aware of the camera, careful to stay out of range of the lens. But after a while the camera had seemed as if it were an extension of his arm and she'd forgotten about it.

This particular shot had been taken outside. The black-and-white film gave it a grainy, vaguely mournful ambiance. With her hair pulled back in a soft twist and the collar of her coat drawn up around her face, she might have been a woman who'd lived fifty years ago. She'd been half turned from the camera.

Looking at it, Mandy knew that the woman in the photograph was her but it was like looking at a stranger. The woman in the photograph had an air of mystery about her, a certain sadness in the curve of her mouth, a vulnerability in the line of throat and jaw.

As a photograph, it was obviously the work of someone who knew how to work with the camera the way an artist might work with a paintbrush on canvas. The lighting, the angle, the delicate contrast in shades of gray—all of it combined to form an exquisite whole.

"Flynn, this is wonderful." There was nothing narcissist in the compliment since she'd already dismissed the fact that it was her in the picture. Herself as subject wasn't what made it a work of art. She handed the photo to Rafferty, who'd leaned forward to get a better look at it.

"Thank you." The compliment seemed to please Flynn. "Do you mind if I use it?"

"No, of course not." She laughed. "That's much too beautiful for anyone to associate with me."

"Anyone would recognize you," Rafferty said, making the words a flat statement so that it was hard to know what to say in reply.

"Thank you," Mandy murmured uncertainly, wondering what had happened to spoil his mood.

Flynn McCallister was what had happened, Rafferty thought sourly. It wasn't that he didn't like the man. As a matter of fact, he liked him a great deal and not just because of what he'd done for Becky.

It was just about impossible *not* to like Flynn. The man oozed charm. And the worst of it was that it was completely natural. Flynn didn't work at being charming and witty and annoyingly amusing. He simply was.

In the more rational portions of his mind, Rafferty was aware that he was being unreasonable, possibly even a bit childish. He knew perfectly well that Flynn wasn't trying to charm Mandy. Flynn was madly in love with his wife and any "charming" going on was just his natural way.

But that didn't make Rafferty feel any better. Without false modesty, he knew that there were a number of good things that could be said about him, too, but doubted anyone was likely to accuse him of having an overabundance of the sort of easy charm that came so naturally to Flynn.

He was, he admitted, jealous. Plain old-fashioned schoolboy jealousy that ill became a man of thirty-six, who was a doctor besides. Admitting to it made the absurdity of it all the more obvious to him and made it possible for him to smile about it.

Whatever lay between him and Mandy—and he wasn't prepared to define what that was—wasn't worth much if it couldn't withstand the presence of another attractive man. Being jealous was actually something of an insult to Mandy, implying that she was shallow enough to have her head turned by a handsome face and a few compliments.

All the same, he would have felt better if Flynn's face weren't quite so handsome and his compliments weren't quite so articulate.

IF MANDY HAD THOUGHT that she and Rafferty might have a chance to explore their relationship once he'd recovered from his cold, she was disappointed. The Christmas rush swept them both up in its frenzy. There seemed to be so much to get done in so little time.

Becky was to perform in her school's Christmas pageant and Mandy was moved to tears when she insisted that Mandy had to be there to see her. It frightened her to realize how much Becky had come to mean to her. She'd wound her way into Mandy's heart so thoroughly that Mandy couldn't imagine a time when she hadn't been there.

She wasn't sure just how or when it had come about, but she was no longer just the housekeeper who kept an eye on Becky after school. At some point she'd grown to care for Becky, not because she was paid to do so but because she loved the little girl.

And certainly her feelings for Rafferty were a long way from being simply those of an employee. She wasn't quite ready to put a label on them, however.

IT WAS, MANDY THOUGHT, somewhat ironic that she should decide to give in to her parents' pleading and go home for Christmas just when they decided that they were going to try a new tactic in their continuing battle to get her to come to her senses.

They were, her mother informed her before she could say anything about coming home, going to Monte Carlo for the holiday. Since she'd made it clear that she no longer cared about her family, they saw no reason to spend a lonely Christmas at home. They were going to take their broken hearts to Europe. Perhaps, once they were no longer there for her weekly phone calls, Mandy would realize just how much she needed them and come home.

Mandy had to bite her lip against an urge to laugh. A few weeks ago, her mother's words would have made her cringe with guilt. Now, the rather heavy-handed attempt at manipulation struck her as funny and rather sad.

Since gambling was one of the few vices her parents admitted to, she decided not to say anything. They might be going to Monte Carlo to make her feel guilty, but she didn't doubt that they'd have a rousing good time while they were there.

Rafferty and Becky were to spend Christmas Day with the family but Christmas Eve was a quieter celebration. Last year the McCallisters had joined them but they were going back to California this year to celebrate a Christmas amid palm trees with Flynn's parents.

It seemed inevitable that Mandy should spend Christmas Eve with Rafferty and Becky. Secretly she had been relieved when her mother unwittingly put a damper on her plans to go home.

The week before, Rafferty and Becky had gone out and found a ridiculously large Christmas tree. On Christmas Eve, Mandy helped them decorate it. They consumed enormous quantities of hot chocolate and argued over where to hang the decorations.

It was not much like the more sedate tree decorating parties she'd grown up with but it brought back enough memories to make Mandy feel slightly misty-eyed. She really did miss her family.

"Homesick?"

The cushion dipped as Rafferty sank onto the sofa next to her. Becky had gone up to her room to get something, leaving the adults alone. There was a fire crackling in the fireplace, the scent of burning wood mixing with the crisp smell of the Christmas tree. Outside a light snow was falling, just enough to add the perfect Christmas touch.

"A little," Mandy admitted, accepting the glass of ginger ale he offered.

"You should have gone home. Becky spends a few days with her grandparents right after Christmas, anyway."

"Well, actually, I'd planned on it." She laughed and shrugged. "My parents wanted me to come home at Thanksgiving and I refused. Then, when I decided to go home for Christmas, they decided they were going to Europe, instead. I suppose it serves me right."

Rafferty leaned back, his eyes on the fire. "You don't talk about your family much."

"Don't I?" Mandy frowned. "I guess I don't. There's not much to say, really. We get along but they're a bit overprotective."

And if that wasn't a masterpiece of understatement, she didn't know what was.

"Is that why you left Philadelphia?"

"Pretty much. When I think about it now, it seems pretty silly, running away from home at my age."

"Just what is your age?" He asked the question so casually, it took a moment for the significance of it to register.

It had been a long time since she'd given any thought to the application she'd filled out and the answers that had been something less than the truth. She flicked him a nervous look, which he met with amusement.

"I'll be twenty-five in January," she admitted uneasily.

"Not thirty?" He widened his eyes in mock surprise.

"No."

"I bet you didn't spend time working as a teacher's aide, either?"

She shook her head.

"Or running a large household, which included the care of two children?"

She shook her head again, nibbling uneasily on her lower

lip. "I was sure I could do the job and I knew I wouldn't get a chance to prove it if you knew I didn't have much experience."

"You're right there," Rafferty admitted but he didn't seem particularly upset. Mandy dared to breathe again.

"I wouldn't have lied if I hadn't been certain I could do the job," she assured him earnestly.

"Like you ran the washing machine? Or the vacuum cleaner?"

She winced but there seemed to be more humor than censure in his questions. "Well, the housework turned out to be a little trickier than I'd anticipated."

"So I gathered."

Silence stretched between them. He finished the last of his coffee and set the cup down before turning to look at her, drawing one knee up on the sofa. "I hate to tell you this, but a blind man could tell that you're not thirty. And the experience you listed would have been a bit much even if you were thirty."

"I was afraid I might have overdone it a little," she admitted.

"Just a little. Didn't it occur to you that I might have asked for references?"

"No." She looked stricken, as if the possibility had the power to frighten her even now that the danger was past. Why hadn't she considered something so basic?

"Why didn't you?"

"Because I was fairly sure they wouldn't check out," he told her. His mouth twisted in a wry smile.

"But you hired me," she protested. "Why did you hire me if you knew I'd lied?"

"I've asked myself that a few times," he admitted, his eyes scanning her face. "More than a few times."

He reached out to catch a soft brown curl between his fingers, his expression vacant. She was suddenly vividly aware that they were alone. Becky was upstairs but she might as well have been a thousand miles away. There was no one but the two of them, alone in the firelight.

"What did you decide?" She had to clear her throat to get the words out.

"I decided that I must have been working on instinct," he said slowly. His fingers slid deeper into her hair, brushing against the nape of her neck. Mandy felt the soft touch all the way to her toes. "Becky liked you from the minute she met you."

"So you hired me because Becky liked me?" She was hardly aware of what she was saying. It was hard to think with Rafferty so close. When had he gotten so close? His hand cupped the back of her head, drawing her closer. Only inches separated them now. When had the room gotten so warm? She felt breathless with the heat. Or was it the look in Rafferty's eyes that made it impossible to catch her breath?

"I hired you because I had to."

He was just a breath away.

"For Becky's sake?"

But he didn't answer with words. His mouth closed over hers with a gentle hunger that stole the last of her breath away. Mandy's hands came up to clasp his shoulders. Her lips parted beneath his, her hunger as great. This was what she needed to be complete. Only this.

One hand buried in the extravagant length of her hair, Rafferty's other hand found its way to her waist, pulling her forward until they were as close as it was possible to get while sitting on the sofa.

Mandy shared his frustration at the awkward position. She wanted to be closer to him. She wanted—

The sound of Becky clattering down the stairs was like a bucket of ice water thrown over the pair on the sofa. When she dashed into the room a moment later, Rafferty and Mandy were sitting at opposite ends of the sofa, their eyes fixed on the fireplace.

If Mandy's hair was a little mussed and her lips a little swollen, the dim light helped to conceal that. And if Rafferty was concentrating just a bit too fiercely on the fire, one could have assumed he was lost in thought.

"I'm starved," Becky announced.

Mandy felt as if she'd been poised on the brink of a scary but exciting precipice and had been abruptly yanked back. Becky crossed the room to lean on the arm of the sofa.

"You can't be hungry," Rafferty told her, nothing in his manner hinting that she'd disturbed anything more than a casual conversation. "You just ate dinner."

"That was *hours* ago. My stomach's growling," she told him, managing to imply that death by starvation was only moments away.

"I think there's some chowder left," Mandy offered, proud of the steadiness of her voice. "I could heat it up."

The chowder was duly heated and consumed, with the adults concentrating on Becky, as much to avoid concentrating on each other as anything else.

By the time the dishes had been rinsed and the last of the wrapping paper picked up, Rafferty announced that it was time for everyone under the age of eleven to go to bed. Recognizing this as clear evidence of prejudicial lawmaking, Becky protested. Her half-hearted whining turned to giggles when Rafferty ended the discussion by picking her up and dumping her over his shoulder.

Mandy refused to interfere in what was a clear case of excessive use of force but she did agree to come up and kiss Becky good-night.

It was a very domestic scene, with Rafferty and Mandy both on hand to tuck Becky in. Anyone watching would have naturally assumed that she was their daughter, though Mandy looked rather young to be the mother of a ten-year-old.

Walking downstairs with Rafferty after Becky was safely tucked in, Mandy was suddenly aware of the quiet house around them.

"It's late. I should probably be getting home." Though there was no one to hear her but him, her voice was hushed.

Rafferty put his hand on her arm, drawing her to a halt in the archway between living room and entryway.

"You could stay here tonight," he said quietly.

Meeting his eyes, Mandy shook her head. Nothing had to be said for her to know exactly where that would lead.

"I don't think that would be such a good idea."

Rafferty glanced up the stairs to where his daughter was sleeping and nodded. "You're right," he admitted ruefully.

They stood there for a moment, both reluctant to see the evening end.

"You're sure you won't change your mind and come with us tomorrow?" he asked at last. "My parents specifically invited you."

"I know. But I think I'd really like to be alone. I have some things I want to think about." At the top of her list was where her relationship with him was headed. And she couldn't think about that with him right in front of her. Maybe he guessed as much because he didn't press her anymore.

"All right. But you can't expect me to let an opportunity like this pass."

His smile took on a wicked edge as he glanced up. Mandy followed his look, her cheeks coloring when she saw the rather moth-eaten sprig of foliage that hung in the archway.

"I didn't hang that there," she protested in a whisper.

"I suspect we have Becky to thank for its presence. She's much too precocious," he added thoughtfully. "Still, it seems a shame to waste it."

Mandy closed her eyes as his head bent over hers. What started out as a relatively restrained gesture took fire the moment their lips met. Mandy's arms came up to encircle his neck as his hands swept across her back, drawing her up on tiptoe, so that she was cradled against his thighs.

Mandy's fingers slid into the hair at the nape of his neck. His hand slipped down her back, pressing her thighs against the hard evidence of his arousal. The feel of him against her both excited her and shocked her with the reality of their actions.

Mandy dragged her mouth away from his, her hands moving to his shoulders, pressing against him in weak protest. Rafferty's arms loosened reluctantly, giving her the breathing room she so desperately needed.

"Are you sure you won't stay the night?" he asked, only half kidding.

She shook her head without looking at him. If she looked at him, she'd probably agree to anything he suggested. "I have to get home," she whispered.

She moved away but he caught her hand before she was out of reach. "Becky is going to be staying with my parents for four days after Christmas. You could take the time off, if you wanted." His fingers tightened, urging her eyes to meet his.

"Is that what you want?" she whispered, half-frightened by the desire she saw in his gaze.

"No." His answer left no room for equivocation. His eyes left no room for pretending that she didn't know exactly what he was saying.

He wasn't worried about floors being vacuumed or dishes being done. He was telling her that they'd have four days without the distraction of a small pitcher with big ears and even bigger eyes. Four days to themselves.

"I'll see," Mandy finally said, unwilling to commit herself, even though she knew, deep in her heart, that she'd be here.

Without giving him a chance to say anything more, she murmured a good-night and slipped out the door. Rafferty stood in the hallway until the sound of the car had faded into the distance.

On the landing above him, Becky eased back from the railing. She'd been too far away to hear what her dad and Mandy were saying but she'd seen the kiss and she didn't need words to interpret that. Her friend Cindy Radizill had suggested the mistletoe as a surefire way to get two people together. She'd have to tell her how right she'd been when she got back to school.

Chapter Ten

Spending Christmas Day alone, contrary to Mandy's somewhat mournful imaginings, was not the lonely, regret-filled day she'd half anticipated. She did feel a pang of self-pity when she woke in the morning and remembered what day it was and thought about the fact that everyone else in the city, if not in the entire state, was spending the day with family and friends.

But the mood soon passed. She'd been the one to choose to spend the day alone. She could have been a part of the Traherne's celebrations. For that matter, she didn't doubt that her parents would have canceled their trip to Monte Carlo if she'd told them she wanted to come home.

She spent the day pampering herself, taking a long bubble bath and not getting out until her hands and feet were decidedly wrinkled. She'd bought a game hen for her dinner and she served it with as much ceremony as she could manage, considering her stock of fine china was limited to a few plates she'd bought at the supermarket.

Eating the deliciously moist bird, it suddenly struck her that, a few months ago, she had barely known how to boil water. She might not be Cordon Bleu standard yet but she could hold her own in the kitchen. Except for the dishwasher. She frowned. Maybe she should make that her New Year's resolution—to master the dishwasher.

Mandy had planned to spend the day thinking about her

relationship with Rafferty, deciding whether or not she was ready to take the next step. She had no doubt that, if she went there tomorrow, she was going to end up in his bed. The tension had been building between them ever since that first kiss. Maybe longer. Maybe it had started the moment she'd seen him standing in the doorway, those gray eyes seeming to see through to her very soul.

They hadn't talked about it. There'd been no intimate discussions in which they'd bared their souls to each other. Maybe she was being a fool to even consider sleeping with a man before having lengthy discussions about what they meant to each other or what their relationship might mean in the future.

She had no experience to guide her, no years of dating to help her make a decision. Was she a fool to think he felt something more than simple lust? Was she reading something deeper into the way he looked at her? The way he kissed her?

She scowled at her half-eaten dinner. Just how much good would experience do her anyway? From what she'd seen and read, all the experience in the world didn't mean much when it came to falling in love.

Falling in love.

Was that what she was doing? Had already done?

Did she love Rafferty Traherne?

He made her heart beat faster whenever he entered a room. Just thinking about him made her feel warm inside. He made her laugh and he made her feel protected but not smothered like her parents had often done.

They hadn't talked about his wife. About why she'd run away. She hadn't told him about her heart or the fact that her legs sometimes gave out on her if she got too tired. Since he was a doctor he'd surely understand those things. But what he could accept in a patient might bother him in a lover.

A lover.

She was already thinking of him as such. A lover. A mate. *A husband?* The thought made her flush. It was too soon to be thinking in those terms but the thought persisted. What would it be like to be married to Rafferty? To share his life?

She shook her head. She was daydreaming like a foolish teenager. She should be trying to think logically, consider the commitment she might be making, decide whether he would make an equal commitment.

But all she could think about was how wonderful it felt to be in his arms. How right it felt when he kissed her.

In the end, it wasn't a matter of logic. It was a matter of gut instinct, of knowing it was right, even when she couldn't explain why it was right.

MANDY HAD NOT YET ARRIVED when Rafferty left for work the day after Christmas. He tried to control his disappointment, telling himself he'd been a fool to count on her being there. But he had counted on it. Counted on it so much that he'd made arrangements to take the next three days off to spend with Mandy.

Obviously she'd opted for caution and was going to take him up on his offer to take a few days off. Not that he'd had any intention of her spending those three days cleaning house. But she'd known that.

Maybe he'd been too obvious, seemed too sure of himself. As a matter of fact, he wasn't at all sure of himself but she might not have realized that. She might have thought he was being arrogant, expecting a little too much, a little too quickly.

After all, they hadn't had much time together. Not *together* together. Becky was usually there, if not actually in the room, then at least within earshot. He and Mandy had never really been alone, never had a chance to exchange all the intimate confidences one was generally expected to exchange with someone before getting involved.

What had made him think she'd want to become his lover?

His lover.

God, the word made him ache. He'd never in his life

wanted a woman the way he wanted her. Not even poor sweet Maryanne, who'd been his wife. He'd cared about her, loved her, in a way. But he'd never felt this passionate need for her, not even when they were first married.

No, the feelings Mandy brought out in him were nothing like what he'd felt for Maryanne. He'd felt protective toward Maryanne. She'd been so helpless, so in need of care.

As Claire had said, she'd been another wounded bird that he'd brought home. Only he'd tried to help her by marrying her. A mistake. He doubted that the marriage would have lasted, even if she hadn't run away.

At first glance, Mandy seemed as fragile as Maryanne had been, just as much in need of protection. But she had a core of strength Becky's mother had never possessed. He felt protective toward her but it wasn't because she needed it. It was more a primitive male reaction to caring for someone that he—

No, he wasn't going to think in those terms. Not yet. He wasn't rushing into anything this time. Not that he had to worry about rushing things. It was hard to rush this sort of thing all by yourself.

He pulled the Jeep into his parking place and stared glumly at the building that housed his practice. She wasn't going to show up and who could blame her? Why hadn't he told her how he felt?

Because he didn't know *how* he felt, damn it all! How could he tell Mandy how he felt about her when he wasn't sure himself?

Rafferty slammed out of the Jeep and marched into the office, sure that he was going to have a thoroughly miserable day, which was, he thought, all he deserved.

The day didn't quite live down to his expectations. In fact, its worst aspect turned out to be boredom. Aside from a panic-stricken mother who brought her son in convinced that ingesting a small metal part off his brother's new toy was going to be fatal, the day couldn't have been duller.

The X rays showed that the offending part was likely to pass through the boy's digestive system without causing

any damage. Rafferty told the worried mother to watch for
the brightly colored piece to reappear as it almost certainly
would and call him if any further problems developed.

When she left with the toddler in her arms, he could hear
the older brother demanding to know when Billy was going
to return the part he'd stolen.

On one of the only days of his entire career when he
would have welcomed an excuse to stay late, the patients
refused to cooperate, leaving him no choice but to go home
on time.

Despite the fact that it was still quite early, it was almost
completely dark, a condition helped along by the heavy
cloud cover that pressed down from above the mountains.
Snow started to drift down as Rafferty pulled out of the
parking lot. The weather report was promising a lot more
where that came from and Rafferty felt his mood slip even
lower.

Great. He was going to be snowed in with nothing more
entertaining for company than a stack of old medical journals. Why had he agreed to let Becky stay with his parents?

"Because you thought it would give you some time
alone with Mandy," he muttered to the softly falling snow.
"Fool."

By the time he pulled the Jeep into the driveway, the
snow was coming down in earnest. It was a good thing it
had held off until the day after Christmas. This kind of
weather on Christmas Day, with everyone trying to get
home after eating and drinking too much, would have been
a recipe for disaster.

The garage door eased up in answer to the opener. The
Jeep's headlights illuminated a familiar scene of old bicy-
cles and assorted clutter.

And the car Mandy had driven home on Christmas Eve.

For several seconds, Rafferty didn't move. He stared at
the light blue Chevy, aware that his pulse rate had just
increased out of all proportion to the effort needed to push
the button on the garage door opener.

After a moment, he pulled into the garage and shut off

the engine. In the sudden quiet, the whine of the garage door shutting sounded unnaturally loud. He got out of the Jeep and shut the door with considerable care.

She'd come.

He'd been so sure she wasn't going to be here. But here she was. Of course, he couldn't assume too much. She hadn't necessarily shown up because she wanted the same things he did. And even if she did want the same things, she was probably going to want to talk a lot. It seemed that women generally did want to talk a great deal.

That was fine as long as she didn't want him to try to explain how he felt. Because he knew he couldn't do that. His feelings for her were so tangled. Affection. Need. Desire. None of them quite explained what he felt. But he wasn't yet ready to put a more powerful word to his feelings. Not yet. Not until he was sure he knew what they were.

MANDY TURNED as he pushed open the kitchen door, hoping he'd attribute her flushed face to the warmth of the kitchen. She'd heard his car pull into the driveway and it had seemed to take forever until the garage door shut and then another endless wait for him to turn the knob of the inner door.

She'd been so sure she was ready for this. So sure that she'd made the right decision, that she could handle this in an intelligent, adult fashion. Whatever might come of it, for the moment, they were doing nothing more than starting an affair. No lifelong commitments. No deathless promises. Just a simple affair.

That was all she expected. All she wanted. After all, she was mature enough to have an affair with no strings attached.

But she didn't feel mature. She felt nervous and giddy. Terrified and excited. She couldn't wait for him to walk through the door and at the same time she couldn't bear to see him. She wanted to run to him and she wanted to hide.

All very logical and intelligent, she thought, suppressing a nervous giggle.

Rafferty pushed open the door and the urge to laugh disappeared. For a blind instant, she felt nothing but panic. He was so large, so male. She hardly knew him. She was crazy to think of putting herself in his hands.

"I didn't think you'd show up." The plain statement told her that he wasn't any more certain of the wisdom of what they were doing than she was. She felt the panic recede.

"I wasn't sure I would," she admitted, her smile hesitant.

"I'm glad you did." He shut the door behind him, closing them into the warm kitchen together. "Whatever you're cooking smells wonderful."

"It's nothing fancy." Mandy tried to follow his lead, keeping the conversation casual. "I was a little worried about you when I heard the weather report."

Rafferty followed her gesture to the window. It was full dark out now, the snow visible as a ghostly white blur against the darkness.

"We may be snowed in by morning, at least until the snowplows get through." His eyes were on her as he spoke, gauging her reaction to his words, the implication that she'd be here in the morning.

"That's all right," Mandy said quietly, giving him the answer to the question he hadn't asked.

Rafferty felt the tension leave his shoulders. She was here and she was planning to stay. He smiled at her, feeling suddenly younger and more carefree.

"I guess we can find something to do if we're snowed in," he said, his eyes warm.

The color rose in her cheeks but her eyes were steady and held a touch of humor. "We could always play Monopoly."

"That wasn't exactly what I had in mind," he told her provocatively.

The promise in his eyes made her face burn. He reached

for her but she spun away, snatching a spoon from the counter as if it were a life raft in the middle of the ocean.

"Dinner will be ready in about half an hour," she said brightly, stirring the contents of a pot more vigorously than necessary.

Rafferty's mouth quirked with gentle amusement. He wasn't particularly interested in dinner and he doubted that she was, either. But he'd give her all the time she wanted. He rubbed his hand over his face, feeling the rasp of a day's growth of beard.

"Do I have time to shower and change clothes?"

"I think so."

Mandy didn't turn to look at him before he left, pretending to be terribly busy with the cooking. She didn't draw a deep breath until she heard him going up the stairs, taking them two at a time from the sound of it.

She set down the spoon she'd been annoying the cassoulet with and pressed her hands to her cheeks. If she had any sense at all, she'd leave now, while she had the chance. But she didn't make any move toward the door.

She doubted if either of them particularly enjoyed the cassoulet she'd spent most of the afternoon preparing. Rafferty made the appropriate appreciative noises but he ate very little and she might just as well have been eating a well-cooked shoe for all the tasting she actually did.

After dinner, Rafferty went to start a fire in the fireplace while Mandy rinsed the dishes. She lingered over the task but she couldn't put off the inevitable. Slipping off her apron, she smoothed her hands over the skirt of her dress. She'd chosen to wear this dress specifically because she felt very feminine in it. Pale pink wool challis formed a softly draped bodice with long sleeves. The same fabric gathered at the waist before falling in rich folds to just below her knees.

Though she made no sound, Rafferty knew the minute she entered the living room. He'd been kneeling on the hearth, staring into the flames that were starting to lick up around the logs. He stood up and turned to gaze at her.

Mandy would never have believed that a look could be as potent as a touch but she felt this look all the way to her toes.

"You're beautiful," he said softly.

"Thank you," she whispered.

She'd stopped just inside the doorway. She was grateful for his approach because she wasn't sure she could have taken another step on her own.

"Dance with me." He didn't wait for her response. His fingers felt warm and strong as he took her hand and pulled her forward. It was only when he drew her into his arms that she realized he'd turned on the stereo. Soft music filled the room, a warm accompaniment to the crackle of the fire. He'd turned on only one lamp, leaving most of the room in darkness.

Mandy was grateful for the dim light and quiet music. If it had been another man, she might have felt that he was cynically setting the scene for seduction. But this was Rafferty. If he'd set the scene, it was because he wanted everything to be right. He didn't want anything to spoil the mood.

She couldn't really have said whether or not he was a good dancer. She'd taken dance lessons when she was fourteen but she'd never had a chance to use them. This was nothing like dancing with Mr. Fiorino who'd smelled of breath mints and the old-fashioned hair pomade that made his hair gleam like polished leather.

Rafferty smelled of soap and after-shave. He didn't count under his breath. In fact, he didn't even worry about specific steps. They simply moved in time to the music. Or rather, he moved and Mandy followed where he led.

There was no resemblance to Mr. Fiorino's careful placement of hands in the way Rafferty held her, either. One hand held hers, just as Mr. Fiorino had always done, but the other hand spread across her lower back, drawing her much closer than her dance teacher would have approved of.

Mr. Fiorino's hand hadn't swallowed hers and his shoulders hadn't been so broad. And she'd never had the urge to move closer to Mr. Fiorino and lay her head on his chest, to have him wrap his arms around her and hold her close.

"I've wanted to hold you like this for weeks," Rafferty said quietly, his breath stirring the hair on her forehead.

"Have you?"

His hand left her back to fumble with the pins that held her hair in place. An instant later it tumbled down her back in a rich, dark fall.

"Your hair is so beautiful," he murmured, wrapping his fingers in it. "Like silk. And your skin is so soft."

Mandy let her head fall back in answer to the gentle tug of his hand. Her eyes drifted shut as Rafferty bent over her, his mouth finding the delicate arch of her throat. His hand released hers to settle on her hip. She felt the warm weight of it through the thin fabric of her dress.

She held her breath when his fingers moved upward, brushing against the side of her breast, hesitating for a long frozen moment before closing over her. Her breath abandoned her in a rush. Even through the layers of cloth, the sensation was intense.

His tongue found the pulse that beat raggedly at the base of her throat and Mandy felt her knees weaken. Only the fact that she was clinging to his shoulders kept her from collapsing to the floor.

When his mouth at last closed over hers, there was no need for tentative exploration, no need to coax her response. Her mouth opened to him, her tongue coming up to intertwine with his.

They'd given up all pretense of dancing and stood locked in an embrace in the middle of the room. Behind them, the fireplace crackled and snapped as it consumed the logs. But the heat it generated was nothing compared to the fire burning between the couple standing in front of it.

All the weeks of wanting but not touching, of wondering what it would be like, of dreaming, were suddenly fulfilled. The shyness Mandy had thought she'd feel, the uncertain-

ties, the doubts, all vanished, burned away in the heat of
Rafferty's mouth on hers.

This was the right decision, the only choice. She'd
waited her whole life for this moment, this man.

When he bent to scoop her up against his chest, Mandy
offered no protest. She linked her arms around his neck,
letting her head fall against his shoulder. He carried her
through the dark hallway and up the stairs, pushing open
his bedroom door with one foot. A small lamp burned next
to the bed, leaving most of the room in shadows.

He stopped next to the bed, his eyes locked on hers as
he lowered her to her feet, letting her slowly slide down
the length of his body. Her eyes held his for a long moment
and then she turned her back, lifting the heavy fall of her
hair out of the way. A row of small buttons marched down
the back of the dress, each slipped through a loop of fabric.

There was something at once innocent and erotic about
that row of buttons. Rafferty's fingers fumbled with the first
one, slipping it free at last. The second and third were easier
and the dress opened to reveal the nape of her neck.

Mandy shivered as his mouth touched her delicate skin.
Another button slipped loose and his mouth slid lower.
Each inch of revealed flesh was graced with a kiss. He
flipped open her bra when he reached it, running his tongue
down the length of her spine. By the time the last button
was undone, she felt as if there wasn't an inch of her left
untouched.

Rafferty turned her to face him again. The dress had
fallen only to the tops of her breasts, stopped there by her
hands. He caught her hands in his and pulled them gently
away, holding them at her sides. Mandy closed her eyes,
feeling the cool brush of air on her breasts as the dress
slipped to her waist, taking the lacy bra with it.

"You are so beautiful." The words were no more than
a breath. She shuddered as his hands closed over her
breasts, covering them completely, molding them, coaxing
the nipples into tight peaks.

She was hardly aware of her dress slipping to the floor,

or of the half-slip following it. She heard Rafferty's breath catch when he saw the lace garter belt and stockings and she felt a small, totally feminine smile curve her mouth.

She'd felt wildly sinful when she purchased the garments, even more sinful when she put them on. But she felt his hands tremble against her skin and was glad she'd worn them.

He fumbled with the garters, finally getting them loose, and rolled the stockings down her legs. Mandy balanced herself with one hand on his shoulder as he slipped first her right leg, then her left, free. The delicate lengths of nylon were tossed into the darkness somewhere, the scrap of garter belt following them an instant later.

Rafferty rose to his feet and stood looking down at her for a moment. Mandy felt a flush that seemed to start at her toes and work its way up the length of her body, washing her breasts with delicate color before reaching her face. She knew exactly what he was seeing. A small woman, not too slender but not fulsomely built, wearing nothing but a scrap of pale pink silk.

Without taking his eyes from her, he began to unbutton his shirt. Mandy dropped her eyes to the movement, finding it easier than meeting his gaze. A moment later, he shrugged the soft cotton off his shoulders and she caught her breath. She'd never seen him without his shirt. She was unprepared for the impact the sight of his bare chest had on her senses.

His broad hands closed over her shoulders, sliding down her back to draw her closer. Mandy shuddered as her breasts were gently crushed against the width of his chest. The sensation was exquisite.

Until that moment, urgency had been a distant thing. Now, suddenly, it exploded between them. Someone reached for his belt buckle. Was it her? There was a moment of struggle and she heard Rafferty mutter a curse. Then there was nothing between them but shadows and, in a moment, not even room for those.

The bed was firm against her back, the sheets cool. Or

maybe they only felt cool in contrast to the heat Rafferty was generating, above her, within her. There wasn't an inch of her his hands didn't stroke into tingling life.

Somewhere in the back of her mind, a small voice kept prodding her, hinting that there was something he should know.

"Rafferty?"

"Um?" He was nuzzling her breast, his tongue teasing nerve endings she'd never known existed.

"I've got to tell you something."

"God, you're so exquisite." His thigh slipped between hers, pressing gently upward and drawing a shudder of response that scattered her thoughts in a thousand different directions. "Wait."

He leaned over her, fumbling in the drawer of the nightstand. Mandy flushed wildly as she realized what he was doing. But the moment's delay also gave her a chance to clear her head.

"Rafferty." He was leaning over her, his face intent in the lamplight. "I've never done this before." She brought the words out in a rush, almost stuttering in her haste.

There was a moment when she thought he hadn't heard her and then she saw the shock register in his eyes.

"What?"

She didn't repeat the words, couldn't have if her life had depended on it but she didn't need to. He closed his eyes for a moment and she felt an odd little shudder ripple through him. When he opened his eyes again, they were flat silver.

"You don't have to do anything you don't want to," he said slowly.

Mandy felt tears burn the backs of her eyes. She could hardly have blamed him if he'd been upset with her. Talk about waiting till the last minute to spring a surprise like this on a man. Instead, he was telling her that it was her choice all the way.

She let her hands slide up his chest, flexing her fingers in the thick mat of hair that covered his muscles. "This is what I want,'' she whispered. Her voice was soft but steady.

She saw her words reflected in the way his eyes darkened to smoky gray, in the way his hands gentled against her.

"You won't regret it."

And he'd never given her any reason to, she thought later. If he'd been gentle before, there was a new tenderness in his touch. He didn't demand. He coaxed a trembling response from her, drawing her senses to a fever pitch before finally moving to join his body to hers.

In the end, she couldn't remember why she'd been even momentarily frightened. This was what she'd lived her whole life for—this man, this moment.

would seem to stare. Above him, Pru's voice was still, but ...

She saw her words reflected in the way his eyes narrowed slowly, even in the way his lids barely settled against her.

"You won't leave for ..."

And he'd been given her his mercy ... he thought that if he'd been gentle beyond anyone was a guy conscious on his touch. He didn't understand. He placed a trembling to another than he'd ... only ... if a fever built be ... her, finally came ...

As he ... said, yet the first was why he'd been even passionately frightened. This was what she'd lived for ...

Chapter Eleven

Mandy slept next to him, curled against his side, all silky skin and tangled dark hair. In those first moments of waking in the predawn dark, Rafferty was aware of being at peace in a way he hadn't known for a very long time. Not only had his physical hunger been fed but his emotional aches had been soothed.

She was his.

The wave of possessiveness surprised him. He'd never considered himself a possessive man, had in fact thought he was above such a feeling. He'd certainly have said he was more enlightened than some. But he was learning a great deal about himself lately.

He frowned into the darkness. He'd been fairly sure that her experience was limited. There was an innocence in her eyes, an uncertainty in her response that hinted as much. But he hadn't realized just how very limited her experience was.

Virginity was no longer the prize it had once been. A woman's value wasn't determined by her chastity, any more than a man's was. But knowing that he was the only man to have touched Mandy, to have brought her to trembling release, gave him a satisfaction that had little to do with being enlightened and a great deal to do with being primitively male.

In fact, Mandy brought out any number of feelings he

wasn't accustomed to dealing with. A considerable number of which he didn't even want to think about. At least not right now. Not when she felt so right cuddled against him. He wanted to savor the feeling, not analyze it.

IT WAS LIGHT OUT when Mandy woke. The sun was shining through the window, reflecting off the night's snowfall with a clear light. She didn't wonder where she was or why she felt so different. The night's events were crystal clear in her mind.

Rafferty's arm was wrapped around her waist, his chest pressed against her back, his legs drawn up under hers. It was, she decided after a moment's drowsy thought, rather like being hugged by a grizzly bear—large and warm and furry. The image made her smile.

She wanted to stretch, but even more, she wanted to stay exactly where she was. Never in her life had she felt safer or more protected. No one could have been gentler or more considerate than he had been. He'd soothed her nervousness and brought her tingling to life in ways she'd never imagined.

How was he going to feel about her in the cool morning light? She stirred uneasily. Everything had changed between them. This wasn't like a kiss that they could pretend had never happened.

"Are you always this fidgety first thing in the morning?" Rafferty's voice rumbled in her ear, freezing her.

"Sorry," she mumbled, suddenly sure that she could never face him again.

"Don't be. This is certainly nicer than the dream I was having."

His arm tightened around her, turning her onto her back. Childishly Mandy closed her eyes, feeling the color flood her cheeks.

"Why are your eyes closed?"

"Because I'm afraid to look at you," she told him honestly.

"I may not look my best in the morning but I don't think

anyone has ever been turned to stone by the sight of me."
Amusement laced his voice, giving her the courage to open
her eyes.

He looked sleep-warmed and tousled, his hair lying in a
thick silver wave on his forehead. The humor she'd heard
in his voice lit his eyes and she felt some of her nervousness ease.

"Did I become an ogre overnight?" he questioned softly,
one hand coming up to stroke her cheek.

"No. It's just that I haven't had much practice at this.
Actually I haven't had any practice at all."

"So I suspected. I don't think there's any official pro-
tocol."

"No, but there are probably terribly clever things I
should say."

"Like what?" He lowered his head to nuzzle the soft
skin beneath her ear and she felt her thoughts scamper in
fifty different directions.

"I don't know," she said shakily. "Like what a lovely
morning it looks to be."

His teeth nibbled at her earlobe.

"Or have you read the latest Far Side cartoon?"

She gasped as his tongue traced the delicate shell of her
ear.

"Or would you like some coffee?"

She felt herself sinking fast. Languid hunger was stealing
over her, making it difficult to think. Impossible to do anything but respond.

"Tea?" She got out as his mouth changed targets.

"Just you," he said, his lips closing over hers.

She didn't have to worry about clever conversation for
quite some time.

BY THE TIME they got out of bed, the sun was high in the
winter-blue sky. There was not a cloud in sight. The light
was thin and weak but the snow reflected it back onto itself,
making it seem brighter than it was.

It occurred to Mandy several times over the course of

the day that there were surely things that should be said, important things. But she was no more anxious than Rafferty seemed to be to start such a discussion.

They ate bacon and pancakes, arguing amiably over whether the meal should be considered a late breakfast or an early lunch. Then Rafferty suggested that the snow was simply too perfect to be left that way and they bundled up to go outside.

Stepping outside, Mandy's eyes were dazzled by the way the sunlight reflected off the snow. A pristine blanket of glittering white stretched from the back door, turning the yard into a fairy-tale place. Shrubs and plants were mysterious mounds of snow. The pathway had vanished.

"It's beautiful," she breathed.

"Very," Rafferty agreed, his eyes on her profile. He tried to remember the last time he'd seen someone so dazzled by something so simple. Becky, maybe, the first winter after they'd been reunited. She'd thought the snow absolutely magical. Maybe that was part of what drew him to Mandy. She hadn't lost that childlike ability to take pleasure in simple things.

Uncomfortable with the direction his thoughts were taking, Rafferty swooped, startling a cry from her as he caught her up in his arms.

"The only way to really appreciate snow is to get right out in it," he told her, picking his way down the steps and wading out into the field of white.

Mandy threw a glance in the direction he was going and saw a deep snowbank built up against the side fence. Her arms, made clumsy by her thick coat, clamped around his neck.

"Don't you dare drop me in there." Her fierce tone was spoiled by the giggle that followed it.

"I'm only doing this for your own good," he told her very seriously, his eyes sparkling with laughter. "You'll thank me for it. Really you will."

"I'll get you for this, Rafferty Traherne!" The threat ended in a shriek as he dumped her, seat first, into the snowbank. The snow crunched beneath her, absorbing the shock of her landing. Despite the cushioning effects of the snow, the fall was enough to knock the breath momentarily from her.

Even as she was falling, Mandy was planning her revenge. Since she could hardly expect to best him in any trial of strength, she'd have to be sneaky about it. Accordingly she lay still, just where he'd dropped her, her eyes closed, one arm flung out to the side.

Rafferty's chuckle faded when she didn't move. "Mandy?" There was no response. Feeling his heart catch, he bent over her. "Mandy? Are you all right?"

What she lacked in strength, she made up for in speed. One hand came up and caught the front of his coat. Leaning over as he was, he was already off balance. She caught a glimpse of his startled expression as she yanked on his coat with all her might and then he fell face first into the snow.

Laughing with triumph, she scrambled to her feet. But Rafferty was too quick. One long arm came out, catching her around the hips and tumbling her back into the snow. Her struggles were hampered by the thickness of her clothes, as well as her own laughter. In a matter of minutes, he had her pinned down, looming over her with a fierce frown.

"That," he said heavily, "was not a nice thing to do."

"And dumping me in the snow was?" she questioned, arching her eyebrows.

"Certainly. It's an old Colorado custom. It's for good luck."

"Whose good luck?"

"Mine, of course. And it looks as if it worked," he said with exaggerated smugness. "I've got you trapped and at my mercy. You'll have to pay a forfeit before I let you up."

"Of course," she said meekly. She let her body go soft beneath his, linking her arms around his neck. Rafferty's eyes sparked with interest when she gave him what she hoped was an inviting smile. "How about this?"

His answer was a startled bellow as she shoved a handful of snow under his collar. In the ensuing pandemonium, she made good her escape. Stumbling to her feet, she ran a few feet and then paused to watch his contortions as he attempted to rid himself of the rapidly melting snow.

Giving the attempt up as hopeless, he stood, giving her a pathetic look. "What was that for?"

"You're much too big to whine successfully," she told him without sympathy. "And that was an old Pennsylvania custom. It's for good luck."

He arched his eyebrows in haughty challenge. "You realize, of course, that this means war."

Without taking his eyes from her, he bent to pick up a handful of snow and began packing it between his gloved palms. Realizing his intent, Mandy squeaked and turned to run for cover. The first snowball flew over her left shoulder. The second would have caught her right between the shoulder blades if she hadn't dodged behind a tree.

She'd never been allowed to have snowball fights when she was a child. But she soon discovered it was a game that was easy to master. The trick was to pelt your opponent with snowballs while remaining relatively unpelted yourself. In realizing this goal, she was aided by Rafferty's size. Those broad shoulders made a wonderful target. Unfortunately he was also very quick and her aim was not terribly good.

His aim, on the other hand, was. She quickly developed guerilla tactics. She hid behind something, only coming out for a quick strike and then dodging back into cover. It worked reasonably well, except that it didn't take him long to circle around and smoke her out of her current hiding place.

Laughing and dodging, she lost track of time. She was having so much fun that she didn't notice how tired she was getting. Slogging through the knee-deep snow put strain on muscles completely unaccustomed to the effort.

Rafferty had just forced her out of her hiding place behind the toolshed and was stalking ominously toward her.

Mandy backed away, holding out one hand for mercy, a plea slightly spoiled by the laughter that insisted on bubbling out.

One moment she was standing in the snow. The next her legs had collapsed under her and she was falling. It wasn't the tumble into the snow that made her heart beat double time. It had been so many years since anything like it had happened, she'd almost forgotten the awfulness of feeling her legs fail to support her.

Rafferty must have seen the terror that flickered across her face and known that she wasn't playing any kind of game. He was beside her almost before she'd had a chance to realize what had happened.

"What is it?"

"My legs," she whispered, fear choking her voice.

"Are you hurt? Can you move them?" The doctor in him took charge as he reached for her, easing her back until she lay flat, straightening her legs.

"It's...it's an old injury," she got out. "I'll be all right in a minute." She prayed that that was the truth.

"Can I move you?"

"Yes."

He scooped her up, his hands so gentle it made her want to cry. Holding her carefully, he picked his way across the yard and up the steps. The warmth of the kitchen made her face tingle.

"Shall I put you down here or do you want to be in bed?" he asked.

"Here is okay."

He settled her in a chair. Straightening, he jerked off his gloves and shrugged out of his jacket, dropping both on the floor. His fingers went to work on her coat, after first tugging her gloves off.

Mandy knew she should say something, should reassure him. But she couldn't quite make herself believe it. Was that really the feeling coming back in her legs or was it just what she desperately wanted to believe?

"Can you feel anything?" he asked, the brisk tone concealing the fear that threatened to choke him. When he'd seen her fall, seen the look of terror in her eyes, it had been like feeling a hand clamp around his heart.

"I...I think so," she said slowly.

"Can you move your legs?" he asked as calmly as if she was a patient in his office. As if he hadn't slept with her in his arms last night. As if at least a portion of his heart weren't already held in her slender hands.

For a moment, she was afraid to try. What if she couldn't? What if the old nightmare started all over again? She couldn't expect to beat the odds twice.

But there was no arguing with Rafferty's tone. She'd spent too many years following doctors' instructions not to respond to that voice. Her eyes clung to his face as she tried to straighten her leg. She knew from bitter experience that the body didn't always do what she thought it was doing. She felt as if she was moving her leg but maybe she wasn't.

The relief that flooded his eyes told her that she hadn't imagined the sensation of her leg straightening. The muscles felt weak and tired but that wasn't unexpected. She'd overtaxed them.

Leaning back in the chair, Mandy closed her eyes and let thankfulness flow over her.

Rafferty remained where he was, on one knee in front of her, letting his heartbeat slow. He didn't try to speak until he was sure that his voice would be steady.

"You want to tell me about it?" he suggested, standing up. To give his hands something to do, he picked up the tea kettle and began to fill it with water.

"I was in an accident when I was sixteen," Mandy said slowly. She was reluctant to tell him the whole story. Since leaving Philadelphia, she'd almost managed to forget that she was anything but normal.

"What sort of an accident?" He put the kettle on the stove before turning to look at her. Leaning one hip against the counter, he folded his arms across his chest, the position making it clear that he wasn't going to be satisfied until he'd heard the full story.

"A car accident. I'd only had my license a few weeks. There was a little boy who chased his ball into the street."

"And you smashed the car trying to avoid hitting him," Rafferty prompted when she stopped.

"No. It was a truck that swerved to avoid him and crossed onto my side of the street. We hit head-on."

He winced. "Not a pretty picture."

"No. It was nasty, all right. Luckily the little boy wasn't hurt and the truck driver came through with fairly minor injuries."

"But your injuries were more than minor?" he questioned gently.

"There was considerable damage to the spine," she said without inflection. "The doctors thought I might not walk again."

"As a general rule, the medical profession likes nothing more than to be proved wrong in predictions of that sort. You obviously did that."

"Yes. Actually it was my grandmother who browbeat me into not giving up. I'm not sure I'd have done it if it hadn't been for Gram."

"From what I've seen, you've got a considerable backbone. I suspect you could have done it on your own." He turned as the kettle began to whistle and fixed two cups of tea. Neither of them spoke until he set a steaming mug in front of her.

"So what happened today?"

Mandy cradled one hand around the mug. "Sometimes, when I try to do too much, my legs give out and for a few minutes I can't feel them."

She glanced at him, expecting to see pity.

"From the sound of it, you're pretty lucky that the weakness isn't more than it is," he said briskly.

He didn't seem to feel the need to shower her with reassurances, nor to reproach her for overtaxing herself as either of her parents would surely have done. He simply accepted the fact that her legs weren't as dependable as most people's and acted as though that was the end of it.

Mandy sipped the hot tea, feeling vaguely annoyed. His reaction was exactly what she'd always wanted from people. Hadn't she left home, in part, because she was tired of being treated like an invalid, pampered and fussed over?

So why was she sitting here, feeling piqued because he hadn't fussed?

She smiled into her tea, amused by the total illogic of her feelings. A classic example of the perversity of human nature. She'd spent most of her life wanting to be treated as if she were normal. Now she was annoyed because that was exactly how she'd been treated.

"You want to share the joke?"

She glanced across the table to see Rafferty watching her, one eyebrow raised in question.

"I was just thinking that humans aren't terribly logical."

And with that, he had to be satisfied.

BECKY WAS TO SPEND four days with Rafferty's parents. For three and a half of those days, her father and Mandy managed to pretend that there was no tomorrow.

They talked, but not about the future. They talked about the past, about what it had been like for Mandy to think she might never walk again. About how Rafferty had felt when Becky's mother had taken her from him.

"I don't think I was sane for the first year. All I could think about was finding her, making sure she was safe. It's probably just as well I didn't find them at first. I might have throttled Maryanne."

They were stretched out on the sofa in front of the fireplace, Rafferty's head in her lap, her fingers idly stroking his hair.

"What was she like?" Mandy remembered hearing his sister say that she looked like Rafferty's late wife, that that was the reason he'd hired her.

"She was sweet," he said slowly, his eyes on the fire. "Sweet and helpless. She was born late in her parents' lives and I think they treated her as if she were a miracle. She had no understanding of the real world. I don't think she even wanted to understand it.

"I met her not long after her parents died and she seemed so fragile. She was pretty and I was young and thought I was in love with her."

"Were you?"

He shook his head. "I don't think so. I think I was going through my Albert Schweitzer phase. Only instead of going off to Africa to save the natives, I married Maryanne."

Mandy smiled, just as he'd intended her to but there was an underlying seriousness in his words.

"You must have felt something for her," she couldn't resist probing.

"I did. Once the paternal glow had subsided, I felt affection for her. By then she was expecting Becky and the idea of being a father held enormous appeal."

"What happened? Why did she leave?"

He rolled so that he was looking up at her. "What if I told you that I frightened her out of her wits and she ran away because she was afraid of me?"

"I'd say you were either lying through your teeth or that she was hallucinating," Mandy told him without hesitation.

His eyes remained watchful for a moment and then he gave her a slow smile.

"Thank you."

"You don't have to thank me. No one could spend as much time with you and with Becky as I have and believe you'd hurt anyone."

"Thanks. But your analysis is not entirely true." He sat up and then stood, moving over to the fireplace to add another log to the already crackling fire. Frowning down into the flames, he continued, "I did frighten her. And she did run because she was afraid of me. But I never lifted a hand to her."

"I know that," Mandy said calmly. "What happened?"

"She wasn't very well suited to being a doctor's wife. I think when we got married, she had this image of having tea with other doctors' wives and sitting on the boards of various charities and wearing pearls and little white gloves. Maryanne would have been perfectly at home in the fifties. She actually *owned* white gloves.''

He said it as if he still couldn't quite believe it. Mandy said nothing, remembering the several pairs of white gloves she'd left in a drawer in Philadelphia.

"What she hadn't counted on was the fact that I was still working at the hospital. My hours were erratic. I was getting called out at night, much more than I do now. She'd cook dinner and I wouldn't get home until midnight." He shrugged.

"It might have helped if she'd yelled at me. If we could have quarreled, it might have cleared the air. Maybe I could have made her understand that it wasn't going to be quite so bad forever. But she didn't know how to quarrel, I guess. She whined. At least that's what it seemed like to me.

"She didn't complain that she was feeling neglected. She'd fuss because her dinner had been ruined. She didn't tell me that it was time I cut back on my hours and spent more time with her and the baby. She was upset that I couldn't take her to a play.

"If I'd been more mature myself, I would have been able to read the signs better. But I was a selfish swine, like most men at that age are." He ignored Mandy's murmured protest. "And I was so filled with self-righteousness at the worthy job I was doing that I didn't see that her dinners and plays were as important to her as my patients were to me.''

He stopped, his expression pensive as he looked back on those months.

"So what happened?"

"She had a dinner party she wanted to go to. It was at the home of a senior doctor and I think she saw it as a chance to get to play doctor's wife at last. She made me swear I'd be home in time to get changed for it."

"And you weren't?" she guessed, when he stopped.

"What? Oh, no, I got home in time. I had a patient in

the hospital. She was very ill and I was worried that I might lose her. I'd already warned Maryanne that I might have to stay with my patient. But her condition seemed to have stabilized and I knew how much Maryanne was counting on me to go to the party.

"So I came home to change. She was so pleased and excited. Like a little girl. She had a baby-sitter for Becky and she was dressed and ready even before I got here. I showered and changed and we went to the party. My beeper wasn't working but since I knew exactly where I was going to be, I wasn't worried. I'd told Maryanne to call the hospital and leave a number where I could be reached, in case my patient took a turn for the worse.

"It was a nice dinner party, and it seemed like a good sign that nobody had called. I reckoned everything must be fine at the hospital. Only when we got home, the baby-sitter told me the hospital had called half a dozen times, trying to find me. Maryanne hadn't called the hospital to leave the number. She hadn't even left it with the baby-sitter."

"She'd forgotten?" Mandy suggested softly, knowing that wasn't the case, even before he shook his head.

"No, she hadn't forgotten. She admitted as much. She was tired of me always being dragged back to the hospital so she'd made sure they wouldn't be able to find me."

"The patient?" she questioned, half-afraid of his answer.

"She came through," he said. "No thanks to her doctor."

"It wasn't your fault you weren't there." She came to his defense with a speed that made warmth curl in his chest.

"It didn't matter, really, except to me. Maryanne was waiting up for me when I got home. If she'd gone to bed, I'd have cooled off by morning and the whole thing would have blown over. But I was still furious."

"What happened?"

"Oh, nothing all that dramatic. I said some things I probably shouldn't have. I have a pretty nasty temper when it finally breaks, I guess. I was younger, more hotheaded. I accused her of not caring about Becky. Hadn't it occurred to her that, if something had happened to Becky, the baby-sitter had no way of getting ahold of us? I think I said something very dramatic, like she was an unfit mother.

"She started to cry and I stormed out of the house and spent the night at a friend's. I went to work from there.

"I guess by then, I'd realized that the marriage wasn't really giving either of us what we wanted but I figured we'd find a way to work things out.

"Only, when I got home, she'd taken the baby and disappeared."

He picked up a poker and jabbed it at the fire, the force of the gesture telling its own tale. The firelight cast odd shadows over his face, drawing deep lines around his mouth, making his eyes seem sunken.

Mandy tried to imagine what it must have been like, especially in those first terrible weeks. She'd seen him with Becky and knew how much he loved her. He must have gone through hell. The sleepless nights, the calls to police stations and hospitals, none of them doing any good.

"It took me a while to figure it out," he said, setting the poker down and straightening away from the fire. "Why she'd left, I mean. I don't think anyone had ever spoken a harsh word to her and I spoke more than one, I'm ashamed to admit. I think she panicked and took the baby and ran away. God knows what was going through her head. Maybe she thought I was actually going to strike her. Or she thought I'd gone crazy. I guess I'll never know exactly what was in her head at the time."

Mandy got up and went to him, sliding one arm around his waist and leaning against him. His body felt rigid, as if from the effort of remembering all the old pain. She wanted to be able to say something that would take away that pain. But there was nothing that could be said, just as there was nothing that could give him back the years he'd lost with Becky or give poor Maryanne back her life.

"You can't blame yourself, you know," she said at last,

knowing it must have been said to him a hundred times before. "You couldn't have known she'd run away."

"Couldn't I?" He put his arm around her shoulders, pulling her close but there was still a tension in him. "She was my wife. It seems to me I should have known."

"Hey, I thought you said you were going through an Albert Schweitzer phase." She leaned back to look up at him, a teasing smile tugging at her mouth. "Albert Schweitzer was a lot of things but I don't think he ever claimed to be able to read other people's minds."

"Point taken." He tugged on a strand of her hair, and she could see some of the shadows leaving his eyes.

FOR THREE DAYS they pretended that the outside world didn't exist. Mandy didn't go back to her apartment, Rafferty didn't go to work. The rest of the world cooperated by not calling or visiting, allowing them these few days all to themselves.

It was only on the last evening, when Becky called to make sure her father hadn't forgotten that he was to pick her up the next day, that they had to give up the fantasy that they were isolated from the rest of the world.

"We need to talk," Rafferty said abruptly.

"I know."

Becky had called more than an hour ago and they'd been pretending that the call hadn't burst the little bubble they'd been living in. But Mandy had spent fifteen minutes pushing her dinner around on her plate without really tasting it and Rafferty hadn't done much better.

"We need to talk about Becky. About what we're going to tell her." Rafferty pushed his plate away and leaned his elbows on the table.

"I know." Mandy sighed and pushed her own plate to the side.

But neither of them knew where to start. Rafferty frowned at the saltshaker. Mandy stared at her hands, linked together on the table.

"I don't know what to tell her," he admitted at last.

"Why tell her anything?"

His eyes swept up to meet hers. "You mean, pretend that nothing has changed? That we haven't become lovers?"

Just hearing him say the word sent shivers of awareness down her spine. How could she possibly pretend nothing had changed when all he had to do was walk into a room to set her every nerve ending quivering? She swallowed.

"That's the simplest solution," she said, proud of how calm she sounded.

"Maybe." He sounded doubtful.

"What else do you suggest? If we tell her that we-'re...that we're lovers—" She felt the color rise in her cheeks but forced herself to continue evenly. "If we tell her that, it's going to make things awkward. What is she supposed to say to her friends? 'This is the housekeeper, who also happens to be sleeping with my father'?"

Rafferty winced. "That makes it sound rather tawdry, don't you think?"

"What else could we say?" she asked softly.

She wasn't looking at him but she felt the glance he threw her. She didn't know what she wanted him to say. That they'd tell Becky they were madly in love? There'd been no talk of love between them.

"It won't be long before she's ready to start dating," Rafferty said, seemingly at random. "I don't want to send her any mixed signals at this point."

Mandy had no trouble following his chain of thought. "You can hardly tell her that she should wait until she has a strong emotional commitment before sleeping with a boy if you don't follow the rules yourself, you mean?"

His chair scraped across the floor as he stood up. Shoving his hands into his pockets, he strode to the window and stared out at the darkness.

"God, that makes it sound like there's nothing between us but sex," he said harshly, speaking as much to himself as to her.

Mandy stared at her hands, feeling every separate beat

of her heart. She wasn't prepared for this conversation, for the emotionally loaded questions it brought up. She'd been living day to day, not thinking about the future and suddenly the future was looming up in front of her, posing questions she couldn't answer.

"*Is* there more than sex?" she asked him slowly.

"Yes. God, yes." He spun away from the window, his eyes stormy gray. "Of course there's more than that. I just...don't know what it is, yet." The words were almost angry but his eyes were pleading with her to understand.

She did understand. He, even more than she, had reason to be wary of strong attractions, of mislabeled emotions. If she wasn't ready to put a name to what she felt, why should she expect him to be any different?

"If it wasn't for Becky, things could be different," Rafferty said restlessly. "But I have to consider her. She's lost a lot in her life and I don't want to see her get hurt again. She's grown to care for you and I don't want anything to jeopardize that bond."

"Neither do I." Mandy ran her thumbnail along the edge of the table, her eyes following the aimless movement. "Little girls can be very possessive of their fathers. It might upset her if she thought we were getting involved and leaving her out. Sometimes children see that kind of thing as a threat."

"Maybe we need to approach things more slowly, give her a chance to get used to the idea," Rafferty said.

Mandy felt a wave of relief wash over her at his words. She'd wondered if he might suggest that they'd made a mistake altogether. That there was no reason to tell Becky because their relationship wasn't going to continue.

"That sounds like a good idea." Maybe something in her voice gave away her thoughts because Rafferty's gaze sharpened on her face. He covered the distance between them in two long strides, grasping her hands and drawing her to her feet. Mandy stared at their clasped hands, afraid to meet his eyes.

"Mandy, I don't regret what's happened between us. Not

for a minute. If it wasn't for Becky, I'd be happy to let the whole world know we're involved. But I have to think of Becky first. I have to protect her.''

''I know that,'' she said quickly, lifting her head so that their eyes met. ''I want to do what's best for her, too. I guess I'm just feeling a little shaky at the moment. I keep wondering where this is all going.''

''I don't know where it's going.'' He set her hands against his chest and slid his arms around her back, drawing her close. ''I know I like where it's gotten us so far.'' Mandy flushed at the warmth in his eyes. *She* liked where it had taken them so far, too.

''Let's just take it a day at a time and see what happens, okay?''

''Okay,'' she whispered, tilting her head up for his kiss.

Chapter Twelve

The thing Becky had never understood was why adults always believed they were so good at keeping secrets. Take her father and Mandy, for example. They thought she was too dumb to figure out that something must have happened between them while she was staying with Grandpa and Grandma.

She frowned down at the horse she'd been drawing before picking up the eraser and applying it to a lopsided ear. Mandy was supposedly doing the dishes but she spent more time staring out the window than she did washing plates. It was odd how she never used the dishwasher, Becky thought, momentarily distracted. Of course, considering what had happened with the washing machine and the vacuum cleaner, maybe it was just as well she stayed away from it.

Mandy sighed unconsciously and dragged her attention back to the plate she'd been running the dishrag over for the last three minutes.

Becky began penciling in a new ear, her thoughts returning to the important issues at hand. Even if she'd been blind, she would have sensed the change. Oh, they thought they were being clever about it, not looking at each other and hardly even talking to each other. That alone was enough to alert anyone with a brain to the fact that something was going on.

But then there was the way her dad looked at Mandy when he thought no one would notice. Becky couldn't quite put a label on that look. To tell the truth, it looked suspiciously mushy to her. It bothered her to think that her own father was capable of looking all calf-eyed at anybody. But Cindy said that even the best grown-ups did that sort of thing when they were in love so maybe he couldn't help himself.

And if there was one thing Becky was sure of, it was that her father and Mandy were in love. What she wasn't at all sure about was whether they knew it. Adults could be amazingly stupid sometimes.

She caught her lower lip between her teeth as she sketched in a bridle. She wasn't too worried about her dad and Mandy figuring things out. They were smarter than most grown-ups she knew. And if they didn't figure it out pretty soon, maybe she'd have a talk with her dad, sort of point him in the right direction.

RAFFERTY WOULD HAVE BEEN grateful for anything that helped point him in the right direction, though he didn't consider the situation quite as clear-cut as his daughter did. This uncertainty was new to him. New and unwelcome.

All his life, he'd known where he was going. Even when he'd taken a wrong turn, he'd been able to get back on track as soon as he realized the need.

For the first time in his life he felt as if he were stumbling in the dark, groping for the right door. He couldn't find it in himself to regret sleeping with Mandy but it had made his life more complicated than he'd planned.

When he'd suggested it, it had seemed like a simple enough idea to just go on as if nothing had changed. He'd even thought, heaven help him, that it would give them a chance to take stock, to consider the next step. God, what a pompous fool he'd been!

How could he possibly consider anything except how much he missed the feel of her in his arms. In his bed. He'd slept in that bed alone for nearly eight years. He'd *liked* sleeping alone. No cold feet, no complaints if he hogged the covers. So why did the bed feel so empty now? She'd shared it with him for only a few nights and managed to leave her scent on the sheets. Even when he knew the linens had been changed, he still seemed to smell her on the pillows.

When he saw her in the morning, he wanted to pull her into his arms and kiss her. He wanted to feel her melt against him, hear that little sound she made in the back of her throat that told him her knees were dissolving under her.

He'd thought, naive fool that he was, that they'd have a little time together, even with Becky home. After all, Becky wasn't going to be in the same room with them every minute. And she wasn't. But she was always in the house. And, somehow, Mandy simply wasn't the sort of woman a man dragged behind a door to kiss.

The same problem arose when it came to getting a chance to talk. He'd never realized just how omnipresent a ten-year-old could be. Becky seemed to have the most incredible talent for popping up just when he was about to tell Mandy that they couldn't go on like this, that they had to talk.

It might have been easier if he never saw Mandy. But he did see her, every morning and every evening. Looking cool and undisturbed, as if nothing really had changed. Sometimes, in his more feverish moments, he wondered if he'd had an attack of malaria after Christmas and imagined the time they'd spent together.

But just when he was about to succumb to that theory, he'd catch a look in Mandy's eyes that told him it hadn't been a delirium-induced dream he'd held in his arms.

He wanted her. He wanted her like he'd never wanted anyone in his life. The very intensity of his desire made him uneasy. He was no longer a hormone-driven teenager who could let lust order his emotions as easily as he let school order his life.

How could he possibly feel such intense physical desire

for Mandy if it wasn't grounded in a strong emotional base? Like love. That was the big question, the one he admitted, to himself, at least, that he was afraid to face. That was the reason he didn't figure out a way to find some time alone with Mandy, even if it meant sending Becky off to stay with his parents again.

He'd thought he was in love once before and he'd been wrong. His marriage had shaken his belief in his ability to trust his own emotions. And this time he had Becky to consider. Whatever he did, he wouldn't see her hurt again.

By the middle of January, frustration had made his temper roughly equivalent to that of a grizzly bear awakened too early from hibernation. He wasn't sure what annoyed him more: the undeniable sexual frustration that made him want to ravish Mandy every time he saw her or the frustration of not knowing his own mind.

It was an unfortunate coincidence that his mood should reach its absolute lowest ebb on the same day that Mandy decided to master the dishwasher.

It had been her one New Year's resolution and nearly three weeks into the new year, she was still eyeing the machine as if it might jump up and bite. Besides, she was beginning to appreciate just how inaccurate the ads were that made doing dishes sound like a beauty treatment for your hands.

She loaded the dishwasher carefully, glasses on top, silverware in the little basket and plates on the bottom. Since Rafferty had no fear of the dishwasher and used it on the weekends when she wasn't there and occasionally didn't empty it before Monday morning, she'd been able to study where things went.

Satisfied that everything was just where it should be, she filled the little cup that said Soap up to the top. It didn't occur to her that the soap she used to do dishes by hand might not be the right soap for the dishwasher. She shut and latched the door and turned the knob to start.

The machine began to hum immediately and she could hear water rushing into it. Satisfied that she'd done the best she could, she gave it a small pat and left the kitchen. She'd promised Becky that she'd help her with her homework.

Becky generally did her homework on the dining-room table. From there, Mandy could hear the dishwasher chugging through its cycles. Maybe it was her imagination that made her think it sounded contented, as if it might be glad that she was finally willing to trust it.

When Becky's homework was conquered and she'd run off to watch the afternoon cartoons, Mandy approached the kitchen to find that her trust had been woefully abused. While she'd imagined it to be cheerfully cleaning the dishes, leaving the glasses spot-free and the plates shining like mirrors, the dishwasher had been taking an evil pleasure in making the most of her one big mistake.

The soap she'd used to fill the dispenser advertised mounds of suds. And mounds of suds were precisely what she found when she returned to the kitchen. Half the kitchen floor had vanished under them. Fluffy white puffs of foam drifted across the tile like clouds sailing through a patterned sky.

At another time, she might have laughed before getting out the mop to clean the mess up. But she'd been finding laughter a hard thing to come by lately. Ever since Christmas, in fact.

For weeks now Rafferty had been stalking around like a lion with a thorn in his paw and her own emotions were about as stable as a roller coaster gone wild.

The clouds of suds oozing across the floor made her want to burst into tears. But crying wasn't going to get the mess cleaned up. With a sigh that threatened to become a sob, Mandy started toward the broom closet and the mop.

She was only halfway there when the garage door was pushed open. She'd been so absorbed in contemplating the sea of suds in the kitchen that she hadn't heard the Jeep pull into the garage, hadn't realized Rafferty was home.

He glanced up from the envelopes in his hand, his eyebrows hooking together in the frown that seemed so habitual with him these days. Before she could warn him, he'd taken one long step into the kitchen. His foot landed in the midst of a mound of foam.

In a movie, it would have been funny. His foot started to slip. His expression reflected his shock. He threw out his arms for balance, envelopes flying in all directions. But it was futile. His body hit the floor with a resounding thump. For a stunned moment, Mandy could only stare at his sprawled figure.

"Oh my God. Rafferty, are you all right?" She hurried toward him, slowed by the necessity of picking her way gingerly across the slippery floor. "Are you hurt?"

Rafferty just sat where he'd fallen, his hands braced on either side of him, his expression reflecting stunned disbelief at finding himself in such a position. He said nothing.

"Are you hurt?" she asked again. She'd almost reached him.

"I think I'm reasonably intact," he said slowly. He drew his feet under him and began to stand up, using considerable caution. He looked at the envelopes that lay scattered and soaked on the floor. He looked at the slowly dispersing mounds of foam. He twisted around to look at the huge wet stain on the seat of his pants.

"I'm sorry. It was the dishwasher. Maybe I did something wrong. Are you sure you aren't hurt?" Mandy was aware that she was babbling.

Rafferty studied the scene of the disaster again and then looked at the bottle of soap she'd left sitting on the counter.

"Is that, by any remote possibility, the soap you put into the dishwasher," he asked in a voice so calm, it sounded ominous.

"It's dish soap," she offered meekly, sensing that she'd made an error.

"It's *hand* dishwashing soap," he told her with forbidding emphasis. "When you put *hand* dishwashing soap in a dishwasher, it creates suds. Lots and lots of suds."

"Oh."

There didn't seem to be anything else to say. It was clear that he wasn't taking this well. She couldn't entirely blame him. No doubt the fall had been painful. A man of his size didn't hit the floor that hard without getting some bruises.

"Oh?" His eyebrows arched over eyes gone stormy-gray. "Is that all you can say?"

"I'm sorry you fell?" she offered, already sensing that it wasn't going to be enough to calm the wrath she could see in his eyes.

"Did it occur to you to read the directions on the soap?" he inquired, managing to imply that only a total idiot wouldn't have read the directions.

"It's dish soap," she pointed out. "I didn't realize that the dishwasher took a different kind of soap."

"Have you been doing the dishes by hand all these months?"

"Yes."

"Let me guess. You've never used a dishwasher."

She lifted her chin. "That's right." She'd already confessed to lying about her experience in the housekeeping department.

"Any halfway intelligent person would have asked how to run the damned thing first." He'd dropped any pretense that he wasn't upset. "I don't know how in the hell you've managed to survive as long as you have when you don't know the first thing about running a house."

The strain of the past few weeks had worn on him, making his temper sharper than normal. At another time, he might have picked himself up off the floor and shared a laugh with her over how silly he'd looked. Nothing had been damaged beyond his dignity.

The weeks since the holiday hadn't been easy for Mandy, either. She had many of the same questions and doubts that Rafferty did. And she had also had her first taste of sexual frustration and was finding that she didn't like it at all. If asked, she would have said that she didn't have much of a temper. But Rafferty had just managed to find it and set a spark to it.

Her chest tight with anger, she drew herself up to her

full five foot and one-half inch and matched him glare for glare.

"If you had the intelligence of a gnat, you would have noticed that the floor was wet. You stalked in here like a bull charging into a china shop and fell flat on your butt and now you want to blame me for it. Well you can take your blame and your damn dishwasher and its stupid soap and you can...you can sit on them!"

Rafferty's eyes had widened in surprise at her attack but Mandy was in no mood to wait for his reaction. Her plan was to spin on her heel and make a dignified exit, leaving him to ponder how unfair he'd been.

That was the plan.

But she'd forgotten just what had sparked their quarrel. She took one step and felt her foot slide on the slick tile. Seeing her start to fall, Rafferty reached out to catch her. In the process, his own feet slid out from under him. With a startled cry from Mandy and a resigned grunt from Rafferty, they landed on the floor in a tangle of arms and legs and drifting soap bubbles.

Rafferty's hold had ensured that she land sprawled across his lap, an undignified position but more comfortable than direct impact on the floor. After a stunned moment, Mandy scrambled away, only to slip again and wind up sitting on the floor with a damp plop.

For a moment, there was stunned silence. Neither of them could absorb what had just happened. Rafferty couldn't believe he was sitting on his kitchen floor for the second time in five minutes. Mandy couldn't believe she was there at all.

She lifted her hands, staring at the water dripping sluggishly off her fingers to splat on the damp floor. She lifted her eyes slowly, afraid of what she might see in Rafferty's face. If he'd been angry the first time, there was no predicting his mood now.

Rafferty looked at her and then at himself. His eyes swept back to her and his mouth twitched. His expression was sternly controlled but his eyes began to twinkle. Mandy bit her lower lip, trying not to notice that his tie was tossed over one shoulder, as if he'd been caught in a windstorm.

Their eyes met and the battle was lost. She giggled. He smirked. Within minutes, the kitchen was filled with laughter.

Becky, drawn by the sound of their laughter, stopped in the kitchen doorway. With more prudence than either of the adults had shown, she eyed the slick floor and chose not to venture onto it. Her father and Mandy both sat in the middle of the floor, laughing hysterically, water seeping through their clothes, envelopes scattered around them.

She tilted her head to one side, puzzled over what they found in the situation that inspired such humor. They *did* look rather silly but not silly enough to cause quite so much laughter. Still, it was a nice change from the way they'd been pretending not to notice each other lately.

Hearing the sounds of her cartoon returning after an advertisement, she trotted back into the living room. She was going to have to ask Cindy if she'd ever heard of falling down together as a good way to get people to admit they were in love.

THE INCIDENT in the kitchen hardly solved all their problems but it went a long way toward easing the tension between Mandy and Rafferty. Becky's request to spend the night at her friend's house went even further toward soothing stretched nerves.

Mandy happened to be there at the time the request was made and, as her eyes met Rafferty's, she knew he was thinking the same thing she was. Becky spending the night with a friend would give them a chance to be alone.

Rafferty gave his permission, wondering if he was an unfit parent for being glad his only child was going to be gone for the night because he quite desperately wanted to make love to his housekeeper.

Mandy told herself that she was only concerned with them having a chance to talk. Which was why, as soon as she'd seen Becky off to school, she began planning a wonderful dinner, the sort of food that Becky's chili-dog tastes generally precluded.

Cindy's mother would be picking up both girls at school and taking them home, which left Mandy with an entire day to plan what she was going to say, to try to anticipate what Rafferty might say and, in general, to turn herself into a nervous wreck.

Rafferty didn't do much better. He'd managed to get Mandy alone that morning, just long enough to ask her to stay until he got home. She'd nodded, her eyes reflecting the same nervous anticipation he was feeling. He'd risked a quick kiss before leaving and he'd paid for it by tasting her response all day.

They needed to talk, he told himself firmly. They certainly couldn't go on this way very much longer. The strain would have been enough to turn his hair prematurely gray if genetics hadn't turned it that color already.

Running through his thoughts was a conversation he and Becky had had the night before when he'd tucked her in. She'd seemed more pensive than usual, her eyes following him as if she had something she wanted to say.

Rafferty knew his daughter well enough to know that she wouldn't tell him what it was until she was ready. He'd lingered, without making an issue of it.

"Do you like Mandy?"

He hadn't been anticipating the question and it took him a moment to choose an answer.

"Yes. I like her a lot. Why do you ask?" Had she sensed something between them? Did it upset her to think of him involved with someone?

She shrugged. "No particular reason. Just wondered."

She fell silent but he was sure she had more on her mind. He sat on the edge of her bed, waiting. His patience was rewarded.

"You know, I wouldn't mind if you wanted to get married again." Her tone was elaborately casual, as if the thought had only just occurred to her. "I mean, I wouldn't be jealous or nothin'."

"You wouldn't, huh?" Rafferty's tone concealed his shock.

"No. I mean, it might be kind of nice, having a mom again."

He reached out to stroke her bangs back from her face, feeling his heart twist.

"You miss your mom, don't you?"

"Yeah." Again, she hunched her narrow shoulders to show that it was no big deal. "Not as much anymore. But sometimes."

"You know, if I were to get married again, it wouldn't be like having your mom back." He followed her lead in not mentioning any names. "Even if you loved her and she loved you, it wouldn't be exactly the same."

"I know. I'm not a baby, you know." Her tone was so disgusted that Rafferty had to bite his lip to hold back a smile.

"I know you're not, but fathers have this really weird tendency to think of their daughters as babies, even when they're not. I guess you'll always be my baby, at least in some ways. Think you can live with that?"

"I guess." She looked rather pleased with the thought, as if she wasn't really in quite such a hurry to leave her childhood behind as it sometimes seemed.

"Good." He bent to kiss her and her thin young arms came up to encircle his neck in a fierce hug. Rafferty was unashamed of the stinging in his eyes as he returned the hug. He'd missed out on three years' worth of hugs. It made the ones he received now all the more precious.

"I love you, Becky." He tucked the blankets around her shoulders, knowing full well she'd push them away the minute he was out of the room.

"I love you, too, Daddy."

He paused in the doorway to look at her a moment before turning off the light. She looked so young. But he knew it would seem like hardly the blink of an eye before she was going out on dates and getting her driver's license.

"Good night, urchin."

"Good night. You won't forget what I said about it being okay if you got married, will you?"

"I won't forget," he promised. "Now go to sleep."

OUT OF THE MOUTHS of babes, he was thinking as he drove home the next day. All day his thoughts had veered between Becky's words and thoughts of Mandy. The two were inextricably intertwined. She might have thought she was being subtle but it wasn't hard to see where his daughter's thoughts were heading.

He should have seen it coming. She and Mandy had hit it off from the start. It wasn't surprising that she should begin to see Mandy as a substitute for the mother she had lost. Now that Becky had said something, he wasn't at all surprised. The wonders of twenty-twenty hindsight, he thought ruefully.

Obviously he and Mandy needed to talk. They needed to figure out just where their relationship was going, if that was possible. And they needed to make sure that Becky wasn't going to get hurt.

Talk. That was what they needed.

Which didn't explain the fact that his heart was beating too fast even before he'd pushed open the kitchen door and seen Mandy standing in the doorway to the dining room.

She was wearing a soft dress of some fuzzy knit that he vaguely identified as angora. It was a warm, neutral shade that hovered somewhere between cream and brown. Combined with her dark hair and eyes and the pale ivory of her skin, it should have made her look dull and faded. Instead, she seemed soft and gentle, a touch old-fashioned, like a sepia print.

The kitchen was redolent of herbs, a warm inviting scent that did nothing to assuage the hunger that had been haunting him for weeks now.

Mandy's eyes widened as he pushed the door shut behind him and started toward her. There could be no mistaking the look in his eyes. Her heart began to hammer in response to it.

"We need to talk," she managed breathlessly.

"Yes." Without breaking stride, he jerked his tie loose, letting it fall to the floor.

"It's important that we discuss things." She took a step backward, seeking the support of the wall because her knees were beginning to shake.

"Absolutely."

He stopped in front of her and time seemed to shiver to a halt. He didn't say anything. He didn't touch her. He didn't have to. His eyes devoured every inch of her.

"We really should talk," she offered weakly.

"We will," he promised, his hands coming up to cup her shoulders. "Later."

He drew her forward as his head lowered toward hers. Mandy's hands came up to grasp the edges of his jacket, needing something to cling to.

"It feels as though it's been years since I've held you," he breathed against her mouth. "We'll talk later, but right now, I want to make love with you."

Mandy couldn't have formed a protest, even if she'd tried. He was right. Talking could come later.

Chapter Thirteen

In Rafferty's darkened bedroom, amid whispers and soft words, they rediscovered the passion that had haunted them both for weeks. Waiting had made the pleasures more intense.

Rafferty wondered how he could have forgotten just how soft Mandy's skin was. Or the way the lamp picked up golden highlights in the darkness of her hair. Or the taste of her warm honey skin and the sound of her gentle sighs.

Mandy hadn't thought it possible that she had forgotten even a single detail of the way it felt to make love with Rafferty. But had his hands been so exquisitely tender before? Had he known just how to touch her, every movement drawing pleasure with it?

She felt more confident now, as if she'd come to terms with her femininity in some subtle way during the weeks since Christmas. There was a delicious power in feeling Rafferty tremble at her touch. Something intensely erotic in knowing that, if she was drowning in pleasure, he was also swept up in it.

Lying in his arms afterward, her head resting on his shoulder, Mandy felt as if she'd come home after being away for a very long time. Rafferty's hand moved across her back, an idle stroking that had nothing to do with arousal and everything to do with the warm contentment they both felt.

They lay without speaking for a long time. Words would have been an intrusion. Around them, the house was quiet. They might have been on a mountaintop, isolated from the real world.

But the real world couldn't be kept at bay forever.

With a sigh, Mandy lifted her head from its comfortable resting place. Rafferty's arms tightened around her when she moved to sit up.

"Where are you going?" His voice was husky and warm.

"I was going to go see if dinner is salvageable."

"You turned the heat off," he murmured, nuzzling her temple.

"Maybe I should turn it back on," she managed, trying to ignore the shiver of awareness that ran down her spine.

"We could turn up the heat right here." His mouth sought out the sensitive line of her jaw.

"But I'm hungry."

"So am I." His kiss left no doubts that he was talking about a different kind of hunger, the kind not satisfied by coq au vin.

Mandy returned the kiss, feeling the warmth of it wash over her. It would be so easy to lose herself in his arms, to pretend that there was nothing to consider beyond this moment.

Rafferty lifted his head, looking down at her with renewed desire simmering in his eyes. The look was enough to make every bone in her body turn to mush. But they couldn't just forget about tomorrow, no matter how much they'd both like to.

"We've got to talk." Her voice was breathless and her eyes reflected how little she wanted to say the words.

Rafferty hesitated a moment. If he kissed her again she'd melt for him. He could feel it in the way she lay beneath him, could see it in her eyes. His arms tightened around her and then loosened.

"You're right," he said abruptly. He rolled away from her to sit on the edge of the bed.

Looking at the muscled width of his back, Mandy was sorry she'd said anything. Her body hummed with awareness. Would it really be so awful to just forget about the rest of the world for a little while longer?

"You're right," he said again, just when she'd almost decided that she was wrong. He twisted to look at her, his mouth curved in a rueful smile. "But if you think I can have an intelligent discussion with you while you're lying in the middle of my bed, all flushed and warm and inviting, you're nuts."

He stood up and reached down to scoop her off the sheets and set her on the floor. Mandy felt her cheeks flush wildly. She was not yet so comfortable with their relationship that she didn't feel self-conscious standing stark naked in front of him.

"Here. Put this on." Rafferty handed her the shirt she'd so recently pulled from his shoulders. Mandy slipped it on, grateful for the covering. Rafferty pulled on his pants. Mandy had to swallow the urge to ask him to put on a shirt. The sight of that muscular chest was too distracting.

"I really should check on dinner," she said. Now that the moment was here, she was anxious to gain a little more time.

Dinner proved to be in fine shape, despite the considerable delay in serving it. More for something to do than because either of them was terribly hungry, Mandy got out the salad she'd made earlier. Whether Rafferty really was hungry or because he also needed a breathing spell, he helped her finish the preparations. They sat down to eat, as if food was all they had on their minds.

"Becky told me it would be okay if I wanted to get married again," Rafferty said abruptly.

Mandy set her fork down, aligning it precisely along the side of her plate. The half dozen bites she'd taken suddenly felt like a lead weight in the pit of her stomach.

"Did she?"

"She assured me she wouldn't be jealous." He'd eaten

only a little more than she had. Now he set his own fork down and pushed the plate away.

"What did you tell her?" Mandy asked, keeping her eyes on the food slowly congealing on her plate.

"I don't know." He raked his fingers through his hair. "I don't really remember. Some nonsense about being glad, I think."

"What sparked her sudden interest in you remarrying?" But she already knew the answer.

"You." Rafferty made the word blunt, almost accusatory.

Mandy lifted her eyes to his face but she saw only turmoil. "Me?"

"She's obviously picked up on something between us." He frowned. "I suppose it was stupid of me to think she wouldn't notice anything. Kids are a lot smarter than most people think."

"And Becky's smarter than most," Mandy said. She shoved her plate out of the way and leaned her elbows on the table, hands clasped together. "Did she ask about us?"

"No. She asked me if I liked you." His voice softened, remembering Becky's carefully guarded question, her obvious attempts at subtlety.

Mandy felt a little stab of pain. *If he liked her.* At Becky's age, that was the big question. Did Joey like Amy or did he like Susy better? The question was simple and straightforward. A long way from the tangle it became when you grew up.

"What did you tell her?" she asked softly, her eyes searching his face.

"That I liked you very much," he said slowly. The words were so anemic. They fell far short of explaining his feelings for her. Yes, he liked her but there was so much more to it than that.

"Mandy, I—" He stopped, groping for words. She waited, knowing what she wanted to hear. Knowing it wasn't possible. Not yet.

"I don't want to lose you," he said finally. "I don't

know exactly where this is headed but I...I care about you. And I've got to protect Becky. I've got to make sure she doesn't get hurt.''

''I understand.''

She did understand. He loved Becky. Wasn't that one of the things she loved most about him?

Her eyes dropped from his, concealing the shock of realization. *She loved him.* All her talk about not being ready to make a commitment, needing time to prove she could conquer the world on her own. That was all nothing but an attempt to avoid facing the truth of her own feelings.

Rafferty stared at her inclined head, wondering what her continued silence meant. Did she think he was wimping out? Using Becky to avoid making a commitment? The truth was, if it wasn't for his daughter, he'd be down on his knees, begging her to move in with him, promising engagement rings.

He felt the shock race through him, snatching his breath away.

My God. *He loved her.*

How could he have been such an idiot? Why hadn't he realized it weeks ago? A room came alive when she walked into it. She was always in his thoughts. How long had he loved her? From the moment he saw her, laughing with Becky? He'd told himself he was hiring her for Becky's sake, because Becky liked her. Maybe he'd been lying to himself even then.

''Mandy, I—''

The sharp ring of the telephone cut him off. Mandy's head came up and they looked at each other. The phone rang again. Rafferty wanted to ignore it. But it was almost midnight.

''It could be Becky,'' Mandy said, reading his thoughts.

''Or an emergency at the hospital.'' He shoved back his chair and stood up.

Mandy listened to his side of the conversation. It was obvious it wasn't Becky. Equally obvious that he was going to have to leave.

"A patient of mine was in a car crash," he said, turning to her as he hung up the phone. "They're going to have to operate. Her parents want me there. I have to go."

"I understand."

"You seem to be saying that a lot tonight." He hesitated. There were so many things he wanted to say. He'd only just realized what he felt. How could he leave without telling her, without asking if she could return his feelings?

But he didn't want to~eram it into a few hurried moments. He wasn't even sure he could have expressed what he was feeling if they'd had all night. The recognition of it was so new.

"We still haven't had that talk," he said at last.

"It'll keep. You'd better get dressed."

Mandy was relieved when he finally turned and left. She heard him take the stairs two at a time. When he came back down, she was sitting just where he'd left her. Seeing him dressed and ready to leave, she stood up, tugging self-consciously at the bottom of the shirt that was all she wore.

"I'm sorry about this," he said, shrugging into his coat.

"It's not your fault. I hope your patient is all right."

"Me, too." He hesitated, looking as if there was something he wanted to say. "I don't know when I'll be back. Will you stay here?"

"Of course. I'll be here in case Becky calls."

"I wasn't thinking about Becky." He reached out and took her hands, drawing her forward until hardly a breath remained between them. "I'd like to think of you here, in my bed, even if I can't be there with you. Okay?"

There was something in his eyes, as if he wanted her to read something more into his words. She knew what she wanted to read into them but she doubted it was what he had in mind.

"I'll be here," she promised softly, wondering if he could see her heart in her eyes.

"Good." He dropped a short, hard kiss on her mouth and then he was gone, striding out the door without looking back.

Mandy didn't move until she'd heard the Jeep back out of the garage. Then she sank slowly back into her seat at the table.

She'd fallen in love with Rafferty Traherne.

What on earth was she supposed to do now?

There was, of course, nothing to *do* about it. After staring at their uneaten dinner for quite some time, Mandy gave up asking the question. She put away the food and set the dishes in the dishwasher—with the right soap, it had turned out to be quite friendly.

Though she couldn't imagine sleeping, she wandered upstairs to the master bedroom. Curling up in the middle of the bed she'd so recently shared with Rafferty, she surprised herself by falling asleep almost immediately. The lateness of the hour and the emotional stresses of the evening combined to provide her with a deep, dreamless sleep.

Rafferty was still not home when she woke up. She showered and changed into the clothes she'd brought with her the day before. She'd felt so deliciously sinful when she packed the overnight bag. Now, she felt confused and uncertain.

Rafferty's receptionist called at ten o'clock to tell her that Dr. Traherne's patient had come through the surgery quite well and was expected to make a full recovery. The doctor had caught a few hours of sleep at the office and was, even now, seeing his first patient of the day. He expected to be home at the usual time.

With Becky at her friend's house, Mandy had little to do all day besides sit around and think about Rafferty. It made for a long and wearing day. By the time late afternoon crept around and it was time to pick up Becky, she was as tired as if she'd scrubbed floors all day.

She was looking forward to getting Becky. It was impossible to remain depressed in Becky's presence. She was on her way out the door when the phone, which had remained stubbornly silent all day, suddenly rang.

For a moment, she considered ignoring it. Muttering about the evils of modern technology, she snatched up the receiver, moderating her voice at the last minute to avoid barking into it.

"Mandy? This is Flynn McCallister."

"Hello, Flynn. Rafferty's not here right now and I'm just on my way out the door to pick up Becky. Shall I have one of them call you back?" She was pulling on her coat as she spoke, cradling the receiver in her shoulder.

"Actually I called to talk to you." He sounded hesitant and rather un-Flynn-like.

"Oh." Mandy wondered what Flynn would want to talk to her about. Only one thing came to mind. "Is it about the photo in the show? I saw it this weekend. Has someone complained about the subject being too dull?" she asked jokingly.

"Not exactly." Again that odd tone. Despite the fact that she was running late, Mandy's interest was piqued. "Look, I've got a couple sitting in my living room right now who claim to be your parents."

"What!"

"They seem to think I'm holding you captive in a basement somewhere."

"Oh my God. How did they end up with you?"

"It seems someone recognized the photograph as being that of the daughter of an old family friend—an Amanda *Bradford*." Mandy closed her eyes at the heavy emphasis on the last name. "Of the Philadelphia Bradfords," he added.

"Oh, dear."

"Yes, well, the family friend called your father—I gather it probably is your father who's steaming in my living room?"

"Yes."

"You don't look much like him. Of course, it's hard to tell what either of them looks like. Your father keeps shouting and your mother keeps crying. Makes it difficult to trace any familial resemblance."

"I'm sorry."

"Don't apologize to me." She could hear the shrug in

his voice. "There've been a few times when I've wanted to run away from my family."

"I told them I was all right."

"Well, they don't seem to believe it. They're actually threatening to call the police."

"Oh, my God." She closed her eyes, her fingers tight on the receiver. "I'm really, really sorry, Flynn."

"Don't worry about it. But do you think you could come over and assure them that I don't have your lifeless body stuffed in a closet somewhere?"

"I have to pick up Becky. I guess I'll just bring her with me. I'll be there as soon as I can."

Her thoughts tumbled one over another during the short drive to get Becky. What on earth were her parents thinking of? She wasn't a child. She'd told them she was safe and well.

Becky accepted Mandy's announcement that they were going to see Flynn without question. Mandy listened with half an ear to the little girl's chatter about what she and Cindy had done the night before. It was lucky that the streets were reasonably clear, though the weather reports were threatening more snow tonight. Mandy wouldn't have been up to handling the car on icy roads.

She stopped in front of Flynn's house but she made no immediate move to get out of the car. She knew what awaited her inside. Her mother would weep pitifully. Her father would look at her with a mixture of anger—how could she do this to them?—and hurt—hadn't they always done their best for her?

"Mandy? What's wrong?" Becky's question roused her out of her thoughts. She turned to look at the little girl, feeling her heart soften when she saw the anxious look in her eyes. She'd really grown to love Becky. It was only now that she recognized part of that love was because Becky was Rafferty's, a part of him. But mostly, Mandy loved her for herself.

"My parents are in there," Mandy said slowly.

"Is that bad? You look unhappy."

"It's not bad. I love them a lot." She sighed, her glance straying back to the house. "But we don't see eye to eye the way you and your dad do. And I'm a little angry with them for coming out here like this."

Becky considered this in her usual quiet fashion. "Are you going to yell at one another?"

"I hope not."

She soon discovered it was unlikely that anything less than shouting was going to allow her to be heard. Flynn met them at the door, looking so relaxed, it was hard to imagine that he'd had a pair of hysterical strangers on his hands for the past couple of hours.

"Hi, Becky." He reached out to ruffle her sandy hair. "Hannah's about ready to wake up from her nap. You want to go get her up?"

"If you want to get rid of me, you should just say so," Becky informed him calmly. Smoothing her hair, she departed with great dignity.

Flynn quirked an eyebrow at Mandy. "I guess I've been put in my place. Your parents are in the den. Ann's out shopping but she should be home before too long."

"I can't tell you how sorry I am that you were dragged into this, Flynn." Mandy shrugged out of her coat, letting him take it and hang it up for her.

"Oh, I don't know. I didn't really have anything else to do today. If you need a referee, I'll be within earshot."

"Thanks."

Taking a deep breath, she pushed open the door he'd indicated.

"Amanda!"

Her mother promptly burst into tears, not the first she'd shed from the looks of her. Her father looked as if he'd just seen his only child come back from the dead. They both surged toward her, enveloping her in familiar scents. Her mother's delicate perfume. Her father's after-shave and the pipe her mother so disapproved of.

"Mama. Dad." Despite her annoyance at the way they'd reentered her life, Mandy felt tears come to her eyes. She *did* love them. And she'd missed them these past months. She hugged them both. But the moment of closeness didn't last long.

Her mother drew back, studying her with critical eyes.

"You're so thin, Amanda. You're not eating well. I knew it, Howard. I knew she wouldn't eat right."

"I haven't lost an ounce, Mama. You look lovely. How was your flight?"

"It was fine. But that's not what we're here to talk about." Clutching Mandy's hand, her mother drew her to the sofa. "You should sit down. You look pale."

"It's winter. I don't get out in the sun much." Mandy sat down next to her mother. Her father chose to stand in front of them.

"You didn't get out in the sun much in Philadelphia, either, but you were never this pale. Have you seen a doctor recently?"

"For what?" Mandy stopped, catching hold of her temper. They were only doing this because they loved her. She forced a smile. "I work for a doctor, remember?"

"Well he can't be a very good doctor if he hasn't seen how pale you are." Pamela Bradford sniffed. "Does he know about your problems?"

"What problems?"

"Don't be rude, Amanda," her father told her. "Your mother has been extremely worried about you."

"I'm sorry. But I told you both there was nothing to worry about."

"Considering your health, that's a foolish thing to say," he told her.

And so it went, Amanda assuring them that she was in smashing good health and neither of them hearing a word she was saying. It was a conversation they'd had many times before. The only thing that had changed was the setting. And her reaction.

Before, she'd felt smothered by their loving concern. She'd always given in, feeling guilty for not appreciating their solicitude. She'd even half believed that they were right and she really *was* little more than an invalid. But that had been before she'd proved to herself that she didn't have to be wrapped in cotton to survive. Before she'd built a life for herself. Before she'd met Rafferty, who treated her like a normal, healthy woman.

She'd changed. She'd grown up and developed a solid belief in herself. This time, she wasn't going to give in to the guilt. She loved her parents but she couldn't remain an invalid all her life just to avoid hurting them.

Mandy tried explaining all this to her parents but the only result was that her mother broke into fresh sobs and her father developed a pinched look around his mouth that bespoke paternal heartbreak. Despite her best efforts, she felt the old guilt creeping in around the edges of her determination.

They only wanted what was best for her. They really did love her. Hadn't they done everything they could for her?

She shook her head and stood up as if she could fight the insidious voices better on her feet.

"I'm sorry if I worried you. But I'm happy here. I've made a life for myself. I have a job."

I've fallen in love. But that wasn't something she could tell them.

"You're not thinking clearly, Amanda," her father told her. "You can't possibly stay here."

"Why not?" Frustration made her voice rise.

"What if something happened to you? Consider your weak heart."

"My heart has been doing just fine. I'm not talking about training for a triathlon, Dad. I'm just talking about building a life. A nice normal, healthy life."

"Are you saying that we don't want you to have a healthy life?" her mother asked tearfully. "Don't you think that's what we want more than anything in the world?"

"I don't know. All I know is that you've never given me a chance to develop one. You protect and shelter me until I feel like...like I'm smothering. Sometimes I think you prefer me helpless."

"Don't talk to your mother like that, Amanda Leigh!" Her father's voice was sharp. "I've had enough of this nonsense." He pushed his hands into his pockets, his feet braced apart in his very best chairman-of-the-board, man-to-be-reckoned-with stance.

"You're coming home with us and that's all there is to it! We're not going to argue about it anymore."

"She's not going anywhere she doesn't want to go."

None of the room's occupants had noticed the door opening.

"Rafferty." Amanda felt a mixture of relief and dread. Here at last was someone likely to understand her side. On the other hand, she didn't like the idea of him being dragged into the midst of a family quarrel.

"Just who are you?" her father demanded with a touch of belligerence.

"Rafferty Traherne." He stepped into the room, leaving the door open behind him.

"This is my…employer." Mandy hesitated over the description. Just how did she describe their relationship? "Mama, Dad, this is Dr. Rafferty Traherne. Rafferty, these are my parents. Howard and Pamela Bradford."

"Bradford?" Rafferty shot her a quick glance, reminding her that he knew her as Amanda Bradley. Mandy flushed but this was hardly the time to explain. Rafferty recovered immediately.

"Mr. and Mrs. Bradford." He held out his hand to her father, who took it automatically. "I'm glad to meet you."

"Yes. Well, yes." Her father had been thrown off stride by Rafferty's presence. It took him a moment to recall just where he'd been before he was interrupted.

"I'm afraid you've interrupted a private, family discussion, Dr. Traherne," he said finally. "I'm sure you won't mind leaving us alone."

"Actually, I do mind," Rafferty said in a tone so polite his refusal didn't register at first. "Unless Mandy wants me to go." He turned, arching one eyebrow in her direction.

"I'd like you to stay." No doubt she owed him an explanation later, but at the moment she needed the support his presence gave her.

"Very well." Her father made no attempt to hide his disapproval. "It doesn't really matter. We've decided that Amanda is coming home with us."

"Does Amanda have a say in this?" Rafferty asked politely.

"Amanda needs people to take care of her. No doubt you're unaware of her health problems. Otherwise, I'm sure you'd see our point."

"If you're talking about the spinal trauma she suffered when she was a teenager, I understand it quite well. From a medical viewpoint, I certainly wouldn't recommend that she take up discus throwing or pole-vaulting but I doubt she needs constant nursing."

"No, I don't. Dad, I—"

"Did she tell you about her heart problem?" Pamela Bradford asked Rafferty.

Rafferty's hesitation gave the answer. He glanced at Amanda before speaking. "No, she didn't. But since she's managed just fine these past few months, I'd still have to say that she doesn't need constant supervision."

"Well, her mother and I have known her a great deal longer than you have, Dr. Traherne. *We* feel that Amanda's health requires considerable care. *We* feel—"

"Does anyone care what Amanda thinks?" Mandy's voice was louder than was strictly polite but she was beyond caring. They were arguing around her as if she were deaf and dumb.

Her words drew all eyes to her. Her father seemed vaguely surprised, as if he'd almost forgotten her presence. Her mother seemed shocked that she had an opinion to express. Rafferty's expression was unreadable.

"I'm a grown woman and I'm capable of making my own decisions."

"Now, Amanda, no one said you weren't grown."

"Your father and I just want what's best for you."

Rafferty said nothing, watching her with those gray eyes that concealed his thoughts.

"I know you want what's best for me, Mama. But you have to be willing to let *me* make those decisions. Even if I came home with you, things couldn't be the way they were before."

"Then you'll come home," her mother said, having heard nothing beyond that possibility.

Mandy cursed her poor choice of words. "I'm sorry, Mama. I shouldn't have phrased it that way. No, I'm not going back to Philadelphia with you."

Her words brought a storm of protest. Mandy struggled to remain firm. It wasn't easy but it wasn't as difficult as it would have been a few months ago. Among other things, she'd learned to stand up for herself.

It was finally left to Rafferty to end the uncomfortable confrontation.

"I suspect the McCallisters are probably more than a little tired of having the lot of us camped out in their den. And it's obvious we're not going to get anywhere arguing like this. I assume you're staying at a hotel here in Denver? Why don't you and Mandy have dinner together? I'm sure you'll find a way to work out your differences."

Mandy noticed how he'd distanced himself from the situation, as if it no longer mattered to him what the result of the discussions might be.

Her parents protested, of course, but Rafferty gave them little choice. His tone remained reasoned and calm. He didn't throw them out bodily, but somehow they found themselves leaving, having agreed that dinner at the hotel was a good idea. Her mother clutched Mandy to her, as if it might be the last time they saw each other. Her father gave her a more restrained hug. Some of his anxiety had been redirected toward Rafferty, who was clearly a dangerous influence, and worse, a worthy opponent.

The silence they left behind was deafening. Mandy had remained in the den while Rafferty saw them out the door. She half expected him to leave right behind them. But he

came back into the room, stopping just inside as if he didn'
particularly wish to be any closer to her.

"I'm sorry about the name," she said immediatel
"When I first left home, I had this hysterical fear that the
were going to put out an all-points bulletin or somethin
It was stupid and melodramatic but I thought Amand
Bradley would be harder to find."

"And it didn't occur to you to tell me about it? Mo
recently, I mean?" His tone was level but she knew hi
well enough to hear the anger behind it. And hurt?

"I forgot."

"Just like you forgot to tell me that you'd had rheumat
fever and that there'd been damage to your heart?"

"I didn't want you to see me the way everyone els
always has," she said. How could she make him unde
stand? "All my life, people have treated me as if I wa
different. That was a big part of the reason I left home.
was sick of being wrapped up in tissue paper like a po
celain doll."

Rafferty stared at the polished wood floor between the
his eyebrows drawn together. He could understand what sh
was saying, sympathize with it, even. But understandin
and sympathy didn't do anything about the knot in h
chest.

She'd lied to him. Not just about the unimportant thing
like how many jobs she'd had or how old she was. Eve
the name was no big deal. She might see her health prol
lems as nothing more than barriers to her being treated
a normal human being. But they'd helped make her wh
she was. She'd been shaped by them, by the way her pa
ents had responded to them. And she'd kept all that fro
him.

"What if something had happened?" he said at las
"What if you'd been injured? What if it had been you
heart that gave out instead of your legs that day? I wouldn
have known anything."

"That was a chance I felt I had to take," she said slowl

"But I didn't know *I* was taking it, too."

His words were still hanging in the air when Flynn's voice interrupted the tense conversation.

"Has either of you seen Becky?"

Rafferty's eyes held Mandy's a moment longer before he turned to Flynn.

"No. Why?"

"I can't find her." Flynn's eyes were worried. "She was in the house earlier."

Rafferty threw a quick glance at the window, confirming what he already knew. It was nearly dark out and snow was starting to drift down.

"Maybe she's reading in a corner somewhere. This house has plenty of those."

But the calm words didn't still the pang of fear he suddenly felt. If something happened to Becky...

Chapter Fourteen

Another search of the rambling house failed to turn up Becky. The three adults gathered in the living room. Flynn had Hannah perched on his hip, a cookie clutched in her small fist. The toddler was the only one who didn't seem worried.

"Where would she have gone?" Rafferty said, asking the question as much of himself as of his companions.

"I don't know." Flynn bounced Hannah absently. "I was getting dinner started when I saw her last. She seemed a little quiet, as if she was thinking about something. Could she have overheard anything that would have upset her?"

Mandy and Rafferty exchanged a quick glance. The discussion with her parents had not been pleasant but there didn't seem to be anything in it to upset Becky. Unless...

"I wonder if she thought you were going to leave with your parents," Rafferty said slowly.

"I don't know." Mandy frowned, trying to remember what had been said. "It's possible. But that wouldn't make her run away."

"Wouldn't it?" Rafferty's voice held cold anger.

He felt as if he'd fallen into the middle of an old nightmare. Becky was gone. His rational mind insisted that she hadn't disappeared forever. But all his emotions were screaming that this was just like before, just like when Maryanne had taken her away.

And just like before, it was his fault. He hadn't understood his wife, hadn't been able to anticipate her actions. He'd let emotion blind him to her instability. He'd repeated the same mistakes by letting Becky form ties with Mandy. The one thing he'd promised himself, over and over, was that he wasn't going to let Becky get hurt again.

"What do you mean?" Mandy asked, reaching out to catch his sleeve when he started to turn away. "Becky wouldn't run away because she thought I might be going home with my parents. She knows I'd be back."

"Does she? How does she know? Have you told her that? Of course not," he answered for her, his eyes steel-gray with anger that was directed as much at himself as at her.

"I don't think this is the time or the place for this, Rafferty," Flynn suggested. He glanced at Mandy's stricken face.

"You're right." Rafferty ran his fingers through his hair, his expression haggard. "We've got to find Becky."

"Maybe she went out to the old barn," Flynn said. "She always likes to hang out in there."

"I'll get my coat."

"I'll go with you," Mandy said, starting forward.

"No." He refused her offer without looking at her. "I can do this alone."

Mandy watched him go without another word but her face must have reflected her feelings. She caught the edge of Flynn's glance and half turned away, blinking back the tears that blurred her vision.

"You know he doesn't mean it," Flynn told her gently. "He's scared."

"I know." But all the effort in the world couldn't keep the bleakness she felt from coloring that knowledge.

Flynn might have said more but the sound of a car in the driveway drew his attention. "That's Ann. I need to tell her what's happened." He shifted Hannah into a more comfortable position, his eyes concerned as he looked at Mandy. "We'll find Becky."

"Of course we will." She forced a smile.

Flynn went to meet Ann, and Mandy turned to stare out the big windows. Becky simply had to be all right. She was probably in the barn, just as Flynn had said. Maybe she'd gone out there to play and had decided to stay there when she realized it was getting dark. Becky had a lot of common sense.

But she was still only a child. What if she had overheard part of the conversation with Mandy's parents? Would she have assumed that Mandy was leaving? And would that have driven her to do something foolish? Surely Becky knew that she would never leave without talking to her first. Even if she did go back to Philadelphia, that didn't mean she'd just walk out of the child's life.

She'd been staring out the window without seeing the dark, snow-flecked landscape. Now a movement caught her attention and she stepped closer to the window. It came again, more a lighter shadow in the darkness than anything clearly distinguishable. But it was a shadow that moved.

Not even bothering with her coat, Mandy grabbed the woolen Indian blanket that lay across the back of the sofa. She wrapped it around her shoulders as she hurried through the kitchen and onto the back porch.

The air was still, with that peculiar quiet that seems to accompany a snowfall. It was cold but Mandy hardly noticed. Snow crunched under the ankle boots she wore under her wool slacks. Walking carefully to avoid slipping on a patch of ice, she made her way across the patio.

Once out of range of the house lights, her eyes adjusted to the snowy darkness. Peering toward the bottom of the yard, she could make out Becky's small figure. Mandy felt a surge of relief. She hadn't gone anywhere. She was here and she was safe.

She started to call out to Becky, tell her to come in, but something in the child's stance made her stop. She didn't think Becky had come out to enjoy the weather. Mandy threw a quick look in the direction of the house. She could go back in and let Rafferty come out and talk to Becky

But if Flynn's guess was right and Becky had overheard something of the conversation with Mandy's parents, then *she* was the one who should talk to the little girl.

Pulling the blanket tighter, she stepped off the patio. The dead grass beneath the snow cushioned her steps. Becky was unaware of her approach. She stood on the bank above the stream, her hands stuffed into her pockets, her shoulders hunched, her whole pose eloquently communicating her mood. Mandy was relieved to see that Becky had taken time to get her coat. Thank God, for it was probably the bright red color that had caught Mandy's attention in the house.

"Becky?"

Mandy's voice was low but Becky started, jerking around to face her a few feet away.

"Go away!" The flat rejection threw Mandy off balance. She hesitated, trying to decide the best way to approach the situation.

"It's kind of cold out here, isn't it?"

"I don't care," Becky said sullenly, half turning away, but not before Mandy had seen the tracks of tears that marked her cheeks.

"Do you want to talk about it?" Mandy asked gently.

"What for? You're going away."

So Flynn had been right. Mandy felt a surge of relief. She could deal with this.

"You overheard me talking with my parents."

"You're going back with them. You're going to go away and leave me, just like Mama did."

There was despair in Becky's voice. Despair and a certain resignation that tore at Mandy's heart.

"Oh, Becky." She stepped forward, only to stop when Becky took a corresponding step back. Mandy caught her breath. "Careful! Watch out for the stream."

"Go away!" Becky was indifferent to her proximity to the edge of the stream. "I don't care if you are leaving. You can go back to stupid old Philadelphia. I don't care!"

"I'm not going anywhere, honey." Mandy had to force the words out past the lump in her throat.

"I heard you. I heard you say you were going back." Becky dashed the back of her hand across her cheek. "And I don't care!"

For the first time since Mandy had known her, Becky was all child. The pseudo-adult manner had vanished, revealing the frightened little girl inside.

"You misunderstood, Becky. I'm not going anywhere." Mandy held out her hand, careful not to move any closer. "Come away from the stream. Let's go back inside and we'll talk."

"I don't want to go back inside." Since Mandy could see her shivering, she knew the words were sheer bravado. "I thought you were going to stay. I thought you and my dad would get married and we could be a family. I thought you liked us."

Mandy stared at her, groping for the right words with which to reassure her. With a child's simple vision, Becky had mapped out their futures. How could she have been so blind that she hadn't realized the fantasies Becky was building up around her relationship with Rafferty? She'd had the same fantasies—but she was old enough to know that wishing for something didn't make it come true.

You couldn't dictate a person's emotions. She loved Rafferty but he didn't love her. From the way he'd looked at her earlier, she wouldn't be surprised if he hated her. She'd lied to him, held back things he thought were important. And worst of all, she'd hurt Becky, no matter how inadvertently. If Rafferty could have forgiven her everything else, Mandy doubted he'd be able to forgive her that.

"I do like your father, Becky. I like him a lot." She drew the blanket closer around her shoulders, trying to suppress a shiver. The snow was falling faster now and it seemed that the temperature had dropped just in the few minutes she'd been out here. And Becky had been outside longer. "Let's go inside. I'll explain everything."

"No. I don't want to listen to you. Not anymore."

Mandy wasn't sure exactly what happened next. Did she start toward Becky or did Becky simply want to put even more distance between them? Whatever it was, the next few seconds seemed to happen in slow motion. Becky turned abruptly but she was closer to the edge of the stream than she'd realized. Mandy saw her feet start to slip out from under her.

"Becky!" She lunged, reaching for the child. She was so close, she could actually feel the rush of air as Becky's coat brushed by just out of reach of her straining hand.

With a shrill cry, Becky disappeared over the edge of the bank. Mandy didn't take time to think. She was only a fair swimmer herself but, weighed down by her coat, Becky would have no chance at all. The blanket was discarded, a bright pool of color on the snowy ground as Mandy plunged feetfirst over the bank.

The water was icy cold. Because of the swiftly moving stream, ice had formed only a few inches on either side. The water was less than hip-deep but the current was strong, threatening to sweep her feet out from under her. The cold was penetrating, numbing her legs instantly.

But there was no time to worry about that. Becky had been unprepared for her plunge into the icy water and she'd tumbled in completely. Hampered by the coat and the current, she'd been unable to regain her footing.

Catching the flash of red as Becky flailed to stay on the surface, Mandy lunged in her direction. Off balance, she was vulnerable to the force of the water, which promptly swept her feet out from under her, dumping her full-length into the water. Gasping, she fought to regain her footing while struggling to reach the little girl.

It seemed like an eternity but was probably only seconds before her hand brushed against Becky's coat. Mandy closed her fingers around the soggy fabric, planting her feet against the bed of the stream as she drew Becky to her.

Choking and coughing, Becky grabbed her around the waist threatening to topple them both as she burrowed her face into Mandy's shoulder.

"It's okay," Mandy told her, hoping Becky could understand the words through the chattering of her teeth. She patted her clumsily on the back, hardly able to feel any sensation in her frozen fingers. "Come on. We've got to get to the side."

Holding Becky to her, she edged toward the bank, hoping she was on the same side of the stream as the Mc-Callister house. The stream rushed by them, maliciously intent on sucking her down.

By the time they'd reached the edge of the water, Mandy could no longer feel her legs. She knew she'd never make the steep climb out. And to slip back in could be fatal.

"Becky, I want you to come around me and grab hold of that rock." She modulated her voice, fighting against the almost convulsive shivering that gripped her. "Have you got it?"

She could see Becky's head move and she hoped the gesture was in the affirmative. "Okay. I'm going to give you a boost out. Can you scramble the rest of the way up?"

"Yes." The word seemed to come from a long way away. Mandy forced all her energy into boosting Becky up and out of the water, which seemed to fight her, as if reluctant to release its victim. But it was beaten at last and Becky was standing on firm ground. Mandy felt the strength drain out of her, leaving her with barely enough to hold on to the rock.

"Mandy?" Fear trembled in Becky's voice and Mandy struggled to look as if she didn't share that fear. "Aren't you coming?"

"I can't get out on my own," she said calmly. "You'll have to get your daddy or Flynn to help me."

"Okay." Becky scrambled partway up the slope and then turned. Even in the dim light, Mandy could see her concern. "You won't go away?"

"I'm not going anywhere."

Mandy watched her disappear before letting her head droop. The stream had cut deep here. There was no shallow edge and she stood hip-deep in water. Her fingers were clamped around a ridge on the big rock that jutted out into the stream. The rock was large enough to create a small stillness next to it, where the current was forced around its bulk.

It was such a little way up onto solid ground. A little bit of a scramble. But she knew she'd never make it. There was no feeling in her legs. She wasn't even sure they were still supporting her. Maybe they were just dangling in the water and only the grip of her hands on the rock was keeping her above water. She was numb all the way to the bone. The shivering had stopped and she was starting to feel a lassitude that should have been frightening. But all she felt was a kind of calm acceptance.

How long would it take Becky to get back to the house? The answer seemed vague and unimportant. Becky was safe. Rafferty wouldn't lose his daughter again. She'd made sure of that. She'd never see that bleak, frightened look in his eyes again.

She couldn't feel the rock under her fingers anymore. Only by looking could she tell that she was still holding on. Mandy knew, with a sudden frightening clarity, that she might die. All her hopes and dreams could end right here. The thought sent a wave of adrenaline through her, driving away the calm acceptance. She tried to force her legs to move but there was no response from them. It was as if they weren't even there.

"Mandy?" The cry held a note of anguish that penetrated her fear.

She tilted her head back but the bank above her was empty.

"Mandy!" It was Rafferty and he was trying to find her. She had to try twice before she could find her voice.

"Rafferty! Rafferty, I'm here! This way." The call sounded pathetically thin to her ears. Not even enough to reach the top of the bank, surely. She listened but there was no response. He hadn't heard her. He was leaving, going some other direction. The thought sent panic sweeping through her.

"I'm here. Rafferty, I'm here." The words choked on sobs as she fought to drag herself out of the water. "Don't leave. Oh God, please don't leave me."

And then his hands were under her arms, lifting her easily, as if she weighed nothing. The water, which had seemed such an implacable enemy, gave her up without a whisper. Rafferty's arms were around her, hard and warm.

"I've got you, sweetheart. I wouldn't leave you." He held her close for a moment, squeezing her so tight her breath was momentarily cut off. But breathing didn't seem all that important compared to being held close to him.

"Becky?" she got out.

"Becky's fine. Ann's got her in a warm bath by now. Which is exactly where we're going to get you." He was shrugging out of his thick coat as he spoke and he wrapped it around her, trapping her arms inside. Mandy could feel its warmth but it seemed to be a very long way away, as if it were trying to penetrate a thick layer of ice.

"Cold," she mumbled.

"I know, honey. Hang on."

An instant later, Mandy found herself over his shoulder. She heard him say something and realized that Flynn must be on the bank above them. With Flynn's help, Rafferty scrambled up the bank. Once up, he shifted Mandy so that she lay in his arms.

"Is she all right?" That was Flynn, his eyes narrowed on Mandy's limp figure. Vaguely, Mandy thought that she should reassure him, tell him she was fine. But she couldn't seem to find the words.

"She's going to be fine." Rafferty said it fiercely as if the very force of his desire could make it so.

It seemed as if she'd only blinked when suddenly she opened her eyes to dazzling lights. She didn't remember Rafferty carrying her through the snowy night, didn't remember arriving at the house, but suddenly they were there.

Ann met them in the kitchen, her eyes going over Mandy with professional concern. "Becky's fine," she said immediately. "I've got her out of the bath and the tub's ready for Mandy. Becky's wrapped in a couple of blankets and I've got her drinking broth. I told her I'd let her know how Mandy was.''

"I don't know," Rafferty said shortly, moving past her with his burden. Mandy wanted to reassure Ann, tell her that she was just fine, but her mouth didn't seem to be connected to her brain.

"You want me to take care of her?" Ann asked.

"I'll do it. Keep an eye on Becky, will you?" He strode into the huge old bathroom and thrust the door shut with his elbow. He set Mandy down on a wicker chair next to the full tub and knelt to tug at her boots.

"We've got to get you out of those wet clothes and into a tub. The water is just warm, though it may feel hot to you."

Mandy managed to nod her understanding. She lifted her hands to the buttons on her shirt but her fingers were too cold to manipulate them through the buttonholes and she had to wait for Rafferty to do it for her.

He stripped her efficiently. No one watching would have been able to guess that he knew her body in any way other than that of doctor and patient. If it hadn't been for the stern set of his face, Mandy might have thought he'd forgotten just how well he knew her.

He lifted her in his arms, then slowly lowered her into the big claw-footed tub as if she were an infant. Mandy gasped, feeling tears spring to her eyes as the water lapped over her chilled flesh.

"I know, honey. I know." Rafferty's voice was a raspy whisper, as if he felt her pain. "It's going to hurt like hell but we've got to get you warmed up again."

Mandy gritted her teeth and allowed him to lower her the rest of the way into the tub. She'd have walked on hot coals to hear him talk to her like that. Leaning back against the tub, she endured the pain, vaguely aware of Rafferty kneeling beside her as if he was afraid she might black out and drown. She didn't know how long it was, but gradually the burning in her arms and legs faded to a more tolerable tingle.

"Do you feel better now?" Rafferty stroked the hair back from her forehead. His eyes were still dark and concerned.

"I'm sleepy," she murmured.

"Don't go to sleep. I want you awake a little while longer." He reached into the tub and caught her under the arms and lifted her onto the thick bath mat. Mandy didn't get a chance to feel chilled since he instantly wrapped a huge towel around her, pinning her arms to her sides. He began rubbing her dry, his movement brisk but gentle.

There was a tapping at the door and then Ann poked her head around, her frown changing to a smile when she saw Mandy.

"You look better." She slipped into the room, a thick velour robe draped over her arm. "I just pulled this out of the dryer. Put it on while it's warm. Becky's asking for you, Rafferty. Why don't you let me get Mandy into bed?"

He hesitated, looking at Mandy. "Are you going to be all right?"

"I'm fine." His concern did as much to warm her as the bath had done. "Go to Becky."

He lingered, looking doubtful but Ann shooed him out, shutting the door behind her before returning to Mandy.

"Honestly, you'd think I didn't know how to get you into a robe." She held up the thick garment, helping Mandy into it. The warm fabric felt heavenly.

"Is Becky all right?" Mandy asked as she tied the belt with fingers that were still a little clumsy.

"She's fine. Once Flynn assured her that you were going to be all right, she was okay. But I think she needed her father to tell her the same thing. Rafferty must love you a lot."

The casual words hit Mandy with the force of a sledgehammer. "Rafferty doesn't love me," she said, aware that her voice fell short of the casual tone she was trying for.

"No?" Ann arched one eyebrow. She urged Mandy

down onto the wicker seat and began combing out her damp hair. "He's doing a pretty good imitation of a man in love."

"He's just concerned, that's all."

"He looked a great deal more than concerned when he brought you in. He and Flynn were just about to go out looking for the two of you when Becky stumbled into the yard. When she told him that you were still in the water, he looked absolutely panicked."

"I work for him. I'm sure he feels a certain responsibility toward me. That's all it is." Mandy pleated the skirt of the robe. She wanted to believe what Ann was saying, wanted it so much she didn't dare let herself.

"Look, this is none of my business." Ann set the brush down and her eyes met Mandy's in the mirror. "I don't know exactly what happened here tonight. Flynn didn't get a chance to fill me in on the details. But I do know that Rafferty is in love with you. As in love with you as you are with him," she added, forestalling Mandy's protest. "I don't know what the problem is but I'd suggest you talk it out."

"There's nothing to talk about," Mandy mumbled without looking at her.

Ann had simply mistaken Rafferty's very natural concern for something more. Mandy refused to let herself even hope that she might be right.

She allowed Ann to tuck her into the huge bed in one of the guest rooms. Rafferty was still with Becky in another room. Flynn brought in a cup of warm broth and sat with her while she drank it. Her friends' concern warmed Mandy more than the thick blankets.

Flynn was in the midst of a story about his show when he glanced up and saw Rafferty standing in the doorway. He broke off without apology.

"Well, I'd better go check on Hannah. I'll see the two of you later."

Mandy hardly noticed him leaving. Rafferty came farther into the room, pushing the door shut behind him. Neither of them spoke. Mandy turned the empty cup around and around between her hands, groping for words.

"How's Becky?" she asked at last, breaking the silence.

"She's fine. Worried about you. She told me you saved her life."

"Anybody would have done the same." Mandy shrugged. The last thing she wanted was his gratitude.

"You could have died."

"So I should have let Becky drown?" She shot him a look, feeling anger surge to life inside her. "Should I have just stood there wringing my hands and crying? I am not helpless, Rafferty. And I am not some child you need to take care of. That's one of the reasons I didn't tell you about my heart. I wanted a chance to prove, to myself as much as anyone else, that I could take care of myself.

"I think I've proved that. And I don't think you have any reason to think I'd let Becky drown without doing anything to help her. I may not have told you the whole truth about some things but I love Becky and I'd sooner die than let anything happen to her."

She hadn't been aware of how agitated her movements had become until Rafferty crossed to her, catching her hands in his as he sank onto the edge of the bed. He took the mug from her and set it on the nightstand.

"I know you love her."

"You sounded surprised that I'd risked my life to save hers." She tugged on her hands but he refused to release them. She gave up trying, but she refused to raise her eyes past the level of his throat. Not for anything would she let him see how his doubt had hurt her.

"That wasn't surprise. It was—I don't know. Awe, maybe. Remembered terror. When Becky told us you were still in the water—" He broke off, his hands tightening on hers. "I thought I might have lost you," he said, almost to himself.

Mandy felt her heart lurch. Was it possible that Ann was right? She chewed at her lower lip, gathering her courage.

"The only way you're going to lose me is if you send me away," she said in a whisper.

There was a moment of silence and she wondered if she'd just made a total fool of herself. Maybe he'd only been speaking in the abstract, not losing her personally, but losing someone he knew. He was probably trying to find some way to let her down easily.

"I love you."

His words were so simply said that it took several seconds for them to penetrate through the turmoil of her thoughts. Her breath caught, her hands suddenly clutched his. She was dreaming. She wanted to hear the words so badly that she must have imagined them. She lifted her eyes to his face, afraid of what she might see there.

She saw all her dreams there, everything she'd longed for was there in his eyes.

"Oh, my." The exclamation was all she could manage.

Humor flickered through the tension.

"'Oh, my?' Is that all you can manage? Couldn't you come up with something more reassuring? Like you'll give me a chance to show you how much I love you, give yourself a chance to love me, maybe?"

There was an unfamiliar uncertainty in his voice and she realized suddenly that he needed to hear the words as much as she had. She'd thought her feelings must be so obvious that he wouldn't have to ask how she felt.

"No." Hurt flickered over his face and he moved as if to withdraw. Mandy held his hands, keeping him in place. "I mean, I don't have to give myself a chance. I already do love you."

The look in his eyes told her that he hadn't been sure of her feelings. Told her, too, how much her answer meant to him. "Are you sure?"

"I'm sure."

He drew her forward to meet his kiss. It was a kiss that held promises. Promises for the future that was suddenly opening before them. Somewhere in the middle of the embrace, the promise gave way to a passion that was made sharper by the knowledge of how close they'd come to losing each other.

There was so much to say, so many questions to be answered. When had he first known he loved her? How soon would she marry him? Was tomorrow too long to wait?

"Do you think Becky will mind?" Mandy's head was tucked against Rafferty's shoulder, his fingers tangled in her hair.

"I think Becky will be delighted," Rafferty said. "She may be a little surprised but she loves you."

"Maybe we should put off getting married, give her some time to get used to the idea," Mandy suggested. It occurred to her that she was talking about becoming a stepmother. Even when the child was Becky, the thought was a little intimidating.

"Why don't we wait and see how she reacts? If she's as pleased as I think she'll be, then I'm not waiting a minute longer than the law allows." Rafferty drew her up for another kiss.

A long time later, Rafferty leaned back against the headboard. Mandy, still wrapped in the thick robe, was cuddled against his chest. Desire hummed gently between them but the urgency was softened by the knowledge that they had all the time in the world to explore it.

Mandy still didn't quite believe how quickly everything had changed. A few hours ago she'd been almost certain he hated her. Now they were making plans for a wedding.

When the door opened, she lifted her head from Rafferty's chest. Becky stuck her head around the corner, her eyes widening when she saw the way her father was holding their housekeeper. Mandy would have moved away but Rafferty's arm tightened around her, holding her where she was. He held his other arm out to his daughter.

"Come here, urchin. How'd you like to be a bridesmaid?"

With a squeal, Becky launched herself across the room, only slightly slowed by the necessity of holding up the hem

f her nightgown so she wouldn't trip. She hit the bed with
a thud, burrowing against her father's side.

Rafferty laughed and dropped a kiss on her tousled head.
'I take it you'd like to be a bridesmaid?''

"Actually, I think I should give Mandy away," Becky
said, after a moment's consideration. "I'm the one who
ound her. *I* knew she was perfect for us from the beginning. It took you guys ages to figure it out."

There was a moment of stunned silence and then Rafferty
began to laugh, the deep sound blending with Mandy's soft
chuckle.

Becky arched her eyebrows. Really, adults could be so
foolish sometimes. What she'd said was no more than the
truth and they thought it was hilarious. Well, they could
laugh all they wanted. It might have taken them awhile but
they'd finally figured out what she'd known all along.

The three of them would be a terrific family.

Harlequin Romance®

Delightful

Affectionate

Romantic

Emotional

Tender

Original

Daring

Riveting

Enchanting

Adventurous

Moving

Harlequin Romance—the
series that has it all!

HROM-G

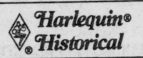

LOOK FOR OUR FOUR FABULOUS MEN!

Each month some of today's bestselling authors bring four new fabulous men to Harlequin American Romance. Whether they're rebel ranchers, millionaire power brokers or sexy single dads, they're all gallant princes—and they're all ready to sweep you into lighthearted fantasies and contemporary fairy tales where anything is possible and where all your dreams come true!

You don't even have to make a wish...Harlequin American Romance will grant your every desire!

Look for Harlequin American Romance wherever Harlequin books are sold!